To Cherish

M.L. Pennock

To the East Yates Center Road girls:

The Barbieri sisters are all of us. Thank you for more than 30 years of being the Stephs to my Stella, and the Stellas to my Steph.

I love you forever,

- M

Table of Contents

To Cherish

Prologue

There was a time when I had my life planned out. I'm notorious for being organized to a fault. Even when I thought my life was a mess, it was an extremely put together one.

Then I met her.

Things got a little crazy.

Everything got twisted and turned upside down.

As for the plan … what plan?

M.L. Pennock

To Cherish

Chapter One

Sutton

"Are you sure?"

"I'll check again, but this is measuring closer to thirteen weeks."

"She's only eight weeks pregnant, though."

No. No, no, no. I can feel the tears burning in the back of my eyes. This can't be happening. This is fucked up. This baby ... isn't Tommy's. There's no way it could be if I'm already three months along.

"Heart rate is 137. That's good," the ultrasound tech says to us, but I'm not sure what's good anymore. How can he say that? Nothing is good. This is devastating.

Everything I read said morning sickness started basically as soon as a pregnancy test turns positive. I had a period before we slept together. I mean, it was super short, but it was there.

A tear rolls out of the corner of my eye as I stare at the screen.

I can't be with Tommy. I can't let him raise another man's baby.

~*~*~*~

He asked questions during the appointment. He kept his head held high. He didn't once say the baby isn't his.

Because he's Tommy, and Tommy sticks by people he cares about.

But now we're in the parking garage and we're sitting in silence. The chill in the December air floods the inside of his car and wraps around us. I'm not sure if the stinging cold creeping up my spine is from 30-degree weather or because I feel my heart freezing in my chest with the thought of what I'm about to do.

"We can work through this. It doesn't change how I feel about the baby or you," he says, though his tone conveys all the pain he feels. He believes his words but his words are hollow by the time they register on my side of the car. He hesitated slightly when he got to the "or you" portion of his declaration and that's enough for me to know what I'm going to do is the right decision.

I watch his jaw tighten and spasm slightly where it comes together just below his ear. He rubs his left hand against the stubble peppering his chin. I notice everything about him all at once. I notice everything and nothing at all. I immediately miss him despite us occupying the same small space.

A sob climbs up out of my chest and falls at his feet as his reaches my ears.

God, this hurts.

I try to catch my breath, clutching my purse to my abdomen, wishing we had met sooner. Wishing ...

Chapter Two

Jacelyn

"How'd your appointment go?"

She's been quiet since she answered. I thought she would be bubbly after the initial shock of what is very much an unwanted pregnancy. Sutton never planned on having kids and now she's about to be in the trenches. It's weird to think of my best friend as a mom, but I'd be a hypocrite if I said I'm glad it isn't happening to me.

"It went. Things aren't looking good ... I don't want to talk about it, Jace." I hear the sob from across the country.

"Oh, Sutton, I'm so sorry. Do you need me to come home? Give me five minutes and I'll book a flight," I say. With the exception of me leaving New York a decade or so ago to attend college in California, we've been inseparable since we were kids. I'll drop everything to be there for her.

"No! No, you don't have to come home. I'll be okay, I just need to get over ... the loss. It's going to take time to cope, you know? I need to figure things out," she says.

"If you need anything, please call me. I'll be on the next flight to Rochester."

Maybe I should pack and go anyway. I'm sure she could use some help with the bookshop. It's not enough for me to send flowers. This isn't a hurt that can be cured by lilies and roses. I understand this hurt.

"I'll let you know, cross my heart," she says before ending the call.

~*~*~*~

I was young and stupid when I moved here. There was a guy — there's always a guy — and I was infatuated with everything listed on his Internet dating profile. It was the 2000s and being on my own away from home for the first time, well, let's just say I was easily intrigued. Plus, he was older and beautiful and lovely and an artist. I'm an artist, but his art was overpowering. Somehow.

So, I decided I could try to be in love and let him talk me into moving in together. My brother reminded me regularly that I was being too carefree at a time when I shouldn't have been, and maybe I was, but I wanted to fit in with the other people in my academic program. I was looking for my tribe.

My tribe turned out to be filled with angry artists who cut one another down in a futile attempt to climb to the top. The chief became my husband, and as "his queen" he cut me off at the knees every chance he got. I think he was confused about how the worshipping the ground I walk on thing was supposed to work, but I digress.

Today, I find out, he hit a last resort.

"So, what you're telling me is, my entire savings was withdrawn?"

The bank teller nods as my words register. Slowly the chipper demeanor melts away.

"My. Entire. Savings. It's gone?" I ask her the question very slowly. She nods again. "Everything?"

"It appears all but three hundred dollars was withdrawn yesterday." I cock an eyebrow. That's a strange amount to leave me with, three hundred. "In order to not be charged a fee we require at least three hundred dollars in the account."

"Well, that's fantastic." I smile. I should try to find the silver lining. "At least I still have that."

There really is no silver lining. That son of a bitch. This is the final straw.

"You didn't withdraw the money from your account?" As if she actually needs to ask that. She picks up the phone in her workstation and calls one of the cubicles across the lobby. Speaking into the receiver, I hear, "Can you come here? I'm having an issue with an account."

"Oh, you don't have to do that. I know where it went. He's on the account, so he didn't even do anything illegal, right? Technically?" My ears are on fire. "Let's just hope he doesn't want to fight me when I find him and tell him we're getting divorced. Then I'm selling his Camaro. Last, I'm going to burn all his crappy paintings."

I smile at the bank teller, offering her my thanks. I'll come back and change my account information another day. He's already taken what he wants. Thankfully, I didn't tell him about Grandpa's life insurance policy or that would have been gone, too.

In retrospect, those early pieces of his I found titillating actually lacked in all areas. Heart. Originality. Vision. Maybe the lack of things was what was overpowering. Infatuation is what got me here. I won't let it get me again.

Chapter Three

Sutton

Weeks have passed, weeks I've used to begin readjusting my life without his knowledge. I reach in the drawer and pull out the mismatched pairs of socks I've stored here. I turn and place them with care in the bottom of my bag. He touches my arm in a futile attempt to make me stop, make me look at him.

I can't look at him.

"You don't have to do this, Sutton. I don't care. I'll love this baby anyway. I already love him, or her." His voice wavers. That's why I have to do this. Tommy is trying to do what he thinks is the right thing, but the right thing is to let me go. Tommy does not love me. He loves the idea of love.

I turn back to the dresser. He gave me a drawer. I pull the few tops from its depths and lay them atop the socks in the duffle bag on the bed before walking in a haze to the bathroom. Reaching for the extra toothbrush I brought over and rarely used, I breathe in deeply, steeling myself against the emotions coursing through my veins.

"Please. We should talk about this."

"What do you want to talk about, Tommy? Do you want to talk about how you want to raise another man's kid? Or do you want to talk about how stupid I must be to have not known I was pregnant when we started seeing each other?" My voice drops low and my head hangs wearily of its own accord. "I'm so, so stupid."

I finally did some additional reading. That period I thought I had? It was because the baby was hooking itself to the inside of my uterus. I should have known something wasn't right back then. I need to call Rob. He needs to know. It's been long enough. It's time to tell him.

"You aren't stupid. You'd broken up with him. How were you supposed to know?"

I glare at him, pinning him with my gaze. How was I supposed to know? It's my body. I should have known.

"It doesn't change things. I'm sorry," I say, refusing to give in to his attempt at love.

Tommy can't love me. I won't let him.

This ... this too shall pass.

M.L. Pennock

Chapter Four

Jacelyn

"Pick up," I say as the line rings once again. "Pick up, pick up, pick up. Damn it, Sutton."

It's done. I've told him we're done. There's no getting my savings back because he spent it. All of it. I don't even know how someone can spend thousands and thousands of dollars of money that isn't theirs without feeling any remorse. He has no soul and I have no trust.

"Hey, it's Sutton. Leave a message and I'll get back to you soon!"

Voicemail. Again. She never calls back, though. I've been trying to call her for weeks. The last time we actually spoke was the day she told me she lost the baby. She's replied to text messages, but the replies come hours later and are usually one- or two-word answers. Open ended questions? They don't even get a response. I know she's going through a rough time, but I'm starting to feel like my best friend has turned her back on me. She has no idea how much I've needed her or how poor my mental health has been, and she certainly has no idea how much it hurts that she's been acting like she doesn't need me in return. My brother hasn't even seen her. He's purposely gone to her bookstore to try to check up on her for me and she's never there. Her mom is always there instead and seems to have taken over the daily business in her semi-retired state. She won't give up any information about Sutton no matter how hard Fisher tries to get even a tiny morsel of detail out of her. It's like she fell off the face of the earth.

"Where are you? Do you not have cell service there? You haven't sent me a text back since I told you and you aren't answering your phone. I'm worried, Sutton. Please call me back. I'm going to start my drive home a week from Tuesday. I told my brother he has that long to convince me he can save the restaurant without my help. Plus, I need to finalize a few more things before taking off from here," I say. "I'm going to take my time driving back to New York so I can stop and see the sights. It'll probably be a couple weeks before I get there. Okay? Okay. Call me back. Please."

M.L. Pennock

Chapter Five

Sutton

I watch as her name disappears from my phone and the call goes to voicemail. I let Jacelyn believe I lost the baby, and if I talk to her on the phone I'll break and tell her the truth. Jacey had the perfect parents and the perfect life. She's smart and pretty and loyal to a fault even when I don't deserve it, but I don't want her to know about this.

Months have passed since I actually talked to her. I've resorted to short text answers and a lot of lies about what's going on in my personal life. I listen to message after message that she's left me, but haven't built the courage to call her back. I've used Tommy as a scapegoat when necessary. I've made him out to be a bad guy when all he's ever been is a gentleman. I'm not deserving of a gentleman and he won't stop being one.

That's part of the reason why I'm leaving. Knowing Jacelyn is coming home is one of the motives for not coming back anytime soon. She should be here tomorrow, and I'll be long gone by then. I found a place down by the city. It's near my brother. He's done well for himself since leaving Rochester and has a storefront with apartments above it in a cute little community. He is willing to rent a unit to me and the store so I can run away with the intention of opening a second bookshop. That's what I'm going to attempt anyway. Who knows if I'll find even an ounce of success in this venture. At the very least, my mom is going to take over managing the store in Brockport while I "expand" the business. That's the story everyone has been told.

The baby ... he's going to have an awesome family who can love him.

It just won't be my family.

"Are you sure you want to do this?" he asks from the kitchen doorway. "We could still make it work. You can still back out."

"No," I gasp. "No. I can't do that. They've been waiting for him their entire lives. I can't take that away from them."

All these months and he's still trying to convince me this could work. This can't work.

My decisions have been mine and mine alone. Rob had so little to say when I told him, practically nothing at all. Nothing except, "I don't want it."

It.

This child isn't an "it."

This baby is going to make someone proud. He'll know love.

I wish it could be my love.

Maybe someday it will be.

"I have to go. My brother is waiting," I say as Tommy pushes off from the doorframe, shoving his hands in the pockets of his jeans. He slinks toward me. He scuffs his feet on the hardwood as he comes up to me, my belly pressing gently into him and he wraps me, so tenderly, in his arms. It's an embrace that says, "I love you anyway." It's a hug that says, "How could you do this to me?" It speaks when he can't. His nose in my hair, breathing in the scent of my shampoo, talks when words won't come to him.

The tears crack through the barrier and roll lazily down my cheeks as I lean into his arms.

"I have to go," I whisper once more before turning out of his arms, out of his life.

Chapter Six

Jacelyn

I'm here. Home. This time I don't have a return flight or enough oomph to drive the almost three-thousand miles back to California.

I open the door and slide my aching body out of the car. While it's way more comfortable than it looks, she wasn't made for a cross-country trip. I certainly wasn't going to hitch her to the back of a U-Haul when I don't even have enough belongings to fill the smallest moving truck. Leaning against the fender, I look at the front of the house before me. It hasn't changed much in the years I've been gone. In the last decade, I've come home on rare occasions, flying in only for a weekend here and there but never seeing more than family for the most part because my time in town was so short. The last time I stepped foot inside the house was right after graduation when Sutton's parent's downsized, moved to a townhouse closer to Rochester, and started renting the house to students at the college. I was surprised when Sutton told me she'd moved into the house. For a small-town kid, she never wanted to live the country life. She was always running to "the city" as soon as we could drive.

The warmth of the sun heats my face as I prepare to surprise Sutton. No, she hasn't returned my calls and her last text message was cryptic, but I'm hopeful as I push off the car and walk to the front door. I knock twice, then ring the doorbell, and wait. My back is to the door as I take in the view of my little town with its tree-lined Main Street when I hear the door open. My hands, pushed into the back pockets of my jeans, clench as anticipation suffocates me. It's been so, so long since I've seen her.

The smile on my face widens more as I spin around, but nothing could prepare me for what I met at the threshold.

"Can I help you?"

First, I hear the southern accent. Then, I see the smile lines, tousled blonde hair, and eyes that remind me of Archer, the Siberian Husky I had as a little girl. Not that this man reminds me of a dog, just his eyes. They're fiercely blue and kind.

"You aren't who I was expecting."

His smile wavers. He swallows and the dimple disappears.

I cover my mouth as quickly as I can and immediately feel like an asshole. "I'm sorry! Oh my gosh, that's so rude of me. I just … I was expecting someone else, but maybe I have the wrong house?" I quickly scan the front of the home. "It's a different color than I remember it, but I'm pretty sure this is the house."

His smile returns, "If it looks like the right house, then it probably is. It's vacant now. The last tenant just moved out yesterday." He holds his hand out for me to shake, "I'm Brian." He peers around me, looking at my car, filled to full with what was left of my California life. "I was just helping get the house scrubbed so it can be rented out again. The owners have their hands busy with other things at the moment. And you are?"

I reciprocate, smiling and placing my hand in his. "Jacelyn. The person who did live here, do you know where she moved to?"

He watches me questioningly, then chooses his words carefully. "It's my understanding she relocated downstate to be closer to her brother."

"Oh," is all I can say as I feel the gap in my friendship rip wider. She's never been very close with her brother, but she chose the week I move home to leave without bothering to tell me. There was never any mention that she was moving. Ever. Even with how scattered I've been, that's something I would have remembered. "Well, thank you. It was very nice to meet you."

I turn to walk back down the stairs, intent on finding my brother so I can crash on his couch for a few hours, when Brian calls out, "I see you have out of state plates. Any chance you're looking for a place to live?" I turn my head and look at him over my shoulder before cocking an eyebrow and gazing up at the large Victorian-era house. He can't possibly think I want to rent here? "I know," he says, noticing me scanning the house. "This place is huge for one person, but there are some apartments available in town. Here's my card. If you're interested in checking them out, stop by the coffeeshop and I'll give you the tour."

Taking the card between my middle and forefinger, I make the decision to take him up on his offer. Anything would be better than living on Fisher's couch for the foreseeable future.

Chapter Seven

Tommy

Make the coffee. Check the oven. Email a press release.

A week ago, I started working mostly out of the back of the coffeehouse again. My office is thirty-seven feet away, if I could walk through walls, and I don't want to go over there. I even hung a sign on the door saying I was at the coffeehouse in case, by chance, someone dropped by. Steph is there in the afternoon usually, so it's not as though the business is totally abandoned. Plus, Brian is in need of more hands on deck and until he finds reliable help, I'm it. That's why I moved up here in the first place — to help him and his best friend, Greg, with the coffeehouse. My own business was a small afterthought.

I swivel in Brian's office chair to find him leaning against the doorframe. Sitting back, I try to prepare for another one of his big brother speeches — "You need to stop doing this to yourself. She's not the one for you. You knew she was leaving."

It doesn't come though.

"I met the girl of your dreams this morning," he says instead.

I narrow my eyes at him. "Have you been huffing paint fumes?"

He laughs, shakes his head, and says, "She's new in town. I think. Her car had California plates and I'm showing her the apartments next door this afternoon."

"You didn't answer my question. I know you're helping Sutton's parents get the house ready to rent out again, so if you're feeling a little loopy from painting that tiny bathroom over there, I will not judge you," I say, placing a hand on my chest. "Cross my heart, Bri."

He ignores me and continues, saying, "She's probably five-seven, dark brown hair, I'm pretty sure her eyes were green. What? Why are you looking at me like that?"

I reach for my coffee mug, stand up, and push past him. "You're incredible."

"Why, thank you, I do like to think so," he replies, missing the sarcasm in my voice.

"Brian, she just left. No, I wasn't head-over-heels in love with the woman, but I did care about her and that baby," I say. Pouring another cup of coffee and grabbing a muffin from the display, I head back to his office. "Give me a little time before you sign me up for the dating service, will ya?"

"But —"

"Back off, or I'm telling Mama you won't quit."

He holds his hands up in surrender. It never fails he'll leave things be when I threaten to bring Mama into the conversation.

Chapter Eight

Sutton

"You moved. You forgot to tell me that was happening."

Her message doesn't surprise me. What does is the lack of hysteria, her calm tone, the way she says it like she nearly expected it.

"I met a guy named Brian at the house when I stopped. He said you were going downstate to be closer to Rick, which was weird since you've always been emotionally detached from him."

The pause is deliberate. I hear her groan and swear under her breath. I deserve that, though, because she's right. I've never run to my brother for anything.

"Call me back, okay? This me calling you and you giving up on our friendship for whatever reason is really starting to take its toll. I don't know what I did, Sutton. Maybe it's something I didn't do. You haven't told me and I'm at a loss. Call me."

I'll call her. Just not today, I say to myself, placing my phone in my purse.

"Sutton?" I hear the nurse say my name from the door as Silas squeezes my left hand and Daphne takes my right.

"Are you sure you want me to come back with you and Daphne?" Silas questions.

"Absolutely. This is your baby, too," I say, as they help me to my feet.

I didn't plan to agree to an open adoption, but there was something striking about this couple. They're best friends, they welcomed me with open arms after I chose them and agreed to the terms of the adoption, and every interaction with them since our first has been beautiful. I didn't tell Tommy the details. They don't concern him. I have no intention of bringing him back into my life as more than a guy I once dated, so he has no need to know.

I won't return calls to Jacey until after the baby is born. It'll be easier to talk to her when he's not part of me in so many ways. I'll call her in a few weeks.

Daphne wraps her arm around my waist as we walk toward the door separating the waiting area from exam rooms, leaning in briefly to remind me, "He's all of ours, Sutton. We're so happy to have you as part of our family."

Putting him up for adoption is easier. Isn't it?

M.L. Pennock

Chapter Nine

Tommy: Eight months later

I stand up at my seat, reach across the table to take her hand in mine, and smile a thousand watt — nearly panty-melting — grin.

Mama raised a gentleman. Just ask anyone who knows me or my brother. We are gentlemen and we pride ourselves on holding doors open for the gentler sex. That sounds really bad. Let me rephrase that. It's not that women need men to hold open doors and help them out of cars — my last roommate would have castrated me if she'd ever heard me refer to her as the "gentler sex" because, frankly, Steph is one tough cookie — but I like to think that my southern ways are a sweet change of pace for the women up here. Too many of them that I've met have gotten used to being used and tossed away, like plastic silverware you find in the trash after the county fair.

Her firm grip is a touch unsettling, like she's challenging me to an arm wrestling competition instead of giving me the opportunity to buy her a nice steak and a few beers. It catches me off guard, as does the flaming red hair. Her profile picture was the same face but her soft features were surrounded by a mane of blonde hair, not a crimson pixie cut.

Instead of acting offended by the unannounced hair change and Hulk handshake, I simply make a note that this is one profile I might not explore for a second date. "It's nice to meet you, Lena. Were you able to find the restaurant without much trouble?" I question, my accent heavy from nerves and, perhaps, a tinge of fear.

"You chose a place in the middle of nowhere. I'm lucky my GPS knew where it was and that I had enough gas to get here," she deadpans, rolling her eyes at me while spreading the nicely pressed cloth napkin in her lap. There's no doubt in my mind that she's serious. "Do they even serve bottled wine in this dump or does it all come in a box?"

Suddenly, I'm not feeling so gentlemanly. In fact, I almost don't give a shit if I offend this woman. Inconspicuously, I lift my hand as though I'm itching my temple, alerting the waitress that it's time she brings me another bottle of beer. The young brunette arrives with another drink just as my date begins a revival rant about how long her drive was. And she doesn't stop talking. Not when food arrives and she picks at it. Not when there's food in her mouth and I get a glimpse of her tonsils. Not even when I attempt to interject with my own thoughts.

Her profile never alluded to her narcissism. This is a nightmare. I just keep nodding my head like I'm listening. I'm trying to listen, but her voice is just ... I think she just started talking about her ex-boyfriend. She's actually comparing me to her ex right now. How is this my life?

"And he used to take me to all these fancy restaurants, not a hole like this. Did you know ..." *No. No, I didn't know Al Capone started one of the first soup kitchens or that it was during the Great Depression*, I wonder as she continues talking. "I mean, what's a man like him doing helping people? And soup kitchens? Gross. Like they couldn't have cooked for themselves, but still I imagine it was something like this place. Are you sure the health department has inspected the kitchen here recently? Excuse me a minute. I need to use the restroom."

"It's out by the entrance, to your left," I say, standing briefly and holding my tie to my shirt so it doesn't fall into my mutilated, half-eaten porterhouse steak. As soon as she's out of sight, I pull at the knot at my neck to loosen the fabric and push my hand up through my blonde hair. It's longer on top than I'm used to, but it gives me something to pull on in frustration. I'm frustrated.

"She's a fun one," the husky voice behind me says quietly. "You'll have to bring me up to speed on how you found her after she leaves."

Chuckling, I lace my fingers behind my neck and, dropping my head back, catch her eye. "What makes you think I won't be leaving with her?"

"Oh, please, Tommy. I've been watching this whole thing play out all night. You're going to walk her to her car, tell her you had a nice evening, that you'll call her — but you won't — and send her back to her rich bitch neighborhood. Or hell. Whichever one she came from." The teasing tone draws a grin from me, breaking my somber mood. She's right. She's watched this happen time and again, so why wouldn't she know how this one will end, too?

The sigh escapes me as Lena strolls around the corner and Jacelyn goes back to being our waitress. Setting the guest check holder on the table before walking away, she says the customary, "I'll take this when you're ready," while clearing plates. She gives me an ego boosting wink before turning and heading back to the kitchen.

"Well, well. Seems I'm not the only one into blondes," Lena huffs out, her eyes trailing after Jacey's hourglass figure. Reaching across the table, she traces her finger possessively over the backs of my knuckles. It would be a turn on if the rest of her wasn't such a turn off. "Hurry and pay so we can get out of here. She's been eye fucking you all night and she needs to know you're mine."

I feel my eyebrow raise quizzically and unintentionally. Does she really think I'm going to go home with her? She can't. This has been the worst date in the history of first dates.

"Uh, yeah. Let me take this out to the bar while you get your jacket," I say, stunned still that she's assuming I want to sleep with her. She licks her bottom lip in a manner I believe was meant to be seductive, but it's not. She's not. Grabbing the bill from the table, I stand and make a beeline for the bar where I know Jacey will be waiting. She's always waiting for me and as soon as she comes into view I feel relief.

"Save me," I mouth as I step up to the bar. "Please."

"But, don't you want to see how much saliva you can swap with Red?" she whispers back, a coy smile playing on her lips as she reaches for my credit card. "It could be a fun night of trying not to contract a slew of venereal diseases."

She swipes my card, I sign my name, ask her to pull a fresh beer from the cooler for me and head back to my torturer.

Date. I meant date.

"You ready?" I question from behind Lena as she stands at the coat closet. She hands me her jacket and autopilot turns on as I help her slip her arms into it. I hold the door open for her. I walk her to her car. She paws at my shirt, tugging on my tie, and says there's a motel a mile up the road that she remembers passing on her way to dinner. I should meet her there. I decline and her face contorts like she's just bitten into a sour apple.

"I'm sure there's someone out there you're perfect for, but it's not me. There's no chemistry here," I wave my hand in the space between us. "But, hey, it was nice to meet you and thank you for letting me buy you dinner."

It's the first time all night she's been silent longer than the time needed to take a breath between complaints. Not sure what else to do, I hold my hand out for her to shake and she looks down at it, confused.

"You ... don't want to sleep with me?"

"Nope."

"Why the hell not?" Her anger makes me laugh, but that must not have been the reaction she expected. I have to duck out of the way when her perfectly manicured hand attempts to make contact with my five o'clock shadow.

Pushing my hands deeper into my trouser pockets, I remain composed and remind myself I was raised a gentleman. "For starters, doing something like that. But mostly it was the chewing with your mouth open, talking incessantly about yourself, and your shitty attitude about anything and everything. All of that? It's a turn off. At least for me it is. Maybe someone who just wants arm candy would be a better suitor for you, but I'm not that guy." I speak slowly and deliberately hoping I won't have to repeat myself. Letting her digest my words, I nod once in her direction before continuing. "So, have a good night, Lena. Drive safely."

Strolling back to the building, I hear her cuss at me as she climbs into her way too nice car and slams the door. The engine purrs to life. She hits the gas forcefully and the squeal of the tires is cringe worthy. I reach the door to the restaurant and turn to watch as she whips out into traffic, cutting off cars in the oncoming lanes. Horns blare as she speeds away after nearly causing a three-car accident.

I don't think she understands the concept of "drive safely."

~*~*~*~

"Nothing ever goes as planned, Jacey. I should be used to that by now considering every plan I've recently made has been obliterated beyond belief." I attempt to make an explosion sound and do something ridiculous with my hands, but all I get from her is a half-smile when I want her to double over with laughter. I need to feel useful. Her whole smile would make me feel useful.

"Aw, Tommy, don't look at it like that. She could have been the girl of your dreams. Take away the wrong color hair, the horrendous attitude, the bad manners ..."

Looking up into her innocent face while I peel the label from my beer, I raise an eyebrow and wonder where she was planning to go with that line of thinking. And I wonder why she's working at a bar. Even more than that, I'm curious why she's single. Girls like Jacelyn don't stay single forever.

"Why haven't we ever gone out?" The words are out of my mouth and I can't grab them back. I feel the shock making its way across my features and press my lips into a thin line, holding my breath while hoping she doesn't take me seriously despite just how serious I am. I've been wondering it for months now. The first time I saw her at the coffeehouse, I knew she was the girl Brian talked about in April, but I didn't tell him I felt anything toward her aside from thinking she's a nice woman who orders fancy drinks I need to Google. Inside, though? There are butterflies and I'm dying over the fact I keep going on these horrible dates instead of trying to date Jacelyn. Now, because of my stupid mouth, I'll find out why we haven't taken the step from budding friendship to blossoming … more than friends.

"I'm more than you can handle, that's why." But she winks. "Nah, actually, it's probably because I see the types of girls you do take out and I'm nothing like them."

Pulling at the label a little more, I contemplate her words and how correct they are. Jacelyn Crocker is nothing like the girls I seem to attract. She's quick-witted and fun-loving. She likes intellectual conversation. She's interested in me for me, not what I can offer.

Taking another quick sip of my lukewarm beer, "Jace, I don't know what I'm doing. I've got this great little business that Steph and I have built from the ground up over the last couple years. I had a girl, a dream, the picket fence life started. Now?"

Why did I just go there? I haven't talked about Sutton in weeks. I'm past the relationship we had; the hurt is still a little raw, but vastly diminished compared to where I was eight months ago. The healing happened even faster after meeting Jacey and building a friendship with her.

She shrugs and continues wiping water from the clean glass in her hand. She searches my eyes from across the bar before she speaks, because she speaks her mind.

"Now? You just keep searching, Tom. She's out there. Will you find her using that handy dandy search engine dating thingamajigger? Probably not. Those things aren't designed to help you find your soulmate as much as they are to help you get laid."

"Please, tell me how you really feel about online dating," I scoff.

"It's how I met my husband," and my jaw practically comes unhinged. When she catches my expression, I gleefully watch her roll her eyes. "*Ex*-husband. He kept his crazy hidden long enough to wipe out the savings account. After that? I swore I'd never date someone again based solely on a profile picture."

Draining my beer and setting the bottle back on the bar, I look at her again while shaking my head. A smile creeps across my lips, chiseling away to find the hideaway dimple in my left cheek. My southern drawl comes out as thick as honey as I say, "I can't believe Miss Jacey was married. Or that you kept it from me this long."

"Yeah, well, believe it and forget about it. It was a long time ago. All I'm saying is not everyone on those sites is actually looking for love. Stop trying to find it there. Obviously, it hasn't worked out so far. How long has it been?"

Too long, at least that's how it feels. Steph's husband Max, who is one of my closest friends, and Brian convinced me to set up a dating profile six months after she left. They thought it would help me get over losing her. I was already "getting over" Sutton, but since I was once again the only single man in our entourage I allowed them to live vicariously through me. It's been nothing short of torture, especially since I see Jacey's face fall just a bit every time I come in with one. But I come here because I'm comfortable here and, if I'm being honest, because I know she'll give me her opinion. Her opinion usually consists of not liking my dates for one reason or another, and I secretly enjoy that she doesn't care for them.

"Eight months since she left. Two months doing this meet-and-greet bullshit with random women." I stare down at my fingers, laced together. My thumbs caress one another because I don't know what to do with my hands. "I don't want you going into counselor mode, though. It's safe enough to say it's been a pretty rough twelve or so months. What time are you done tonight?"

"I close tonight, so not for a few hours. You coming in tomorrow with clients?"

"Are you keeping track of my schedule?"

"Maybe. Are you worried I'll embarrass you?"

"Slightly. You worried I'll grab your ass in front of a full dining room again?"

"Nope, but I often wonder when you're going to do it for real instead of for the shock factor."

I marinate in the thought. Roll around in it for a solid minute even. She's either really good at this game we play or she's actually starting to flirt with me in earnest and I'm not quite sure which one it is. I slide from the stool I've perched myself on. Grabbing my tie from the counter and hanging it in place around my neck, I give the girl behind the bar half a smile.

Tipping my head in her direction, I lower my voice and say, "Goodnight, Miss Jacey."

A sincere blush touches the tops of her cheeks as she flips the towel over her right shoulder and shyly smiles. "Goodnight, Thomas Stratford."

Chapter Ten

Jacelyn

The first time I met Tommy, I had moved into the apartment a few weeks prior and was quickly becoming a regular downstairs at the Jumping Bean. I walked in and ordered my usual, but in my half-awake state didn't realize the muscular, blonde-haired, blue-eyed, dimple-cheeked man staring at me with a cocky grin wasn't my landlord-slash-caffeine-dealer.

Brian attempted to give me a job on top of a place to live because his brother was getting busier with his own business and able to work the coffeehouse less and less, but I kindly turned down the offer since I already had something lined up with Fisher. Tommy seemed to have a hard time admitting he needed to pull back from the coffeehouse and, instead of using his own office next door, worked for his marketing clients between customers at the Bean.

I'm pretty sure I heard angels sing the moment I came face-to-face with Tommy Stratford. There wasn't a whole lot going on in my life that was worth laughing about, but he pulled genuine glee from me when he plucked his phone from his pocket, leaned across the counter, and proceeded to search for a recipe for my drink like he'd never heard of it before.

He's the stuff of romance novels, so I was floored when he asked tonight why we've never dated. The answer is so much more complicated than me being "more than he can handle." Wouldn't it be easier if it was simply because I'm not his type? Except every time he looks at me, I feel like I am his type and he's the one who doesn't realize it. He has a very obvious thing for blondes. However, I am not a blonde, so I'm fucked in the heroine category. That won't ever stop me from hoping he changes his mind about brown-haired women, though.

I sigh a little too loudly and then hear my brother clear his throat as if to tell me he heard that.

"He's the kind of man who will flirt with your grandma to make her smile after a bad day, and it works," Fisher says from across the room. "That's just how he is."

"Thank you, Fish. I wasn't already feeling like the 'always a bridesmaid' type. I'm glad you cleared this up," I throw in his face.

"I didn't mean it that way. I meant, he likes to make people happy. He likes seeing you happy, that's for sure. Any idea why he keeps bringing his dates here? Other than to flaunt his conquests in your face, that is," he jabs.

I shrug, because I don't have an answer. "Maybe because he likes the food. The steak looked choice tonight."

Without hesitation, my brother leaves my lack of love life alone and starts talking about changing meat suppliers. It's very much like most conversations I've had with Sutton since she started returning my calls again. Five minutes of me telling her I'm doing well and forty-five of her talking about her apartment, the new bookstore, and how nice it is to finally have a relationship with her brother and his family.

As he continues talking about visiting organic beef farms, I wipe down my bar and cash out the drawer while wondering how I went so wrong with my life. I must have screwed something up to wind up back home talking about slaughterhouses and longnecks in the middle of the night with Fisher.

Chapter Eleven

Tommy

I pull up in front of the house and park. I sit with the engine idling as I watch the darkened windows where once there was a smiling blonde-haired girl. Once upon a time, she had a growing belly and widening hips.

Then it was ripped away. By her. She tore it away from me.

A knock at the driver side window pulls me from my thoughts — thoughts I wouldn't even be having if I hadn't put myself in this mental space when I was talking to Jacelyn earlier. The conversation has brought back some of my bitterness about my last relationship, but I know sitting in front of the house won't exorcise the lingering anger. It'll go the rest of the way on its own. I glance out, seeing just a dark uniform from waist to chest and take a deep breath before rolling the window down. It's a hand crank. I have plenty of time to calm my nerves, though I have nothing to be nervous about even as I watch his hand come to rest on the butt of his sidearm.

Slowly, I lean over the passenger seat, reaching for the registration, while pulling my wallet from the back pocket of my pants with the other hand.

"Was I doing something wrong, officer?" I question as I move to sit upright again.

"I don't know, T. Were you?" His face is right next to mine and startles me before I realize it's Max propped up in my window. "Creeper. What are you doing out here? Put your registration away. I'm not on duty."

I drop my head against the back of the seat and close my eyes. "Fucker."

"Yup. Turn her off and come on in."

~*~*~*~

"Again, Tommy? You've got to let. Her. Go. Let her go," she says. "She let you go a long time ago, so stop doing this to yourself."

I stare at Steph standing in her cozy, comfortable kitchen, my heart breaking open just one more time because she has what we didn't. I'm not missing something I did have, but rather the idea of what I could have had. I could have had a family.

"It wasn't your fault," Max chimes in.

Lifting my cup of coffee, I pause just before it reaches my lips. "I know."

I haven't even talked to Sutton since she left and it's not for lack of trying. Time and again I've called, messaged, tried to bribe her mom for details while I'm at the bookshop on business. Nothing. Not even so much as a, "She's doing well." My romantic feelings for Sutton may have waned, but, as a human and a friend, I'm concerned about her and want to make sure she's doing well.

"But, really, Tommy, it wasn't your fault. You tried to hold on. She's the one who didn't," Steph continues, the words coming out quickly as though she's rehearsed for this exact confrontation and just wants to be done with it.

"I know."

I haven't heard this speech in several weeks. They don't realize I haven't pined over Sutton in months. Tonight, is merely the result of a lot of emotions with no outlet.

"But, T ...," Max's voice trails off and I catch him looking out the kitchen window to the house next door. The house with windows black as the night. The house empty and void of happiness. It's been vacant since she left. He sighs, because he knows I know and he's getting tired of talking about it. Again. It always sneaks into the conversation somehow and I need it to stop. I'm rarely even the one sneaking it in.

"I went on a date tonight," I say nonchalantly, catching the hopeful look in Steph's eyes. I'm going to squash that hope. "It was shitty and horrible and this woman was the antithesis of everything I want in a partner." She looks crestfallen. Hope officially squashed and because I need just a tiny amount of humor, I'm going to make it awkward. "Instead of sucking it up, enjoying my sexy bachelor status, and leaving her sated and satisfied in some swanky hotel in the middle of the night, I had one of my post-date powwows with Jacey and then parked my car in front of Sutton's house wondering how I ended up there. I don't even know how I got there."

But I went on a date. I got myself back out there, and that's the important part. Two months running and I'm starting to tire from the games women play, though. It's exhausting. This is why it was easy to almost fall in love with Steph when we lived together right after I moved up here. She was there and I got to knew her quirks. There were no games once she laid out the ground rules. Max was a much better choice for her anyway – her nightmares about a past abusive relationship and his demons that followed him from his first marriage created this amazingly strong couple whose relationship I look up to and respect like I do Brian and Stella's and my parent's. They have the kind of love I want.

"I'm glad you were able to talk about your crappy date with Jacey. She's a good friend," Steph says, touching my forearm gently, as though it may break if she presses too firmly. Looking me in the eyes, she says, "You don't always end up in front of Sutton's. Remember that. Someday you won't at all. It'll happen. Tonight was just a glitch, right?"

Her words are encouraging, soft and kind, but her eyes hold nothing back. She's frustrated with the thought I haven't fully moved on and would much rather slap me senseless. Draining what's left of my coffee, I nod my head. I'm going to try to believe her. Eventually, she'll see I've quietly been moving on for a while.

"I know."

~*~*~*~

"Mama?" I shouldn't call so late. She's going to think I'm in jail or the hospital or …

"What happened, Tommy? Are you alright?" she asks. I hear the sleep still heavy on her voice. "If you need bail money, I'll have to wake your father."

I sit in the dining room chair, my elbows on my knees, one hand with the phone to my ear while the other cradles my forehead. "No, Mama, it's nothing like that."

"Girl trouble?"

The emotion wells up and catches in my throat. I have trouble fighting it back down where it belongs and instead it erupts.

"Why wasn't I good enough, Ma? I could have loved her, given her a good life, raised him like my own …," I let my voice trail off as I press the palm of my hand against my eye. If I hold it there long enough, maybe the tears will just disappear. I wanted so badly to be a dad.

In the distance, I hear the bed creak, she mumbles something to my dad, and then the line is quiet for a beat. "Thomas. Sweet, sweet Thomas," she whispers. "You will find someone who deserves all of that with you. I'm not saying Sutton couldn't have been 'the one,' but, baby, she wasn't the one."

But, what if … I try to argue. She stops me again.

"What if she had stayed? What if she decided to keep the baby? What if you finally fell in love with her? Tommy … what if this is exactly what was meant to happen? Don't mess with fate. You can't force yourself to fall in love and you can't force others to do the same for you," she says.

"What do I do now, Mama?"

"Now? You just keep searching, Tom." Her words echo in my ears. Jacey said the same exact thing earlier and it strikes me as odd that Mama would use identical phrasing. She rarely calls me Tom. But that's not the uncanny part — Mama has always been the one to tell me to stop looking for love; it's supposed to find me when I'm ready for it. "You'll find her, sweetie. For all you know, she's right in front of you."

Chapter Twelve

Jacelyn

"He looked ... sad." What else am I supposed to tell her? Every week it's the same conversation. She calls on my day off if I don't call her first and we exchange town gossip. Things feel like they're almost back to normal. Except for when she wants to talk about him. "He was having a rough night."

Sutton and I tiptoe around the same topic at the beginning of most of our conversations. She asks questions that test the limits of my newfound friendship with Tommy and acts like it won't tear me apart to be in the middle. I hate the middle. It's always riddled with tension and leaves a bad taste in my mouth.

"Was he there with clients?" She always asks, and I just don't want to keep answering. It's not my place to tell her his every move, but this time her voice conveys her weakness. She's worried he wasn't there on business and I can't tell her. I can't tell her again that he's attempting to move forward from the disaster she left behind. I can't even tell her he's never actually spoken her name to me, or that he has no idea I know her.

"I think, if you really wanted to know that, you would just come back and find out for yourself."

The line goes quiet. There's a slight crackle in the air between my apartment in Brockport and her apartment in Nyack. I lick the peanut butter from the spoon in my right hand and flop down into the oversized armchair I found last week at an estate sale. I look around my living space and for a brief moment feel like it's starting to come together. By Christmas it might feel like home.

The sigh I release is so forceful the rush of it leaving my lungs blows the hair out of my face, only for the strands to land in the peanut butter I'm coveting. It's my stress food and now it's in my hair, which makes me even more stressed. I'm a mess.

"I don't want to know."

"You're a shitty liar," I accuse while attempting to wipe my hair clean.

Quietly she begs for me to answer, "Was she pretty? Did she treat him well?"

Mumbling through the paste in my mouth I remind her, "I won't do this with you. You say he crushed your heart, so just stop already. There's no point in playing this game." She drops the conversation and gives up trying to pry information from me until next time. We revert to safe subjects like the bar business, if I've killed the plants she left at the bookstore with notes indicating they were for me, and if the store is still standing with her mother at the helm.

The bar is fine. I'm everyone's therapist.

The plants are fine. I'll tell them she said hello.

The bookstore is doing great. I leave out the part about Tommy trying to bribe her mom. His bartering system almost worked once — free marketing for six months in exchange for unlimited information about Sutton and her new life without him. Her mom told me all of it when I stopped in a few months ago to see what she had for art books. It was weird to hear about him asking for info. For a guy who supposedly did the heartbreaking, Sutton's mom made it sound like he still had a vested interest in her wellbeing.

Some things just don't add up with the two of them.

"How's the new store?" I attempt to keep the momentum of our conversation going, but a lack of caffeine drags a yawn from me despite it being only mid-morning.

"New store is good. Business has been good down here, it's just different. It's not home, but it can work," she says warily. "Look, I don't want to keep you. I know it's your day off and you probably have a list of things you want to accomplish. I'm at the shop, anyway, trying to get caught up and someone just came in, so I should let you go."

I heard the clang of the bell through the phone before she confessed to being at work. She doesn't have to tell me she's burying herself in row upon row of *New York Times Bestsellers* while we talk, but she seems to forget I know her as well as I do and all too often states the obvious.

"Go sell books. Text me later."

"Of course."

She makes a sound like she's blowing me a kiss through the phone and I laugh as we hang up. Then, the guilt of keeping my best friend a secret from the guy I'm trying not to fall for settles deep in my gut.

~*~*~*~

Talk to Sutton, go grocery shopping, start laundry while putting groceries away, prep quick meals for the next several days, eat a salad for dinner, watch Netflix, go to bed with a book.

It's comfortable.

It's always the same.

It's lonely.

Today I changed the routine just enough to not feel like an old lady and now have some color in my hair. No one can see it unless I wear my hair up, but I know it's there.

My phone chimes as I'm climbing into bed.

TStratford: I really need to know ... why haven't we ever gone out?

I smile as I read the message but know I need to put up that wall. He was with her first and he's potentially still hung up on her. I can't compete with my best friend and I don't want to just be a replacement.

The middle. It's turning into high school all over again and I'm the only one who realizes it.

Sitting cross-legged on the bed, I set the phone down in front of me and stare at it, longing for the words to come to me. Contemplating the answer I'll give him this time, I push my hands up into my hair, hold it at the nape of my neck, and consider not texting him back.

TStratford: Is it because I'm too tall? Some women have trouble dating tall men.

Where does he come up with this nonsense?

TStratford: If it's my height that has you worried, I'll just buy you hooker boots. Then you can be tall like me.

I finish reading the message as his face lights up the screen. My laughter is lighthearted and honest as the call connects. He has a way of making mundane amazing. Today suddenly feels a little amazing.

"So, you want the hooker boots?"

"What the hell are hooker boots?"

"You know. The ones Julia Roberts wears in *Pretty Women*."

I smile on a sigh. Oh, *those* boots. The line is quiet and I wonder why he called.

"It isn't because you're too tall." My voice comes out shy. That's not at all as I intended. I don't want to have feelings for this man. I don't want this man to have feelings for me.

"I know it isn't. But there's a reason, and I don't think it's because you have an ex-husband or you work strange hours," he drawls into my ear and I feel a blush tear through me all the way to my toes. "I'll figure it out, Jacey Crocker. If it was something simple you would have told me by now. I reckon it's far from simple."

My throat feels suddenly dry and I try to swallow, but it's like choking down a mouthful of dirt. I should tell him.

Perhaps the biggest problem is, I didn't know who Tommy was when I met him. At the time, he was just a beautiful man who occasionally made my coffee and came into the restaurant frequently, each time with someone different. It was always a business matter. I paid no more attention to him than I did the people he was working for and with. They were tips and a paycheck while I put my career on hold and tried to get my bearings back working at the family business. Not to mention, this time I'm back also as co-owner with my brother, though that hasn't really been made public yet. Never once did I make the connection that "Thomas Stratford" on the credit card was "Tommy," impregnator and former love interest of my best friend. Their relationship was short-lived to the point Sutton never even sent me pictures of him. It wasn't until I boldly mentioned to Sutton that I had noticed a very handsome blonde-haired regular patron that I connected the dots.

I mean, I kind of had to put a lid on any sort of feelings I was developing for the Flirt Master after Sutton broke down weeping in my ear when we realized I was talking about *the* Tommy. There was no way I could water and fertilize that seed of hope once Sutton knew he was using my barroom as a base of operations for all of his Rochester-area clients.

I feel like I'm keeping a dirty little secret by not telling him about my connection to Sutton, but I don't want to shatter and knowing how he might react would break me. I'm fragile right now and I'm trying to be gentle with myself. It's been an extremely long time since I felt comfortable around a man, but it has been so easy to fall comfortably into him and his life, even if just as a friend. The reluctance to share the truth with him is greater than the need to tell him I know Sutton.

Not just know her. She was like a sister to me growing up.

Our friendship has always seemed unique compared to other girls we grew up with. If I wanted to pursue something with her ex, I would normally just tell her how I feel and we could have an adult conversation about it over a couple beers and pizza if we were in the same zip code. Growing up, that was never a problem. She didn't date anyone who was my type, but the talk about dating each other's former boyfriends still happened so at least we had some ground rules. For others, it's taboo and written down in the friend handbook from the word "go" with a big red circle and slash through it — no dating your friend's ex, no exceptions.

Their relationship was more than just a few dates, though. They went from zero to "we're living together on the weekend and having a baby" pretty quickly. She had no choice but to tell me how serious things had become. After all, when you're sounding like a sick cat on the phone with someone for weeks on end, you can't keep a lie going and say it's the flu every time.

It's never the flu.

So now, I err on the side of caution.

"It is far from simple, you're right about that, Tommy. For now, I just want to be your friend and friendly neighborhood bartender who also vets your dates for any obvious signs of future stalking," I finally say, and hate myself for not taking what I want. Once again, I'm putting someone else's feelings above my happiness.

I bite my lip and then press my teeth in harder, confident it's the only thing that keeps me from saying something stupid. Something like, "If you'd kept your sperm where they belong, we could date," or, "I'm not blonde. You need to get your eyes checked." But I can't hurt him like that. After all, he's Tommy and, despite Sutton's claims that he's the heartbreaker, I've learned through the grapevine that he's had his heart stomped on time and again. I won't be another in a long line of women to supposedly kick him when he's down.

"You're certain it's not because I'm too tall?" he questions again, hopeful.

"I wish that's all it was," I respond, praying he doesn't hear the hint of agony in my voice.

M.L. Pennock

Chapter Thirteen

Tommy

"I should just cancel. I can't keep doing this."

"No. You, sir, need to go out and take one for the team. This one was Max's pick. You need to at least give her a chance," Brian says as he manhandles the collar on my dress shirt. "Fix your tie. And your hair."

"Damn, Bri. You're starting to sound like Mama." But instead of arguing, he flashes me a smile and watches as I fix my tie and check my hair in the mirror next to the stairs. Glancing up the steps, I nonchalantly mention, "I've been thinking of putting out an ad for a roommate. I'm not home a lot, and it would be nice to have someone to help me with the mortgage."

When Steph moved out because she was marrying Max, I was fine with living alone. I'd been on my own for weeks anyway because she was always at his house. It wasn't a huge deal since I could always count on her to come home for clothes or to check the answering machine or throw out the outdated milk.

Then Sutton was here. We sort of lived between my house and hers depending on what was going on that day. Despite the fact we were "living together," we weren't actually sharing an address. I still got my mail here; hers was delivered a few blocks away. She had a drawer in my dresser. I carried an extra toothbrush in my car. She wasn't even close to fully moved in, but it was enough for the house to not feel empty all the time.

But now it's so quiet and lonely that I'm purposely leaving the television or radio on just for some noise, something to break up the silence. I even started burning candles when I am home because the air is stale without the scent of her shampoo or perfume hanging in every room. I used to rag on Brian and Max about handing over their man cards because of how they were changing for Stella and Steph, but here I am lighting candles at midnight and eating ice cream from the carton while watching Lifetime movies.

Hypothetically.

I'm not actually watching Lifetime.

It's the Hallmark Channel. The fucking *Hallmark Channel*. Those movies are way better, especially at Christmas.

I sigh at my reflection as I consider how very sad I would sound if I opened my mouth and told my brother that's how I usually spend my Sunday nights.

But, I'm not exactly missing her. What I'm experiencing is loneliness. That's what Mama says this is. I'm lonely.

"Male or female?"

"Huh?" I question, raising my eyebrow in suspicion.

"The roommate you're looking for — male or female?" he repeats.

"Employed. I just need someone who can pay rent."

~*~*~*~

I order my usual — the porterhouse steak, baked potato, side salad with honey mustard dressing, and a bottle of Sam Adams. The size of the steak guarantees I'll have leftovers to take home for breakfast. It also helps me weed out the women who are more worried about their waistline than our conversation, vegetarians who lie on their profiles and during the conversations prior to "the date," and women who simply do not know food.

She orders ... not steak. *Well, this just isn't going to end well, now is it*, I judge silently.

It's not that I have anything against vegetarians, because vegetables are amazing and I love them. I just really like a good burger or steak, even properly prepared fish, and I like to share my culinary experiences with people who also enjoy those things. That might be one of the reasons I connect so well with the women in my family. Food is less a social experience and more a spiritual one. We come together in kitchens and dining rooms, those are our gathering areas and where we laugh, talk, yell, argue, and relate to one another.

This girl, she's not looking for a spiritual experience with me. I watch from across the table as she pokes with her fork at the grilled chicken Caesar salad she ordered. Literally pokes at it. My chewing slows as I sit holding my knife in one hand, fork in the other, and I watch as she pushes a piece of chicken through the dressing before carefully cutting a miniscule piece from one end of the tender meat. It's maybe the size of a dime.

A dime!

She lifts the fork to her mouth and takes the bite. Then chews, not just a couple times, though. No. I count. She chews that dime-sized piece of chicken fifteen times.

"What?" her tiny voice breaks my concentration and I swallow the meat I had continued to grind to a pulp between my molars.

"Nothing. It's nothing. So, you work with inner city kids? You mentioned it when we spoke the other day," I say, trying to get my focus off the world's smallest bite of chicken.

"I do. I run the afterschool program. Not nothing, though. You were staring," she says, her voice rising an octave.

I put a normal size piece of food in my mouth, chew while holding her gaze, and once I swallow, I speak. "Why did you say yes to dinner when you don't actually want to eat?"

"I want to eat," she says defensively.

"No, ma'am, no you don't," I say, lowering my voice but feeling bold at the same time. "You want to push food around on your plate and make it look like you ate. Why?"

I pick up my glass of water, eyeing her over the rim as I take a sip, and wonder what the hell is happening to me. I don't get mad at people about their food choices. If she doesn't want to actually eat the food she ordered, why should I care?

That's when I see her standing at the entrance to the dining room. Jacey's watching the entire, awkward interaction with this woman, and I can't tear my eyes away from her. It's the first time I've seen her tonight, and though I've seen her in those jeans a hundred times, I suddenly want to slowly strip them off her. That polo shirt with the restaurant logo embroidered above her left breast would look fantastic tossed over the back of the armchair in my bedroom.

"Meeting new people makes me nervous. I'm actually starving," my date replies, with a quiver in her voice. "My job is stressful, this is the first date I've been on in months, and you make it sound like I'm purposely starving myself."

Giving her my full attention again, I take a really good look at her. "You're, what, twenty-three?" She nods. "You're smart. You're pretty. I imagine you're really great with kids or they wouldn't have you running a program for them." She nods again, but I see the tears making her eyes glisten. I instantly feel like a jerk. "I wasn't trying to imply you're starving yourself. It's just … I like food, and I asked you to dinner so we could have food together and get to know one another."

I glance back over to the doorway, only to see Jacey turn slowly and walk back toward the bar. I can't help but take in the sight of her backside as her figure retreats to the other room. She gave someone else her section tonight and I don't know why. We haven't really spoken much since her day off when I called her at bedtime.

"I promise, I'm not usually an asshole," I admit, and it draws a chuckle from her. Using Max's favorite line, I continue. "Scout's honor. I'm usually a really nice guy. I've just had a difficult few months, so I apologize. How about I tell you something horrible about my life and you return the gesture? Clear the air, so to speak."

She smiles and tilts her head, "Okay. I can do that. Then I'll decide if you're an asshole or just having a bad day."

"Deal." I reach across the table to shake her hand. "Something horrible? I can't remember your name and the only reason I'm using a dating site is because my brother and friend made an account for me." Her eyes widen at the admission, but I'm not done. If I'm going to clear the air, I might as well do a bang-up job at it. "I know. It's an asshole thing to admit on a date, but that's not all. They did it to help me get over a girl, one who thought she was having my baby until our first ultrasound proved there was no possible way the baby was mine."

Her mouth opens but words don't come out. I pick up my beer and take two long sips, feeling the chill and sting of the fluid as it traces its way through my body and hits my stomach. I just told this woman more about my situation than I've shared with anyone outside of immediate family. I haven't even told Jacelyn these details and she's been giving me therapy for the cost of a beer and tip for months now.

"What a horrible thing to do!" She's appalled. Aghast, even. *So am I, girl whose name I can't remember*, I think. "My horrible thing doesn't even come close to yours. How did you know it wasn't your baby?"

This is the question that broke me when Brian and Stella asked it. At this point, though, I've come to terms with it and won't let it twist my heart until it splits open again.

"Babies look more like little babies at twelve or so weeks gestation than at eight weeks." I trail my index finger around the rim of my glass, remembering how a year ago I was exhilarated waiting to see my future son or daughter for the first time. I had started buying all those parenting and dad books, and my Internet browser was nothing but open tabs researching car seats and how to cure morning sickness. "We expected to see a glorified blob, alien-looking thing with a heartbeat, but what we got was a fantastic picture of this perfect little person. A little person I had no part in making."

"That's so sad."

Indeed it is. The ultrasound tech said the measurements and I corrected him, saying she should only be measuring at two months, because that's what eight weeks works out to be, right? I questioned how well he knew how to do his job. It was going to be our first prenatal appointment, so I thought up to that point I knew everything. You know, because I researched it. He redid the measurements just for my sake. I stood by her while we pretended the earth hadn't shaken with the ferocity of that news, like we could ignore the obvious. And we did. At least until we were back in the car after her appointment, an appointment that carried on as normal where she talked about prenatal care and we heard the heartbeat again and we ignored the hell out of the truth.

Back in the car, though? That's when it began to wreck me, rip my heart out, shred the dreams I had of settling down and starting a family because she wasn't the kind of girl to stick with me when she didn't have a reason to. Still, I tried. I wanted it bad enough I was willing to make it work.

"She had just ended a relationship when I met her. The baby is his. She broke up with me soon after we knew the truth and moved downstate right before her due date. She didn't feel right letting me raise another man's child just because he wanted nothing to do with his son, less so when she questioned if she even had feelings for me. Last I knew, she was putting the baby up for adoption."

M.L. Pennock

Chapter Fourteen

Jacelyn

I stand just outside the door, eavesdropping but trying not to, when I overhear the tail end of his confession and feel like I've been punched square in the gut.

Adoption?

I can't breathe as I walk further into the bar, grab my wallet from behind the counter, and make a beeline for the kitchen on the other side of the building. I hurry through the dining room where he sits with his date and focus on the exit. The back door. Outside. I need to get outside. Grabbing the porch railing for support, I dig my cell phone from my back pocket and open the last text message from Sutton.

Me: All these months? Every conversation we've had where you sound exhausted and emotionally obliterated over Tommy?

Me: You should have told me the truth, Sutton. I could have been there for you.

How many lies has she told me? And her mom. I go to the bookstore on occasion and never once has she told me Sutton didn't miscarry. Not once did she mention she has a grandchild other than Rick's kids.

I send the message without thinking. I don't consider the consequences of my rash actions. I don't hesitate. She's my best friend. Instead of being honest with me, telling me she was moving because she likes to run away from her problems, she told me she lost the baby. For months she told me she needed to move on. She told me she couldn't be here near Tommy because it hurt too much. They didn't see eye to eye anymore and she felt he was turning his back on her when she needed him most. Just what did she need from him? She apparently didn't want him to play house with her.

I justified her actions and never once anticipated she was lying to me.

My phone vibrates in my hand minutes later and all the incoming message says is, *Tommy told you?* Followed a short time later by, *I can't talk about this right now.*

Did she think I wouldn't find out? It's a small town. People talk. I can't believe I didn't find out before this with the way some people like to stir shit up. She may have been living in Rochester since we finished high school, but her home has always been here. We have other mutual friends that we both talk to regularly. Did none of them know about this? What about Stella and Steph? The countless times we've all gotten together over the months and never once this came up. I feel like such an outsider still.

I don't calm down and I don't go back to the dining room. Instead I send a text to the rest of the staff letting them know I'm not feeling well and heading out for the night. It's not that I can't physically do my job after those messages between Sutton and me.

It's Tommy. I can't look at him. Looking at him means allowing myself to dream because the things that were holding me back from him aren't even actual issues. Right now, I need to wrap my head around Sutton's lack of honesty. I'm not entirely sure how to handle this situation. If I were a more confrontational person, I would get in my car and drive the five hours from Brockport to Nyack. I would yell at her for feigning concern for him every time we talk. I would tell her she's the reason I haven't attempted to flirt harder and that I haven't gotten laid since California because I don't want just anyone, I want Tommy. I've been denying myself Tommy because of her. Then I would tell her she's a bitch, just to be catty.

It wouldn't solve anything, though. That's never how we've handled our issues and our friendship has somehow lasted nearly thirty years. I hate that I would be willing to destroy three decades of sleepovers and secrets just because I'm mad.

Why am I so mad? Because we tell each other everything. That's why. Because telling your best friend you lost a baby when you actually ran away to put that baby up for adoption is shady and wrong. I'm hurt more than anything and I don't know how to handle hurt.

The last time I physically saw her was when she flew out to California to see me after she left her ex nearly two years ago. He was so forgettable; I can't remember if his name was Steve or John. It was something nondescript. Regardless, she was getting ready to move back to Brockport from Rochester. She'd leased the space for the bookstore the year before and had hardly done anything with it. Steve (or John. Maybe it was Rob? Pretty sure it was Rob.) was doing nothing but taking up space, eating her food, and using her money.

Then she met Tommy, because naturally you choose to pursue the guy who's helping your business grow. His marketing platform and plan for Book Ends must have been enticing.

How could she possibly think I wouldn't find out? I just need her to confirm the truth. It's eating at me already not knowing if she actually put the baby up for adoption. Maybe she lied to me about losing the baby and then lied to him about giving him up for adoption.

Nothing feels right.

I knew something was off about their situation, but nothing could have prepared me for this.

Everything feels like a lie.

I'm having a lot of trouble seeing the good in her right now. I've always preferred to find the good in others, but right now I can't recall a single good thing about Sutton.

I unlock the door to my apartment, unsure how I got from the restaurant to home. My home, my safe place. The day I met Brian, I told him I wanted to see the apartments he had available and when I arrived, I wrote a check for the deposit and first month's rent before he even unlocked the door. The last thing I wanted to do was share living space with my brother. The idea of searching for a place to live was almost as unappealing as splitting chores with Fisher like when we were kids, so it felt like there was a reason I met Brian that afternoon.

I smell the aroma of coffee seeping through the walls from next door and the bass from the band playing. The music isn't very loud, but the walls are thin and a nuance of blues permeates the stairwell and hallway. It's B.B. King mixed with a little Aretha Franklin, a hint of The Rolling Stones, and I remember some of the reasons I loved growing up here. This is a place with soul.

My phone vibrates in my back pocket. Before I look at it, I know.

"Hi, Tommy," I say quietly as the call connects.

"You left. Your new girl doesn't know our routine."

"You were on a date. You should have been paying attention to her," I say, releasing a frustrated sigh. I finish my thought, saying, "Not to me."

Pulling my key from the tumbler lock, I hear the door at street level open. His voice reaches me in stereo as he says, "But I want to pay attention to you."

M.L. Pennock

Chapter Fifteen

Tommy

The phone still up to her ear, Jacelyn turns toward my voice and locks her eyes on me. I make my way up the stairs, taking them two at a time, until I reach her door at the top of the landing. Her hand is poised, ready to turn the knob and get away.

But she doesn't walk through the entrance. She slowly opens the door wide and leans back against the frame, folding her arms across her chest.

"You're supposed to be on a date." But her eyes tell me she's hungry and in need of affection. Her voice makes a sad attempt to hide a pain I can't place. I know I didn't put it there. At least I don't think I did.

"I was. She's young and looking for something I can't give her." I prop myself against the doorframe opposite her. "Besides, she reminds me too much of someone I used to know."

In all the months I've sat and visited with Jacey, I've never once brought myself to say her name. I haven't uttered the name "Sutton" for fear she'd finally cast judgment once she had a name to go with the minimal descriptors I'd given. Blonde hair, petite. I could have been describing half the women in Monroe County, for all she knew, but only one left me feeling devastated.

"She reminds you of ..." Jacey makes an attempt. She's tried before to draw the name from my lips, but I won't crack. This time, though, I get the impression she knows. It's the way she lets the question hang in the air.

Deflect, I tell myself. "So, why did you leave work early?"

She bites the inside of her cheek, pulling the corner of her lip in just enough for me to notice. Then she purses those same lips like she's deep in thought, and I can't help but want to taste them. It isn't heartache twisting in my chest tonight. This time it's need. She needs affection, and I need her. Tonight, Sutton is just a memory. She's not even a memory that hurts. She's becoming just a girl I had feelings for. My past.

Her lips part with her words, glistening in the low light of the hallway, and I almost miss what she says. "I overheard a horrible conversation I didn't like. I needed to get away to think."

My eyes shift and I catch the recognition in her gaze. A conversation. Not just any conversation. A "horrible" one.

I mouth the words. "A horrible one." And then I speak. "That caused you to leave work early?"

"I didn't like the way the story ended."

"I'm sorry. I should have told you everything. It's part of my process, Jace, this whole trying to get over my past by burying it," I say. My drawl sounds a little thicker, my voice a little more gruff. "I didn't want to rehash the past, not with you. I don't care how good a counselor you think you are. I wasn't going to lay it all on you."

She crosses her arms tighter, hugging herself against the truth I'm handing to her on a silver platter. "You could have, you know? You could have told me."

"I know," I say, reaching for her across the threshold. My hand touches her waist, my fingers fitting perfectly against the swell of her hip, and I tug gently. "I know."

She falls away from the wall easily, stepping into my arms. I've never held her like this before. For months, Jacelyn has been standing right in front of me and I've been blind. I've tried to keep myself from having feelings for her, and I can't keep denying myself.

"You're too tall," she says, her tone serious. "Tonight, you're too tall."

She has a way with me and words escape my mouth when I wish they would simply just evaporate.

"Her name is Sutton. She owns the bookstore in town." She tenses against my chest, her hand pressed firmly against my bicep, and I feel her release a breath. It's forced from her as though someone knocked the wind out of her and I look down, watching her face contort in pain. "When I said the other day that things don't go according to plan, I meant it. I was ready to be a dad. She wasn't ready to let me take on that responsibility."

"You don't need to tell me," she says, which leaves me confused.

"You literally just said I could have told you. I'm telling you now," I explain. "You're my friend and I wouldn't mind you being more than that, but not without being honest with you."

Jacey turns her face into my chest, leaning her forehead against my breastbone, as she wraps her fingers around both of my arms. I stand still, my hands resting on her hips, and take a chance — just one quick chance — by pressing my lips into her hair.

"There are things you don't know. Sutton is my best friend." My lips are in her hair and I breathe her in. Not just a little breath. No, it's a deep, replenishing, and renewing breath. But, damn, it hurts, too.

To Cherish

"I'm too tall. You said you wished it was simple. I wish it was, too. I need to go," and I kiss her hair one more time while wondering why I'm walking away when I was finally starting to feel again.

~*~*~*~

No one said a thing as I walked through the coffee house. It's normal for me to walk in at all hours. I'm there all the time. My office is right next door, my brother owns the place, and I help carry the load as much as I can. It's nothing out of the ordinary for me to saunter through on open mic night without saying anything to anyone and hide away in the kitchen.

Tonight, it's different though, and Greg can tell.

I watch him watching me as I work my way through the room. He acknowledges me with a slight nod and brief wave that can't even be counted as a wave before turning his attention back to the teenager belting out gospel like she was made for the church choir.

Pushing through the café doors to the kitchen, I try to steel myself. I encase my heart in iron and pretend not to feel. I've been really good at that for years. I pretended not to feel when Brian became a single dad and Britton's mother decided to confide in me the reasons for leaving my brother and nephew. Emily was sweet, but she gave Bri the impression she was running away from him and the baby. Truthfully, she was running away because she couldn't hurt him knowing the Leukemia she had beaten before meeting him had come back when she was pregnant with Britt and was eating her alive. I kept those secrets from my own blood because I felt like I needed to be loyal to her, because she was dying and needed a friend. That friend happened to be me.

Then I pretended for months that I didn't have feelings for Stephanie even though we'd been thrown together. We were shoved into a house where I'm sure she felt I was more her warden than her friend at first, when all I was trying to do was keep her safe, keep her from harming herself by diving headfirst into a bottle every night. It was so easy to start falling in love with her, but she needed Max, and Steph finding Max meant more loneliness for me.

I found Sutton and for once I was falling for someone who didn't need to be saved.

Turns out I was the one needing salvation.

I didn't pretend I was okay. I got sad and angry. What's worse than finding out your girlfriend isn't pregnant with your baby and is leaving you regardless of how you feel? Your best female friend being pregnant at the same time. That was the hardest part. Steph and Max were expecting at the same time Sutton was and we were all kind of giddy over the prospect of raising these tiny versions of ourselves together, especially since Sutton was living next door to Max. They have their little person, Max has this perfect son, and I have nobody.

Again.

"Okay, what happened? You were supposed to be on a date tonight," Greg asks as he rests his arms over the café doors and stares at me expectantly.

"I did. She was young and unsure of herself. She reminded me too much of Sutton, if I'm being honest with myself." There, I said the whole thing out loud. What's-her-name reminded me of Sutton. "Jacey left work early so I ended my date early and came to track her down. I was worried."

How have I missed that she's Sutton's best friend?

I pull my phone from my pocket and open the last message from Jacelyn. I'm treating her being Sutton's best friend as something horrible, and it isn't. Horrible things happen every day. This is not one of them.

How did I miss it? Am I totally oblivious? I type and send before thinking how I might regret the conversation that needs to happen.

I wait. Seconds tick by. Then a minute. It might as well be five minutes.

"I assume you didn't find her? You don't get that brooding look when you actually get your way," he laughs at me.

She's not going to talk to me in a text message, but I still wait for a response. She knows I wouldn't have gone all the way home after what she said. Jacey knows me well enough to know exactly where I would be.

"He found me, he just had trouble hearing something I needed to tell him," I hear her say sheepishly from the doorway.

Greg looks cautiously from Jacey to me and back. "You two need to talk then. I know when I'm not needed. Yell if you need a moderator, though."

His receding form leaves and it's just the two of us. Jacelyn and I stand staring at one another, the hinged café doors the only thing separating us, as I wait for her to break eye contact first. She doesn't.

"Truth?" she asks, and I shrug in response. "Here's the short version. She never sent me a picture of the infamous Tommy. She never told me your last name. Then, she up and moved as I was trekking my way back across the country. She didn't tell me she was moving. I met you and thought you were ... cute."

She walks through the café doors, pauses and then leans against the counter opposite me, folding her arms across her impossibly perfect breasts. Before continuing, she leads with a reprimand and I'm almost embarrassed to have been caught. "My eyes are up here," she says as a lazy smile twists up the corners of her mouth. Even when she's being serious, she's still genuinely adorable. "I told Sutton about this man who came into the restaurant regularly, and then she spilled her guts and told me all about you. But just you."

"Just me?" I ask curiously, and I know the question lays thickly on the air, like smoke after a fire's been doused with water.

"Just. You." There's more to this, and I wait. Her voice, weighed down by sadness, hits that spot deep inside my chest where my heart is supposed to reside. It seizes up. "She told me after that first ultrasound — the one I overheard you telling your date about tonight — that she'd lost the baby." She speaks slow and deliberately, making sure I don't miss the point. "For nearly a year, I've been under the impression she miscarried and you sort of washed your hands of her, which is why when I first found out who exactly you are I was cautious. I thought you trampled all over her heart after her baby died. She never wanted to talk about it and she never corrected me when we did talk."

She lied to her best friend? Not just a little white lie, but a huge elaborate lie.

"That's not true. None of that's true," I yell angrily, my hands instinctively reaching beside me to grasp the edge of the counter. "I wanted that baby, Jacey. I wanted to be a dad. I didn't care that he wasn't mine, I was ready to be here and help raise him."

"I know that. Now." The anger that flashes in her eyes is unmistakable, but even more apparent is the hurt. "Imagine how I must feel — she didn't trust me enough to tell me the baby wasn't yours, that she was putting him up for adoption, or that she was moving. Instead she said he died!" She spits the words at me, hauling her hurt and hatred up out of the depths to throw it down in the middle of the kitchen floor with mine.

We stand staring at each other, both feeling a sense of loss. With these admissions, the carefully woven strands of friendship are slowly unweaving. I see it in her face, the pain of knowing she wasn't told the truth. That she was led to believe anything other than facts pisses me off and I feel the heat of anger again rising in me like a flash flood.

There's no warning as I step to the side and swing. There isn't any warning as my fist connects with the wooden cabinet twenty-four inches right of Jacelyn Crocker, who barely blinks and doesn't look shocked in the least. I just do it and it almost feels good to get that anger out, that sudden spark of hate that rises up from the deepest pit within me, until I realize it doesn't help at all.

So, I hit the cupboard again, and again. And again. And one. More. Time.

Because I'm past the point of being diplomatic. I'm beyond being nice. I want to break something, not break down.

"Fuck!" I scream and only after I do, do I realize there's silence all around me. Jacey is quietly watching me, her arms still folded across her chest, as she stands stoic and strong in my moment of weakness. Realizing I'm at the coffeehouse is what brings me back, though. The front of the building is as quiet as a funeral parlor at midnight. Looking at my scraped-up knuckles, I quietly curse.

"T? You okay back there?" I hear Greg call from the other side of the café doors, though he doesn't so much as peek his head above them.

"Yeah. Yeah, I'm okay."

"Jacey, you okay?" he asks warily despite knowing I would never hurt her. I would never lay a hand on her.

Our gazes lock and she slowly swallows her emotions before answering. Her eyes never leave mine. "I'm fine, Greg. We just got some bad news. Tommy's got to clean up the cabinet, but we'll be okay."

We listen as he speaks to the crowded coffeehouse, apologizing on my behalf for the interruption. As someone new is introduced to the makeshift stage, I reach out and grab the top of the cabinet I just desecrated. Hanging my head between my arms, I stare at my boots.

"Do you feel better?" she questions, solemnly.

"No. I don't think I'm supposed to."

"It's highly unlikely that's how this is supposed to work," she says. "I think we need to talk to her."

I lift my head high enough to balance my chin on my arm and glare at Jace. "I don't want to talk to her ... which is insane, right? That's what you're thinking? A week ago I was still acting a little heartbroken and now I'm just ... over her."

To Cherish

I'm over her. I can feel it. I've been feeling it for so long now, but tonight it's finally, one-hundred percent real.

Sutton's reign over my heart has ended.

M.L. Pennock

Jacelyn

He's over her, my ass. I'll just lie to myself and believe that's the pain talking.

"I still think we should talk to her," I reiterate.

"I still think I don't want to. What would it solve? She lied to you about the baby, about me, about moving. If I talk to her I'm going to say a bunch of mean shit and she'll cry, probably because she'll agree with me that she's a horrible person for behaving that way. I don't want to put her through that. Don't you think she's probably beat herself up enough over it?"

His words stun me — his defending her — and I stutter through attempting a response. The truth always wins though.

"No." He turns his head to stare at me again. I push away from the counter and uncross my arms. "No. I honestly don't think she's beat herself up. Every time I talk to her she acts like a kicked puppy who wants to come home and beg you to take her back. Now I find out she left you, which gives her no right to sit down there and mope. She shouldn't be allowed to be sad about leaving you."

I pick at my bottom lip, trying to calm myself down by pacing the kitchen, but I'm unforgivably mad. While part of me isn't sure where my anger is coming from or headed to, I know it's there and it's palpable. When my ex-husband took off with all my money, I told her. When I made out with her boyfriend in the bathroom during senior prom, I was honest with her. When I pulled her hair in the fifth grade because she gave my Barbie a buzz cut and started calling her Hank, I forgave her. We have a lot of history. But history can't undo the level of distrust I feel for a woman I've considered family for so many years.

"I'm calling her," I say as I stop pacing and walk out through the front of the coffeehouse, weaving around tables and amid the teenagers and middle age couples on dates. All the happy faces blur together as I shove through the door. Tommy is hot on my heels as I hit the sidewalk and pull my phone from my pocket. She's second in my speed dial and the call is connecting before he can stop me.

The chill of December creeps in through my cardigan as I wait for her to pick up. On the third ring she groggily answers. "Jacey? What's wrong?"

The adrenaline spikes as I hear her voice. "Everything. Why, Sutton? Why would you lie to me? Out of all the people in the universe you could have lied to, why choose me?"

I hear her sigh. "Because you've always forgiven me. And for once, lying was easier than the truth."

"It's never easier," I whisper, the emotion choking me.

"Sure, it is. At least, until the truth catches up with you."

Chapter Seventeen

Sutton

"And when the truth catches up to you, you're fucked six ways from Sunday, renting an apartment from your brother, trying desperately to handle the emotional impact of an open adoption and postpartum depression and loneliness. Jace, it hasn't been easy. Lying was easier than what I'm doing now."

Silence.

"You could have told me."

I wish I could see her, touch her face, make this better. I've never wanted to make things better more than in this moment.

"I could have, but I didn't want to." It's the truth. I didn't want to tell her how I screwed up and made a mess of my life. Getting pregnant by one man and trying to have a relationship with another isn't the worst thing out there, but I couldn't bear the thought that Tommy would feel obligated to be a father just because we were dating. Once we realized there was no way he was the baby's biological father, I made up my mind. I refused to talk to him about it each time he brought it up. Rob told me he didn't want to be a dad, had no interest in raising a baby with me, and to "give it away." So instead of being alone with a baby, that's what I did.

I could have let Tommy do what he felt was right, but I wouldn't tie him down with a child that wasn't his just because he felt some deep-seated need to mature and become a family man. It didn't help that he found out Stephanie and Max were expecting around the same time I found out I was pregnant. That merely made his wanting worsen.

Instead, I researched and found an obstetrician who would act as our intermediary. A couple living near my brother contacted me through the doctor's office. I met them. I spent time with them and we got to know one another. We clicked. We clicked really well. Too well.

"I felt guilty enough without hearing the logical side of things from you. He's with a good family. We get together for dinner a couple times a month," I say as I curl into my pillow, my insides hollow despite the joy I feel at seeing my son with people who love him so much. "They live only twenty minutes away. I've done everything I can to watch him begin growing up from a distance while still being close, because that's what we all wanted."

I don't tell her that I have a freezer full of breastmilk to take to my son's mom because she asked if I would be willing to pump so he could have the one thing she couldn't give him. I don't tell Jacelyn that my fridge is peppered with pictures of him because his mom sends me a new snapshot every few days. It's a small consolation for me giving her the greatest gift.

There's a lot I don't tell Jacey.

Somewhere in the distance, through miles of phone lines and wireless signals, I hear Tommy's voice.

"Can I talk to him? Please?" I ask, fearful she's going to tell me no. She has no reason to let me have my way. But his voice comes on the line and I feel his hurt radiate through the phone.

"You said I walked away from you?" he says, just loud enough for me to hear. "I spent months trying to get you to stay, Sutton. Telling her that doesn't just hurt her, it destroys me. It tears me up to think you'd justify leaving like that."

"I won't ask you to forgive me. I can't ask you to do that. Someday, though, I hope I understand enough to explain why it seemed easier." I sigh deeply, the exhaustion of everything wrapping me tight in its embrace. "I need to sleep, Tommy. Can you please stay by her? I know I've likely ruined the best friendship I've ever had, she'll never fully forgive me, and I don't know how to make it better other than give it time. Neither of you know what the last eight months have been like for me. I'd appreciate if you don't pass judgment."

I'm asking too much of him. He owes me nothing and yet I'm asking him to do more for me.

"Yeah, I'll stick by her. She seems to be processing a lot of new information tonight." He goes quiet before finally saying, "Sutton, you can come home anytime, you know that right? We aren't going to judge. We all have pasts and they aren't all pretty. Jacey might be hurt right now, but she forgives."

That's Tommy. I could feel his hatred for me when he got on the phone, but now it's dissipated. I also hear how much he doesn't care about me anymore. I don't know if I should be thankful or run for cover and use the weight of my shame as a blanket.

"Take care of her, Tommy. Please." I slowly pull the phone from my ear before he can say more and end the call.

I spend the next several hours crying softly into my pillow because there is a lifetime of regret looming over me. A picture of Jacelyn and me arm-in-arm beside a campfire nestled in a frame holding a photo taken at

To Cherish

Thanksgiving last year — me and Tommy, Steph and Max, and Brian and Stella all smiling and content — watch over me every night, but even those images can't chase the demons away tonight. This time might be the last time she's let me break her trust.

M.L. Pennock

Chapter Eighteen

Tommy

I'm not sure what to say to Jacey as I lock the screen on the phone and hand it back to her. Rather than try to make it make sense, I wrap my arm around her shivering shoulders, pull her into my chest, and kiss her hair for the third time tonight.

"We'll get through this," she whispers into my shirt, though I get the impression she's speaking more to herself than to me. "We will. I just need to … process. Like you said, I'm processing new information."

"She's hurting, Jace. I could hear it. Wherever your anger is coming from, wherever mine was coming from, it needs to go back there. This isn't about us," I say, wondering where these words were hiding as I attempted to mutilate the cupboard full of mixing bowls. Maybe I've been listening to Steph and Stella talk for too long.

Our friendship has gone from slow and subtle to fast and furious tonight. We had an ease about us prior to what's come to light since the sun set. Conversation was simple, a brief hug when one of us needed a hug, harmless flirting, a beer among buddies. But tonight? Tonight changes everything.

"You believe me, right?" she asks, tucking herself under my arm as we cautiously make our way back toward the door that leads up to her apartment.

"Of course, I do."

"You have no idea what I'm talking about, do you?"

I shake my head. "Not a clue."

It elicits a laugh from her when I need to hear it most and I feel her shoulders relax, the tension slipping away.

"Me and Sutton. We're going to get through this, right?" She's unsure if they'll make it, and I hear it in the spaces between each word as they leave her lips.

"Friendships are weird, Jace. Do you want to get through it? Do you want your friendship with her to grow from this experience?" I ask. I'm genuinely curious because I've never had a friend for decades other than my brother, and I'm kind of stuck with him. Mama makes us apologize when we fight. When we were boys, she'd even make us hug it out when we were real mad at each other. I don't know how it works with friends who aren't siblings. "Or have you grown apart to the point that this is the thing that finishes breaking the bond?"

She untangles herself from my arm and reaches for the doorknob, opening it and pulling me into the building behind her. As we begin climbing the stairs, she sighs. Not a normal sigh, but one of those that reaches into my heart and squeezes it because I know I touched a nerve.

"I don't like lying, Tommy. That's what I'm having the most trouble with," she says as we reach the top of the stairs. Opening the door she didn't bother locking earlier, Jacey nods and I fall into step behind her, walking into the large dimly lit space she's called home since April.

The entire building was refurbished, room by room, after Brian purchased it. Including my business, Mile 63 Marketing, there's also the Jumping Bean coffeehouse that Brian and Greg, his best friend from college, opened when they moved back to New York, and a currently empty storefront that Jacelyn lives above.

"You should sell some of these and make room for more," I say about the paintings she's completed. Some are more abstract, others more impressionist. I think. I don't know art, but the Internet is an amazing tool and I've attempted to learn a lot about it in the short time I've known Jacelyn. I touch the corner of one of her canvasses with the painted sun setting against the Erie Canal, the reds and oranges searing the rippling water as a Canal Corporation tug boat glides through the ditch. "Why are you working at the family restaurant when you create things like this?"

A wine cork pops in the small kitchen off the living room and I turn my head in time to see her pulling the bottle away from her mouth, her eyes alight with amusement as they challenge me to say something about her unladylike behavior. "Because I'm part owner of the restaurant and this," she says gesturing with the wine bottle to the room around us, "this is just a hobby."

But it's not just a hobby. I can tell by the way she says it that it's so much more. She went to school for this and every fiber of her being goes into creating beauty where most would see anything but.

"Who told you it couldn't be more?" I question.

"Everyone who told me they needed me to come home and help run the family business."

She pours two glasses of wine, but as she walks through to hand me one she forlornly glances at the wall holding her creations. It's the same look I've seen on writers who have bled into their computers for months only to have someone at the coffeehouse ask how their little pastime is going. Her face transforms from sadness to the truly heartbroken gaze of someone who was told too many times she can't make it as an artist. She takes in each canvas, one after another causing her body to tense more, and I wonder who it was that broke her spirit so much because I'd like to have a word with them.

"When were you going to tell me you owned the restaurant?" I ask before bringing the glass to my nose and breathing in the oaky aroma. I raise my eyebrow at her, challenging her for an answer. "That's kind of a big thing to keep a secret."

"Co-owner and not a secret. You just never asked. You assumed I was just the bartender until you found out my family owned it," she quips as she defiantly hooks her right hand over the inside of her left elbow and rolls her eyes at me. "I'm surprised it took you as long as it did, but you were in quite a state when I first came back home. She did a number on you and until now I couldn't figure out why you acted the way you did over her. After all, I was under the impression you broke her heart, not the other way around."

I lift my hand and rub the back of my neck, feeling the tension that's been building for months. I don't remember the last time I felt totally relaxed or at ease.

"Is it wrong of me to wish it had been the other way around? Me breaking her heart? Sometimes I wonder what that would be like," I say. Taking a sip of my red wine, I say into the glass, "What does it feel like to sit on that side of the fence and be the one to say 'I'm done with you' rather than the one who is always being 'done away with'?"

"Oh Tommy, are you really going to go there? Neither side is a good place to be. Unless you're heartless, then both sides would suit you just fine. But you're not heartless, nor are you one to say you're done without giving it all you've got."

She flops down on the end of the plush lavender couch — the centerpiece of the oddly thrown together room — and curls her legs up beneath her. Propping her head in one hand, she carefully balances her wine glass on her knee with the other, tipping it just far enough for the wine to rise almost to the lip before changing direction.

"What's your favorite part of your friendship with her, Jace? Make me understand."

Without looking at me, her eyes drift closed. Her eyeliner and mascara are barely there after a full day of work and emotions. Her lips, though, are naturally tinted the most perfect shade of pink. I'd be surprised if she ever allowed more than lip gloss to grace the surface of such plump, bow tied, pouty ...

"Tommy?"

"Yeah?"

"You weren't listening to me at all were you?" She laughs at me. It isn't a snide, ridiculing laugh, though. She caught me in a moment of testosterone fueled weakness and it amuses her. I enjoy being a source of amusement for her. "Your brain was out in left field. What were you thinking about?"

I'm not ashamed to share. "Your lips, mostly." I watch a blush redden her ears as I take another sip of my wine and watch those lips, those deliciously full lips, part slightly and her tongue dart out to dampen the skin.

"What about them?"

Without realizing what I was doing, I baited the hook and she took it. It wasn't intentional. It just happened. I ponder how to respond, not wanting to come off as needy but also hopeful she doesn't think I'm just looking to score. I mean, it would be great to have sex with her because it's been so long since that happened with anyone, but I don't want it to be meaningless. Worse yet would be if it got weird. I've never been one for sleeping with my friends, and the friends with benefits thing hasn't ever appealed to me because eventually someone always ends up having feelings for the other person.

"They're perfect."

Finishing what's left in my glass, I stroll past her to the kitchen and pour a few more ounces into the bottom of the goblet. I hear her get up from the couch, set her glass on the counter separating the two rooms, and then clear her throat.

"Would you mind pouring me a little more? I want to grab a quick shower and smell less like steaks and salads and more like flowers."

I turn just in time to watch her walk across the room to a doorway that leads to her bedroom and adjacent bathroom. I watch closely as she unbuttons her blouse. It slides from her shoulders and down her arms, revealing the back of a black lace camisole beneath, before she soundlessly closes the door. Minutes later I hear the water turn on and I pull my phone from my pocket, noting it's nearly ten at night before messaging my brother.

Me: Jacelyn is Sutton's best friend. What do I do? I'm at her apartment. She's in the shower.

My phone rings. Rolling my eyes, I answer and say nothing because he doesn't even give me a chance to speak.

"You're joking right? I left you at your house getting ready for a date. How did you end up going home with the bartender instead?"

"Not joking," I say, before launching into the most abridged version of the evening's drama because I know there are only so many precious minutes before Jacey is done doing whatever it is she's doing in the bathroom. No woman ever goes in to shower and only takes a shower. They're always shaving some body part or blow drying their hair. Living with Stephanie taught me that much. "So, what do I do?"

"What any of us would do, Tommy. You need to do this for us," he whines. I hear Stella laugh in the background, though, and know he's full of shit. He doesn't want me to do that.

"You want me to be lonely and depressed for the rest of my life, don't you? You're kind of a bastard."

"You kiss Mama with that mouth?"

"How does Stella deal with you? You act like you want to whore me out," I say. Turning around to face the bedroom door once again, I find it open and Jacelyn standing in the darkened room waiting for me to notice.

"I'm not trying to whore you out, generally speaking. I do, however, think you could use some companionship," he says, trying to hold back his laughter.

A smile creeps across Jacey's face. "Who's trying to whore you out?" she whispers from across the room.

Swallowing, I say, "Brian, I'll have to talk to you later." I don't wait for a response before I pull the phone away from my ear and end the call. Pointing to the counter, I tell her, "I poured you another glass."

I sound like an idiot.

This girl is getting me all tied up in knots when I'm usually the one doing the tying.

She steps further into the room and I feel the corner of my mouth lift without warning into a half-smile. Jacelyn Crocker wears flannel jammies. Not just any flannel pajamas, though. These are hot pink plaid flannel pajamas.

"What are you smiling about?" she asks as she pulls the top closed over the soft pink tank she has on underneath. It's cute how she thinks covering herself even more is going to make my imagination stop cold.

"You look like a sexy lumberjack," I say. I lose my filter around Jacey. It's nice to be myself with her, but when I recount the conversations we have I always wonder how long before she gets tired of my openness.

"And you look like you're trying too hard," she says in retaliation, pointing to my tie and suit jacket. I slide the fabric off my shoulders, lay it across the back of an overstuffed armchair, loosen my tie, and unbutton the top three buttons. I unbutton my shirtsleeves and cuff them to my elbows. She doesn't stop watching my movements until I stop moving. And then I watch her pull her bottom lip into her mouth and dampen it. "That's probably why you bombed your date and came to find me."

I want to get inside her head and figure out her thoughts.

"I did not bomb my date," I mock, pretending to be disgusted while watching her walk through the moderately sized living room to the kitchen. She grabs the open bottle of red wine and her glass before looking back over her shoulder at me, barking out a low laugh that punches me right in the stomach. She gives me feelings I forgot I could have.

"Sure, you didn't. You just ended it early when you realized I wasn't anywhere to be seen, right? You still had half a steak when I walked out of the dining room," she says as she saunters back through the kitchen, stopping only when we're standing shoulder-to-shoulder. Whispering again, she says, "And you didn't bring leftovers with you."

"I might have left them in the car. You don't know my life," I tease. She winks.

"You wouldn't have left porterhouse in the car."

Well, shit.

"Okay, so I may have maneuvered my way out of my date early. I was concerned about you," I say as she shakes her head and continues on to the couch. She beckons to me with a nod of her head and I follow, glass in hand. We sit down on opposite ends of the davenport and, as though we've done this every night for years, she twists her body and thrusts her feet into my lap. Her left arm lifts and falls behind her neck to prop her head up as she brings the glass to her lips, slowly taking a sip, and I watch her openly savor that one mouthful before swallowing.

Her eyes close and I feel her foot flex in my lap, a little too close to home plate. "You know what to do," she says in that deeply sensuous voice I've started hearing when I sleep at night. You know what I'm talking about ... it's the voice that takes every man out of his "we're just friends" mental space straight into "take off all your clothes" mode. I internally reprimand my libido, requesting it to simmer down, and grab the foot closest to my belt before she has a chance to open her eyes or, God forbid, move that foot any closer and find out that I'm not thinking about her in a "just friends" kind of way tonight.

Which fucking sucks because I feel like we still need to discuss what happened with Sutton.

"Why are you so angry with her? Aside from the lying, that is," I say as nonchalantly as possible while I place my thumbs in the center of her left foot and begin rubbing in small, methodical circles. I don't miss the soft, exasperated sigh.

"I don't know. Ever since I moved back home things have been difficult. It's frustration that's been building, obviously since before I knew about all of this. She went from being very open with me about everything — her life, the bookstore, things going on with you — to being totally closed off. That was a year ago, Tommy, and I was so busy trying to figure out my life and plans to move back across the country that I noticed but didn't take the time to care more. By the time I did, she was gone and now ...," she drifts off midsentence. "I'm angry because it's my fault she hasn't been honest with me. How could she be when she probably felt like I was shutting her out? I'm losing my best friend and it's all on me."

Moving my thumbs up under her toes, I work the tension loose. Her eyes open and I find myself staring straight into her heart. And it's breaking. It's splitting open and there's nothing I can do to make it better.

"How were you shutting her out?" I ask, shaking my head, confused why she would turn the blame on herself.

"By being totally consumed with trying to move and get back on my feet after my ex took off with my life savings. I talked about myself a lot. If I went back through my text messages to her, probably ninety percent of them were about myself and not asking how she was doing. I wasn't in a good place, emotionally or mentally."

"So, you're going to take the blame for her not telling you what was going on here because you were going through a rough patch? Okay, I'll buy it for now," I say, but still find her logic flawed. I'm right to be confused. *Women* are confusing.

"The worst part is her telling me tonight she's been dealing with the aftermath of having a baby but not actually raising that baby. I'm angry about everything and she's down there alone being selfless, which is not like her at all," she says, her voice rising slightly. She sounds almost panicked. "Sutton is rarely selfless. She's usually pretty selfish. She's always been okay with using people as long as, in the end, it would benefit her. For as many years as I've known her, she's taken the generosity of others and would do so for as long as she could. Rarely did she offer to be the generous one, and come to find out she's given away a child because someone else wanted one?"

She ends her tirade with a question, chaotic thoughts marring her features, and looks at me as though she believes I have an answer regardless of it being a rhetorical question.

"I'm not sure it's because she was being generous, Jace. We could speculate all we want," I answer to the best of my ability, and my voice trails off when I see her face.

"Maybe she just didn't think she could handle parenthood alone," she says, picking at the fuzz on her pajama pants. "But you were offering to do it with her. I don't understand why she'd not use you."

Sighing, I contemplate making up some elaborate excuse or pretending to be clueless. I can't. I won't lie to Jacelyn. Not because I don't want to and not because she openly admits to really not liking liars, but because I physically cannot lie to her. It makes me ill. Since the day I met her it has made me sick to my stomach if I'm not one-hundred percent truthful with her.

I move forward, speeding on into the land of truth. If Sutton lied to her about everything else, there's no way she told Jacelyn what I'm about to tell her.

"Because she knew if she stayed I'd want to get married. I proposed to her before finding out he wasn't my baby." I release the words and breathe in deeply, the scent of her shampoo hitting all my senses. Her eyes widen. My heartbeat picks up speed. "I was willing to stick by her, for better or worse, and she chose to give him away."

I haven't told anyone I proposed to Sutton. Brian — my brother, my best friend in the entire world — I didn't even tell him. I was going to wait until she said yes.

She never said yes.

"Oh, Tommy, I can't begin to imagine how that feels." Her eyes soften, and I hate it.

"I don't do well with pity," I say, shaking my head slightly as I turn my eyes downward, focusing again on her foot in my hand. "I never have, so please don't pity me or my past. It's the past for a reason."

Chapter Nineteen

Jacelyn

I always forget how good it feels to wake up from a deep sleep and actually be well-rested. It's the coming back to the land of the living part I enjoy the most. When it happens, I get lost in the slow, glorious awakening as my conscious and subconscious minds kiss good morning sweetly before departing for the hustle and bustle of a busy day.

I had that this morning like I've never had before. It was yummy, like blueberry pancakes slick with homemade butter and drowned in fresh maple syrup. It's the most delicious feeling. It's nearly as enchanting as waking up with someone else's heartbeat thrumming against your back because they're holding you so snugly the beats are syncing. For that reason alone, I refuse to open my eyes this morning, because when I finally do, it will all be over. The similes and metaphors and hunger will evaporate. He'll leave my apartment. It'll feel like a mistake. We'll pretend it happened the way it was meant to and that setting off in separate directions was preplanned.

Without warning, though, his arm snakes up around my waist, pulling me back into the scoop of his abdomen. Spooning. It's been such a long time since anyone just held me. I want it to last all day. It's the want that causes my fingers to move of their own accord, reaching for his hand, intertwining my digits with his as his body slowly awakens. It's the want that keeps me firmly planted in my bed when I should be moving his arm and sliding out from under the covers in search of my tank top and pajama bottoms.

"You snore," he whispers, trailing his nose up the back of my neck. "But not in the sleep apnea way. Just wanted to let you know."

I smile into my pillow, feeling his lips fall against the skin behind my ear. He gives me butterflies. I shouldn't let him do that.

"You make coffee in your dreams," I respond, my smile widening before the giggling I can't control tumbles from my lips. He wraps his top leg over mine and pulls me closer yet, grasping my earlobe between his teeth. I gasp, and say, "I'd love to know who you make caramel macchiato for."

"You know who caramel macchiato is," he replies huskily before tipping me onto my back and climbing over me. He pushes the hair from my face and I see the hesitation in his eyes seconds before he lowers his lips and gently brushes them against mine. "California ruined you for real coffee. I had to Google how to make your drink the first time you ordered it."

He has got to be kidding. A coffee guy not knowing how to make that is disillusioning. It's like realizing Prince Charming is actually a self-centered jerk who only married Cinderella for her looks instead of her astute ability to problem solve in a pinch.

"You're joking, right?" I ask him in all seriousness before my mind can wander any further. "I thought you were pretending when you looked up a recipe for it the first time I met you."

"Absolutely not. After that first one, I practiced making them for everyone so I would remember the next time you came in. Now, hush, I'm trying to make you moan and you keep ruining it with your talking." I laugh at his playfulness, but laughing swiftly becomes a deep guttural groan and turns into the moan he was searching for as his tongue teases my exposed nipple. He holds me tight to him as my back arches and my fingers find their way to his hair as he nips and teases my skin.

It's magic, the way I've opened up my life to him, sharing bits and pieces of myself over the last several months. No one has been able to get to me like Tommy and his touch is just as magical as his smile, his personality, his wit and charm. The allure helps me lose myself in him. It's the right combination of traits to unlock my legs as well as my heart, and my knees gracefully fall open when he nudges them silently without breaking eye contact. His hips align with mine as I let out another long-awaited moan much to his satisfaction. The come-hither smile gracing his lips quickly fades away as I wrap myself around him, feeling every inch of his masculinity. His mouth seeks solace against my neck, a breathy groan meets my skin, and the scratching of the last day's growth of beard brushes roughly against me as I welcome him home.

Our bodies rock against one another and the feverish pace feels like an ethereal experience despite having been in this position just hours before. I reach for his face, pulling him to me in a kiss I can feel all the way to my toes just seconds before he takes the lead once more. He entwines his fingers with mine, pressing my arms to the mattress, and intensifies the kiss with a nip at my bottom lip as we move rhythmically.

The pressure builds and it's a beguiling race to the finish line as I pull my right hand free from his and reach between us, crying out pleasurably at the contact. My back arches off the mattress as I try to pull him impossibly closer to me as we crash and break apart in unison.

To Cherish

In the quiet, I hear the galloping of his heart as mine carefully begins skipping a beat.

~*~*~*~

"I slept with Tommy."

As soon as the words are out of my mouth I wish I could take them back. They're out there now, in the wild, and I cannot recapture them. Ever. It's not that I want to take them back, but I am completely confused why I gave up something so intimate so quickly and to someone who knows him so well.

"Slept as in shared a bed with an invisible wall between you?" Steph responds, her eyes growing wide before she looks away. "Or a wall of pillows? A rolled-up blanket?"

"No." The word is clipped. Stark against the truth. Honest.

"Slept, like you gave him a pillow and blanket and sent him to the couch, right?" she asks, refusing to turn her head in my direction.

"No." I look at her incredulously. I know she's playing a game with me because this is a big deal. It's Tommy and therefore a "holy shit" moment for her that she's trying not to acknowledge because … it's Tommy. She's drawing out the inevitable. The moment when I'm supposed to give her details she doesn't really want because that's what friends do. They provide all the little intricacies of their life and willingly give in to judgment. I'm asking Steph to judge me and she's refusing to do that. We've known of each other for years, but haven't known each other all that long, so maybe she doesn't want to be the judgy friend yet.

"You must mean slept together like you had a sleepover and watched movies and ate ice cream," she continues, never once pausing in her task of folding laundry. Her computer and work papers are strewn about the table beyond the pile of towels as she carefully stacks one more on top. "Rumor has it he really likes the Hallmark Christmas movies."

"Steph," I say, getting her attention long enough to make eye contact. "No. Slept as in there was a lot of verbal foreplay which led to physical foreplay which, in turn, led to … you know." I look across the table at a smaller version of Max. Jake's only five months old, but the last thing I want to do is taint the child's mind with some graphic description of what I did with his Uncle T the night before. And twice this morning. He gives me a gummy grin before shying away. I reciprocate, feeling my heart lurch in my chest.

When I look back to Stephanie, I'm greeted with a sincere smile. "And that scares you."

It does. It scares me so much more than I'm willing to admit.

"Why?" she questions. "He's a good man. He's loyal and forgiving. He's like a Labrador, minus the shedding, drooling, and leg humping." I feel my own smile forming as I watch her consider her words before she bites her lip and tries to stifle a laugh. "Okay, not always minus the leg humping. But what's the big deal? You have feelings for Tommy and the two of you acted on those feelings. You're consenting adults. What's the hang up?"

"Sutton," I say, the memory of baring the truth to Tommy flooding back. "Or rather his history with her. My history with her, too. I don't want things to get messy if this turns into more than just ... leg humping." I take a sip of my coffee, realizing I've never told Steph I'm connected to Sutton. She's never once told me she knows Sutton, though it's been implied multiple times simply because of her connection to Tommy. This entire situation is messed up considering all of us girls grew up here. There were just enough years between me and Steph in school that our paths and social circles never crossed in this small town, at least not to the point of needing to interact with one another. We never needed to be friends. I watch as she pauses and considers my admission, cocks her head to the side, and sets her own coffee cup back on the table.

"History with Sutton?" she phrases the sentence like an inquiry, the curve of the question mark hanging in the air, hooked on the edge of my confession and waiting for guilt to fill the expanding silence. She narrows her eyes at me and the chill of the room traces its fingers down my back. I lied by omission. I hate liars. "How do you know Sutton?"

The inborn instinct to fight or take flight is gathering in my abdomen and I hear myself stammering amid the "ums" and every other "uh" until I suck it up. "We're younger than you, but we grew up here. Together. I've known Sutton since we were kids living on the other side of town. She's my best friend, or was. I don't think there's much left of that friendship. I don't deal well with liars. Everyone has their vice, right?" I pick up my coffee mug, slowly bringing it to my lips as I watch Steph absorb, like a sponge, the limited information I gave her. It's only limited for a moment before the questions barrel toward me.

"I know we're in the infancy of our friendship here, Jacey, but ... what the actual fuck? Why wouldn't you say something before now? I mean, I live right next door to the house she lived in." Steph pulls a chair out from across the table and sets herself down, cradling her refilled cup in her hands, and I see in her eyes how desperate she is to understand.

"It wasn't intentional. I didn't even know you knew her until I put it all together that Tommy was Tommy — *Sutton's Tommy* — and that was after I'd been living in the apartment for a while and he was coming to the restaurant regularly. I found out who he was because I started crushing on him, said something to Sutton, and she turned into an emotional basket case on the phone." And there's so much more, I tell her, before elaborating. I spill every tiny detail from the lie about losing the baby to the confrontation I had with her via telephone in front of the coffeehouse.

She asks perfectly normal questions like, "Why would she lie about something like that?"

I give perfectly normal responses like, "Because she thinks I would judge her for not knowing she was pregnant before hooking up with Tommy."

I catch her glancing at the baby, confusion wrinkling her brow. "She gave the baby up for adoption because what's-his-face didn't want him, you know that right? She made the best decision for her and there's something commendable in that."

"Which is why I'm going to try to let sleeping dogs lie. I just can't talk to her right now. Maybe someday that will change. I've had enough time to think about things and I'm proud of her for not staying with Tommy just because he was willing to be a father, but things changed. She's lied to me for months. I don't know what to believe."

Across the table, she bites her lip, worrying it as she quietly contemplates all my words. "I understand. It's easy to not believe people or take them at face value once they break your trust. Before Max and I were serious, before Sutton and Tommy started whatever they were doing, I had concerns about her." As if on cue we each take a sip from our mugs waiting for the other to speak, so I raise one eyebrow and beckon her to go on. "She made him late to our first date. She was moving in and showed up in the garage while he was working on the car, asked him to help her move some furniture, and next thing you know I was sitting at the canal eating a box of cannoli by myself."

Steph rolls her eyes in a way only Steph can. She does it as if to say, "It's ridiculous to get worked up about it again. It's in the past." I feel like it's so much more than that, though.

"I like cannoli," I say, because what do you say when your friend finds out you're friends with the woman who tried to make a move on her would-be husband?

"I started referring to her as 'Max's slutty neighbor' until I found out she was a customer of Tommy's and consequently a customer of mine. Long story short, T handled all the in-person interaction so I had no idea what she looked like and Max failed to say her name until I caught her flirting with him at the gym. It's all so high school and I hate that shit, so I swallowed whatever I had to and attempted to befriend her," she spills. All her words make sense. Perfect sense.

"Drama is stupid. I hate it, but I have a gut-wrenching feeling it's going to follow me around just to spite me." I take an exaggerated deep breath, blow out a sigh, and drop my face into my hands.

"Drama is a dick and it likes to fuck with people, Jacelyn," Steph says, reaching across the table to pat my shoulder. "Brace yourself, honey, because if you're just now finding out about her lying to you, I imagine this is the universe's warning cry. Mercury in retrograde, karma, any cracks in the sidewalk you might have stepped on, all that stuff is going to come back at you now."

I'm not sure how serious she is, but I may as well take it as fair warning.

"What are you going to do about Tommy?" she asks as I stand and walk to the sink. I hadn't thought about what to do about him other than see where these feelings and actions lead, and I tell her as much. "You're not worried that now that she's given the baby up she'll come back and try to win him over again?"

"Well ... I wasn't. Thanks for putting that horrifying thought in my mind," I laugh, but it lacks humor because that's exactly what I'm afraid will happen. I feel like I need to fight to keep Tommy and we aren't even officially a couple.

Right now we're just friends.

We're friends who fell into bed together multiple times over the course of one very sweaty and emotional evening.

Who am I trying to mislead? I'm lying to myself and I know it. This is more than "just friends."

Chapter Twenty

Tommy

"What do you mean you slept with Jacey?"

It's been almost a week since I showed up at her apartment. Almost a week since I felt completely free of my guilt over Sutton.

I've ignored Jacelyn for almost a week because I have no idea what I'm doing.

Christmas is right around the corner. New Year's Eve is coming fast. My gut twists. I feel my insides churn at the thought of not talking to her. Was this supposed to be a one-time thing? I don't want to talk to anyone about it because then it makes it real. It means we've entered the grey area. Friends with benefits? Friends to lovers? Dating? Every time I date it ends badly. And every time dating ends, I find myself trying to reinvent Tommy. Tommy the Good Guy. Tommy the Bad Boy. Tommy the Best Friend. Tommy always has a title.

"Tommy?" Brian attempts to redirect my attention again. I'm doing everything I normally do. I came into the coffeehouse early to help him and Greg. I started baking the things that needed baking. I'm trying to pour a cup of coffee into a mug, but I'm so lost in my own thoughts I overfill the mug.

"My cup runneth over," I say with a forced laugh, but my humor falls short. I should really just go back to my own office where no one will scrutinize my every move. "And what do you mean what do I mean I slept with her? You're the jerk who was trying to get me to get over Sutton with anyone else. I'm over Sutton." I sop up the spilled coffee and try to hide my irritation. "I'm over her. I just don't know if I'm ready to commit to being under someone else permanently."

I want him to drop it so badly I'm willing to make myself sound like a dick. Tommy the Asshole. I'm surprised I haven't given myself an ulcer from all of this, and for what? So Jacey won't want more from me? Because then I won't eventually get hurt by her, too? Pathetic.

"Wait." *Shit.* "You slept with her that night." *Here it comes.* "You haven't talked to her since that night, have you? You're feeling guilty and it's messing you up big time. Stella is going to have a field day with you, T."

How does he know these things? I never once said I haven't talked to her, but he figures these things out like he's an amateur FBI or CIA agent.

"No, she won't, because you won't tell her about this," I say under my breath. *Please, for the love of all that is holy, do not let Bri tell Stella about this*, I silently plead.

"You're right. She'll figure it out as soon as she sees you because she knows you were at Jacelyn's and you've been avoiding her and Steph, and come to find out Jacey too, since that night. This won't end well for you," Brian says as if I'm not already aware of just how screwed I am. The women in this family, they're a little headstrong.

The door to the back of the building slamming shut sends a cold rush through me. "Thomas. Ian. Stratford! Get your ass in here!" Brian raises an eyebrow at me, picks up his coffee, and turns back to the counter where he makes himself busy doing anything but watching his wife figuratively tear me limb from limb.

"I just figured it out, so you know I'm not the one who told her," he says with his back to me.

"I don't want to and you can't make me!" I yell back.

"T. Don't. You pissed off the wrong sister," Brian says without looking back at me. "You might as well go in there and get your ass chewed. Get it over with."

"I really don't want to. I love my sister-in-law, but she's kind of scary when she's mad."

"Then you shouldn't have done what you did," he says, again picking up his mug and paperwork from the counter before walking out to sit at a table in the still empty coffeehouse.

He's right. I hate that he's right. I hate that Stella is going to be right, too, but I grab my coffee and push through the café doors and into the line of fire. What I see standing in the kitchen, though, isn't a firing squad so much as my sister's gentle, understanding face.

"What were you thinking?" she says to me, her eyes filled with concern as she reaches out to hold my face in her hands. "Tommy, don't break that girl's heart just because her friend broke yours."

I say to her, with all the sincerity I can muster, that I'm not trying to break her heart. It's the last thing I want to do. "But she hasn't called me either. She hasn't come in for coffee when I've been here." But I haven't gone to the restaurant. I haven't made the attempt.

Stella's looking at me with sadness in her eyes like she can read my thoughts. Maybe she can. "Go after her," she says. "You're going to regret it if you don't try. We all know what you went through with Sutton and now we all know what Jacey has gone through with her. But, you and Jacelyn? Neither of you know how much love the other is capable of giving each other."

I smile at her while keeping my mask firmly in place. "Who said anything about love? What if we just wanted to have a good time?" My smile falters.

"You're incapable of just having a good time. You, Tommy, are going to fall in love with that girl whether you're ready to or not." She crosses her arms in front of her, squinting her eyes at me like she's trying to figure out a puzzle.

"You put the fear of God in me when you're mad, but this is more frightening. You're up to something," I say, much to her amusement.

"Nope. I'm not up to anything. Just ... thinking," and she smiles one of her smiles that makes everything seem okay before turning to leave through the back door. She reaches for the knob and faces me once more, "Don't forget dinner at my parent's house Friday. Your mama and dad are coming in sometime that afternoon and we want to do a family thing. You're welcome to bring a guest."

Before I can respond, she's back out into the bitter December wind.

"She didn't even come kiss me," Brian says, watching the door close.

"Does she have to do that every time she leaves?" I've never put much thought into how my brother's relationship with his wife has evolved, but I've also never noticed a time when Stella has left the coffeehouse without kissing him or, at the very least, yelling "I love you" through the door loud enough for him — and everyone else — to hear. This time she did neither.

"She doesn't have to, but it's nice. I like kissing her."

"You sound like a fourteen-year-old."

He eyes me while taking a cautious sip from a fresh cup of coffee. "And you sound jealous. You'll get it eventually. When it really means something, you'll get it." And he turns and walks out of the kitchen leaving me to do little more than contemplate way too many feelings way too early in the morning.

~*~*~*~

I could sit here all night and dissect my thoughts, actions, and feelings where Jacelyn Crocker is concerned. I could. Instead, I'm doing shots of tequila and writing an ad for a roommate.

It's the responsible thing to do.

Paying bills and being able to afford my mortgage now that I've bought the house from Stella is responsible.

Earning my keep and keeping afloat. Those are responsible things to focus on.

Property taxes will be due next month. I need to focus on those. It's *responsible.*

What if I don't want to be responsible tonight?

I glance at my phone again. The tequila is trying to talk. It's saying "call her." The not intoxicated part of my brain, which is a miniscule portion, is telling me I really shouldn't do that ... but it's encouraging me to text her.

I'm sorry, I send. I don't tell her what I'm sorry for. Instead I wait.

Miss Jacey: You should be.

I am, I send.

Miss Jacey: Just so we're on the same page, what are you sorry for exactly.

What am I sorry for? I pour myself another shot, because fuck responsibility.

I call her instead of texting her. She answers on the second ring and that voice, her voice, climbs into my heart. I could blame it on the alcohol. I won't though.

"I'm sorry. I'm sorry for not calling you and not taking you out to dinner and not courting you like a proper gentleman," I say as I lay my head down on the dining room table. "I'm sorry I got up and left that morning while you were in the shower. I'm sorry I've been an asshole by not coming around."

She says nothing. I say more.

"I want to know how you feel in my arms without life screwing it up, I just don't know if I'm ready."

"Ready for what?" she questions.

"Commitment. Relationship. More than friends." I punctuate each phrase with a groan because it feels like I'm stabbing myself in the chest by refusing to admit that I could probably jump directly into a living arrangement with Jacelyn and never regret a moment of it.

Again, she says nothing. I roll my head on the table, my forehead and nose flush against the wood, and breathe in deeply, hoping she'll speak before I let the silence bother me. Before I break it with my alcohol fueled babbling.

Still, she remains quiet.

"Everything happened sort of fast and I don't want to go fast with you. We did everything backwards. I always do things backwards. I'm sorry things happened this way," I close my eyes and say. "I wanted to know you before I knew how it felt to be inside you. This would be so much easier if you tried to pick me up on that dating site."

I know I sound stupid, but it really would be easier.

And she laughs. It's a quiet laugh, but it's there. Even though I don't want it to affect me, it does.

"We're still friends, Tommy. We don't have to be more, right? It was one night."

No. No, that's not what I want her to say, I scream without making a sound. *I want you to fight with me about this.*

"It was one really ... amazing night," she says, and I hear her say what I wanted her to say without actually saying it. "I'm off tomorrow. Maybe we can grab a coffee and do something. Like friends would do."

Fight with me, I say inside, but the words never leave my lips. "That would be great," I say instead.

M.L. Pennock

Chapter Twenty-one

Jacelyn

"Well?" Fisher asks.

"I have no idea what just happened." I turn my head to look at my brother as he comes to stand beside me. I set my phone on the bar and place my palms on either side of it. Staring at the blackened screen, I briefly shake my head to clear the confusion. "I think Tommy and I are taking a step backward."

"Which is the exact opposite direction you wanted to be stepping with him," Fisher comments.

"A little."

"Maybe this is a good thing. Let him finish expunging Slutton from his system before you do the horizontal hayride with him again."

Fisher has forever had a way with words. Not necessarily a nice way with them, but he's never led me astray with his advice when he offers it to me.

"When did you start calling her 'Slutton'?" I don't think I've heard that one before and I wonder if I just blocked it from memory because she was my best friend. The expression on his face tells me I'm probably right.

"Since eighth grade." I stare at him. He shrugs. I wait for more, because I know he'll give me an explanation. He rolls his eyes, "Guys are testosterone driven. She developed early. She wasn't popular because she was smart, Jace."

My mouth opens, but I can't get words to come out.

He takes my shoulders in his hands and turns my body to face him. "Jacey, your best friend has slept with half the town. There probably aren't many men you knew in high school who didn't have sex with her. Likely in the back of a pickup truck in the middle of a corn field ... I'm just guessing."

"Fisher!" My eyes grow wide. His ears turn bright red. "Gross."

"Moment of weakness."

I cover my face with my hands and try to scrub my brain from all the thoughts that force their way in. First Tommy and now I find out my own brother had sex with her. I think I'm mortified more at the thought of my brother having sex than the thought of my brother having sex with my friend, but no matter which way it's spun it's still one thing I never wanted to picture.

"I don't want to know," I say through my hands as I peek at him from between my fingers. "A corn field? Really?" I'll never be able to enjoy corn on the cob again.

He shrugs again. "It was a long time ago. I was a stupid kid."

"Stupid doesn't even begin to describe you," I say. "Horizontal hayride is a new one, though. Did you come up with that on the fly just now?"

We move back into clean up mode as he responds, "Nah. I've been waiting for a chance to use it. So, what are you going to do about Tommy and this whole going in reverse thing? Are you okay with that?"

I kind of have to be, don't I? "What other choice do I have? If sleeping with me was a mistake, then we need to push past it to remain friends."

I finish wiping down the bar as Fisher changes out a keg. I place clean glasses on the shelf and he starts going over the lunch and dinner specials for tomorrow.

It wasn't a mistake, I tell myself. Mistakes don't twist you up inside like this. They don't climb in and invade all your senses in the best way.

"And if it wasn't a mistake? What happens then?"

I don't immediately answer him. I don't know what happens. I don't know where we'd go or how we'd start. Where would we end up?

"A happy ending." I don't miss the snicker my brother tries to cover with a cough or the unintentional double entendre, but I choose to ignore it.

"Well, I think everyone wants one of those, Jace," Fisher says, his tone serious as he rounds the bar and sits on a stool directly in front of me. "I hope Tommy isn't a mistake, mostly because you deserve a bit of happiness after your marriage debacle. But, and this is a huge but, if it turns out he's not Mr. Perfect like you think he is, don't let it destroy you again. No man is worth losing your dignity over."

I never said Tommy was perfect, I tell my brother. He's flawed. So very flawed. "I won't let him destroy me. Cross my heart, Fish."

He taps his knuckles on the bar and stands from his perch. Conversation over.

~*~*~*~

The blank canvas stares back at me. The image of Main Street out my second-floor apartment window acts as a backdrop against the stark white surface set on my easel. Everything is dark but for the pools of light from the streetlamps lining the sidewalk. Snow falls like fairy dust, sparkling on its descent to the cement below.

I can't paint, though. It's impossible to capture this moment, so instead I just watch as the snow slowly begins to accumulate just in time for Santa's arrival. Christmas is only a few days away. You wouldn't know that to walk through my door, though, because there's not a drop of Christmas cheer here.

My phone buzzes on the counter.

I don't go to it.

It buzzes again. Persistent. Insistent. In need.

TStratford: Do friends pick friends up to go for coffee? I don't know how that works. Like, do I show up and knock on your door and say, "Hey, I'm here to take you to coffee, friend." *wink* Or ...

He's a very confusing man. He makes things more confusing as three more messages pummel my phone, beating it into submission.

TStratford: Should we just meet downstairs?

TStratford: Am I making it weird?

TStratford: I'm making it weird, aren't I?

I should respond, but I smile at my phone instead. I wonder how much longer he'll continue if I don't say a thing. I wonder how long my heart can take being friends.

TStratford: The longer it takes you to send a message back, the less time it's going to take me to get up these stairs.

A knock at my door tells me exactly what stairs he was climbing. My brain finally tells my fingers to do something useful.

Me: You're a little early for our friend date.

I hit send and open the door as he opens the message.

"Only by twelve or so hours. I can wait out here until you're ready if you want me to," he says. His face is pink from the cold and I resist the urge to place my warm hands against his cheeks to heat the skin. I *resist* because if I don't he will destroy me. I *resist* because if he isn't ready for falling into bed with me every night it'll hurt that much more; it'll feel like that much more of a mistake. "Just let me borrow a blanket and one of those adorable throw pillows you have and I'll wait out here. I even brought a book with me in case you were sleeping." He pulls a tattered copy of "Tuesdays With Morrie" from the pocket of his pea coat and leans against the wall across from my door.

I'm stuck in this moment, standing in the doorway watching the snow melt and drip from his hair as he lowers himself to the floor and begins reading a book that looks like it's been read a hundred times. The cover is torn and tattered along the edges, and when he turns the page I see highlighter marking the paper like he studied every word Mitch Albom carefully placed there. I'm an educated person. I saw a lot of gorgeous, intelligent men walking around spouting off about literature and politics during my days on a college campus.

This ... this is different. This is a gorgeous, intelligent man sitting in the hallway outside my apartment reading literature instead of talking about it. He didn't come here to talk about books; he came here to write his story and I can't even seem to catch my breath.

I turn and walk back toward the couch and grab a blanket along with one of those "adorable throw pillows" he seems to appreciate. As I reach the door once again, I toss them on the floor beside him and smile. I smile through what might end up being pain, but right now it's the wait. I smile through the wait.

"Goodnight, Tommy," I say. Pulling the door toward me, I step back into the room as he looks up, raises an eyebrow, and gives me a sexy smirk like he just won a prize. Silently pushing the door closed, I wait to hear the click of the latch before leaning my forehead against the wood. My phone vibrates in my hand.

I hear him laugh on the other side of the door, but I resist the urge to let it affect me. This was my decision. I said "friends." Repeatedly.

TStratford: *I totally made it weird.*

I don't have the stones to tell Tommy it wasn't him.

It was me.

~*~*~*~

"You need to go out there and tell him to get back in your bed."

I called Steph after texting to make sure she was still awake. She's the only close female friend I have right now and I spend a lot of our conversations lately wishing there hadn't been so many years between us in school. I could have used a friend like her, but hindsight is pointless because I can't change the past.

"You're joking, right? He made it sound like a mistake the first time it happened. He said he was sorry things happened this way, Steph," I say.

She sighs on the other end of the phone and I hear Max in the background asking her if she's coming to bed soon. She tells him she'll be up in a few minutes and then I hear the muffling sound of a hand sliding over the receiver. I don't know what she tells him, nor do I care. I don't care until I hear her say, "Max, this is their business. Give me back my phone."

"Jacelyn, go tell him to come in out of the cold or I'm having Gill swing by and arrest his ass for loitering. Or squatting," Max says into the phone.

"You wouldn't," I say, a little taken aback that he'd ask his former partner to do something like that.

"I would. Go on. I'll stay on the line," he says.

I look at the clock and it's nearing 1 a.m. I groan and tell him fine. I'll go tell Tommy to come in. I push the covers off my legs and climb out of bed, slowly, and make my way out through the living room. I reach the door and unlock it.

I didn't lock it when I went to bed, I recall, feeling my brow furrow. I left it unlocked because he was right outside. I'm not enough of a mean girl to have locked him out and if he was paying attention he would have noticed I didn't turn the deadbolt.

"Never mind, Max, we're good," I say, turning to look at the coat hook that's acquired a grey pea coat and red plaid scarf. My squatter is seated at the counter, his head against the marble and his left hand splayed across the open book beside him. He took the time to put the blanket back on the couch and the pillow in the chair. "He must have come in while I was in the shower and getting ready for bed. Put Steph back on."

He mumbles something about Tommy being Tommy but obliges and says he'll call off the reinforcements.

"One of these days, that boy is going to get himself shot for acting like rules don't apply to him," Steph says.

"He's sitting on a barstool passed out at the counter. What do I do?" I whisper.

"Push him off the stool and see how good his catlike reflexes are."

"You're joking right?" I say. I try to cover my laugh, though. "Because I see that ending really badly."

"You could just paint his nails and make him regret being a jerk."

I don't know if I could do that, I say, but head toward the bathroom to see what colors I have.

"I have some pinks and some nice reds. Orange. There's a sparkly green."

"Christmas colors. Do it. Do it for me," she pleads.

"He must have really hit some nerves with you when you were living together, eh?"

"That's an understatement. Pics or it didn't happen. I have to go to bed now. I'm getting the evil eye from Max," she says and we hang up.

Red and sparkly green it is.

Chapter Twenty-two

Tommy

Her bedroom door is closed still when I wake up, so I don't know if she realizes I came in after she went to bed. She didn't lock the door after closing it, and I can only assume it's because she knew I wouldn't last all night in the hallway. The snow has piled higher on the windowsill and it's dark outside. It will be dark for a while longer and I consider grabbing my coat and going down to the coffeehouse to make breakfast for her, but that might be pushing it if she's hell bent on "friends."

I'm starting to hate that word. I've never not wanted to be friends with someone so much in my life and instead of being honest with her, I told her we were rushing into things. Why would I do that?

I rub the sleep from my eyes with the heels of my hands. The light on the hood unit over the stove is just bright enough to reach me and as my eyes adjust I see my hands.

"Son of a bitch," I say as I hold them closer to my face and really inspect my nails.

I guess dreaming Jacelyn was touching me wasn't all in my subconscious. To know her hands were actually on me at some point last night causes my body to react. It's like I'm a teenager seeing Hustler for the first time again. Except, Jacey is better than Hustler ever thought of being. Her hands are soft and she's gentle. She's all blissful curves and no hard edges. That's all I could think about after our night together, after she let her fingers roam and caress any section of bare skin she could find.

And the way she wrapped her hand around …

At just after six in the morning, Jacelyn and her soft hands walk through the living room, enter the kitchen, and start making a pot of coffee while I'm carefully and consciously stripping her of every shred of clothing in my thoughts.

Boxers and a hooded sweatshirt.

There isn't much to take off her.

The counter is just the right height …

She opens the fridge and reaches in to grab a container of yogurt. She doesn't have to, but she stands on her tip toes and her already long legs appear that much longer and my hips remember the feeling of them wrapped around and pulling me closer.

She plucks a spoon from the drawer and turns to the counter, making eye contact with me. The heat rises up from my collar because all I can think about is how much I want to spend the day tasting every inch of her. She pulls the top from the yogurt and slides the first spoonful into her mouth while she stares at me, suspicion marring her features.

I can't stop thinking about the way she licks her lips.

"It's a little warm in here."

"No. It isn't." Those three words coming from that mouth. "You're thinking about me." She takes another spoonful of yogurt into her mouth and pulls the clean spoon out. She swallows and I want to kiss her throat. "Naked."

I'm transparent. I am horribly turned on by everything about this woman. My friend. A friend with whom I've had relations, no less.

"You painted my nails," I say. I have no idea how to defend myself against her and I find myself changing the subject each time I should.

"You deserved it."

"I did."

"You confuse me," she fires back. The suspicion clears and I watch as the fight in her rises to the challenge. Finally. "You say you don't know if you can do more than friends after we've done things that breach the friend boundary. Then you show up in the middle of the night and station yourself outside my door like an overprotective boyfriend, but you're not my boyfriend and you pretend like you're not sure if you want to be my boyfriend." She's not wrong. "Now, you're sitting there undressing me with a look that melts panties and I know it melts them because I've seen you give it to other women. Is it because you want more than friends or because you want friends with a side of sex? I'm not one of your whore dates who isn't looking for a lasting relationship, you know."

Mama tried to warn me about girls like her.

"This is pretty heavy stuff for so early in the morning," I say, squirming on the barstool. I let out a small, nervous laugh, "Is there going to be a test later?"

My attempt at joking falls flat. It always does. It wasn't even a solid attempt. I'm trying to deflect because she's kind of intimidating when she's heated like this. And it's hot.

"You're doing it again." She pins me with her gaze.

"No, I'm not." I don't know what I was doing.

"We aren't having sex." Oh, I was doing that. I didn't even realize I was looking at her like that again. I can't control how I react to her and it's bound to get embarrassing if I don't get a handle on it. "Not before I have coffee," she says, giving me an ounce of hope. As if on cue the coffee maker beeps and she pours the biggest mug of black coffee I've seen since the days of living with Steph. Inhaling the aroma of beans I roasted and ground for her the other day, she says calmly, "Probably not after coffee either."

Just like that she dumps that ounce of hope down the drain.

I'm still admiring her ability to resist the look as she strides out of the kitchen, back through the living room, and into her bedroom. The slamming of the door closes the discussion and reaffirms the mess I made.

~*~*~*~

It was almost the lunch hour by the time Jacey decided to be nice to me.

I tucked my tail and went home to shower after our conversation. I made sure to take my time because I wanted to give her enough room as possible to stop being upset with me.

She said friends, so this isn't entirely my fault. Sure, I put it in her head and hate myself for doing it because I know I want more than that with her, but I never imagined she would be this angry with me. I just want to make sure this is real.

More than that, I want to make sure she actually cares about me instead of it being some convoluted tactic to get back at Sutton. I don't even want to think about her doing that. Jacey is too good. At the root of who she is, she's better than that and I need to keep myself from thinking otherwise.

"It's twelve degrees out and you want to do what?" I say. "Maybe I should rethink this friendship."

"It's ice cream, Tommy, not a tooth extraction."

"But it's going to feel like getting a tooth pulled because everything is so damn cold. You recall I'm from the south, right?"

She laughs and it echoes against the brick walls of the buildings surrounding us. Taking the alley protects us from the wind, but nothing protects me from her sliding her arm through the crook of mine. Do friends walk arm-in-arm? I want to ask her, but then she'll take it away.

"Yes, I do recall you mentioning a hundred or so times you're from the south. You need to suck it up and deal with the cold, though. I've been in California for the last ten years. I'm a little chilled, too. Besides, your life is here now," she says. I love the way her arm warms mine through the layers of fabric between us and I want to tell her, but I won't. I keep my hand in the pocket of my coat, squeezing it into a fist to tamp down the sudden need to hold her hand in mine. She's gotten quiet, watching the ground as it passes beneath our feet, and I wonder what's on her mind. She lifts her head and sighs, her breath coming out like a puff of smoke. "You wouldn't actually rethink our friendship, would you? I mean, you wouldn't end it because of everything that's happened, right?"

I wait a heartbeat to answer. If it feels to me like I'm waiting an eternity to respond I can't imagine what it must feel like for her, but I need to consider what she's asking. I scuff my work boot through a pile of snow and then say, "I wouldn't end our friendship over something that meant so much to me. I certainly won't rethink it because you like ice cream cones in winter."

I stop and she stops with me, and turning to look at her I don't know what comes over me but right now — right this second — I think I want to eat ice cream in twelve-degree weather with Jacelyn for the rest of my winters.

"What?" she asks quietly. "Why are you looking at me like that?"

I know I'm not giving her the same look she accused me of this morning, but I'm not sure what my eyes are saying to her this time and let my mouth do the talking instead. "Come to Christmas Eve dinner with me? It's informal. It's not even really dinner. We make a ton of appetizers and have shrimp. Lots of shrimp." God, I hope she likes shrimp. Why am I still talking? Why is she smiling at me like that? Why are girls so confusing? I'm acting like a girl. I'm confusing. "And wine. There's always quite a bit of wine."

"What time?"

I wasn't prepared for that. I was prepared for her to be busy, because when I want something badly enough it is never meant to happen. But then she smiles at me and I tell her to come over around three and she somehow smiles more.

"I like shrimp almost as much as I like ice cream," she says as she pulls me down the alley toward Main Street. "Should I bring anything?"

"Nope, just yourself," I say as we ease back into less confusing territory. "Mama, Jenny, Stella, and Steph tend to go crazy in the kitchen when they all get together. You're welcome to ask if they need an extra hand, though. You'd really like my mama. She's got a sweet spot for girls who can put up with me."

"And have there been many of those?"

Pressing my lips together I think hard about my past and how it's littered with meaningless relationships outside of women in the family. There's been the occasional bed partner, but no one important enough to make me want to take her home. I shake my head slowly and say, "No. You're the first."

M.L. Pennock

Chapter Twenty-three

Jacelyn

"Just breathe, Jace. It's just hanging out with friends."

I've resorted to talking to myself in the mirror because I have no one else to talk to. Steph and Stella are hopeful Tommy has removed his head from his rectum and inviting me to Christmas Eve is a step toward a relationship. I'm not as optimistic since I'm the idiot who put it in his head we would be fine as friends. This feels like a set-up, like a pop quiz in high school the first day back from a long weekend. I'm having trouble seeing how this will end on a high note for me and talking to Steph and Stella about my nerves is akin to feeding myself to a pair of hungry wolves.

They will rip my fears to shreds and then I'll just have anxiety left. Fuck anxiety. I can get through this without talking to them about it. It'll be fine. It's just the girls and their mom. And Tommy and Brian's mom.

"Just hanging out with friends," I say once more. I try to build my confidence back up. Everyone sees me as this strong, confident woman and more often than not, it's a farce.

I slide my jacket on and pull my hair from the collar, finally prepared to spend the afternoon feeling like I'm being examined under a microscope by Tommy's mom. Kathryn. Her name is Kathryn and I hope I don't somehow butcher it.

The drive to Jenny and Dale Barbieri's house — the home Steph and Stella grew up in that I drove past a thousand times once I was a licensed teenager — doesn't give me enough time to mentally prepare for this bonding ritual. Nope. Anxiety is officially fucking me. I thought I would be able to have it the other way around, but my confidence has evaporated.

I'm pretty sure I'll be the outcast of the group so when I pull into the driveway and park behind a car with Tennessee plates, it feels like my heart is in my throat. I'm really going to have to meet his mom and it's scary, even if we are just friends. Meeting the mother is always a huge deal. I hope she can't smell the sex on me I had with her son. Moms have a sixth sense about these things.

The rational side of my brain tells me this isn't a big deal. It's been telling me that for days now. I'm kind of beyond being rational, though, because

Tommy essentially told me I'm the first woman he's wanted to bring home to meet his mother.

"Shut up, Jacelyn. You're reading way too much into this," I say to my reflection in the rearview mirror. I take one last deep breath before pushing open the door and scooting from behind the wheel.

"You're kind of cute when you talk to yourself." How I didn't see him walk up to and lean against the back of my car is beyond me, but there he is dressed in distressed jeans and a Carhartt jacket. I thought he looked good in a suit and tie. *I was wrong. So. Wrong.* I try to catch my breath against the chill in the air, but it's useless.

"I wasn't."

"You were."

"I might have been. What does it matter?" I question as I pull my coat tighter around me, locking out the cold and his penetrating gaze.

"It doesn't. I just want you to know they're all happy you came to spend the day with them. Come on, I'll introduce you," he says, stepping away from the car and reaching for my hand.

He's holding my hand and I'm biting my lip hard enough to keep from grinning like a fool that I taste blood.

"We should get you a better car. I don't know how you fit people in there let alone moved across the entire United States in it," he says, shaking his head as he glances back at my most valuable possession.

"What's wrong with Betsy?" I ask, taken slightly aback. I love my Mini Cooper Countryman. She's just the right size for me.

"You named her Betsy?"

"You named your car, I'm sure," I respond. He still has my hand in his, and it is so comfortable. I don't recall the last time I felt this at ease holding hands with anyone.

"I did. But my car deserves a name. Henrietta is special. She's a classic, Jace," he says of the Jamaica Blue Metallic 1970 Plymouth Barracuda. I've done my homework on Tommy's car and committed her image to memory. She's gorgeous and I can't believe he doesn't put her away for the winter. I catch his eye and he winks before continuing, "But I think it's adorable you named your midget-mobile. I'll help you find a real car when spring rolls around."

I act offended as we take our time walking to the house and I want this walk to last just a little longer despite the cold, so I share, "You know, that car is the only thing I bought for myself after my grandfather died. He made me and Fisher beneficiaries on his life insurance because we were his only grandchildren. The deal was to put it toward a down payment on a space for an art studio, but after my ex took off with what money he could get his hands on and Fisher told me he was having trouble staying afloat with the restaurant, I needed to focus on essentials. I needed to get home somehow, so I bought Betsy and packed her full of what I could."

His hand tightens around mine. "What about the things you couldn't fit in there?"

No one has ever asked me that, not even Fisher. I don't guard the information. It's not sacred. It's just something I haven't talked about. Walking up onto the back porch, Tommy and I stop so I can look at him as I say, "I hired a moving company to take my furniture to a local women's shelter. They needed it more than I did. There was a woman who needed a bed, so I gave her mine. Another needed clothes for job interviews and was my size. I sent her my dress pants and button downs," I say. His eyes lose what remains of the playfulness from the beginning of our stroll toward the house. "And I donated ten thousand dollars to the house so they could get a new central air conditioning system. They needed it. I didn't think I would need the extra money."

Silence. In the cold, I hear a tree creak but that's the only sound as Tommy looks at me with the same look he gave me in the alley.

"What?" I whisper, afraid to break whatever spell he's under.

"You're such a good person Jacelyn. I'm so scared I'll ruin you," he whispers back.

His breath warms my lips as his leans into me. It's involuntary that my eyelids flutter shut while waiting for him to place his mouth to mine. But he doesn't and I hear instead, "Don't think your mama don't see what you're doing."

"We aren't doing anything," Tommy says, but his eyes are pleading with me the moment I open mine. It's a silent apology when he has nothing to apologize for.

I smile broadly at the man behind Tommy because it's like looking at his twin, if he had a twin.

"Mmhmm, sure you aren't. Let that poor girl go in the house and get warm, Thomas," he says.

Tommy drops his head to my shoulder in defeat and I laugh, just a little. "It's okay," I say quietly so only he can hear, then push him back off me. "I should go in and see what all I can help with. Bond, bake cookies, and whatnot."

"Whatnot sounds delicious, young lady," a motherly voice says behind me as the door to the kitchen opens. "Come on in here. What were you thinking keeping her out in weather like this, Tommy? Neither of you have gloves on or hats. You're going to catch your death a cold. All of you get in here," she says, stepping back so we can enter. "You must be Jacelyn. My heathen son was too busy trying to grope you on the porch to even introduce his father so I'm sure he'll forget about me, too. I'm Kathryn, that's Ben. Let's cook. The wine's this way."

I toe off my shoes once I'm inside the mudroom. She motions me to follow her and I do, slipping my coat off as I go and with it goes the apprehension, the fear, and the well of panic that had pooled in my gut.

"T, why don't you come out back with me and Dale. Let the women do what they do," Ben says behind us. Tommy says he'll be out in a minute and I hear the door close as his father retreats to the garage in the backyard.

I can see Kathryn, Jenny, and the girls from the open doorway as they pour over recipes at the wide counter jutting out from the wall. It splits the kitchen into two large sections and reminds me of my parent's house. I bite my lip as I feel Tommy come to stand behind me and place his hand on my arm. "You going to be okay without me? I can stay inside if you want me to," he offers. I love that he's offering to be my buffer, but I'm a big girl. I can handle this now. Somehow it all suddenly feels right, like I'm supposed to be here.

"Go spend time with the dads. You never see your parents and I'm sure your father would love to catch up with you." I smile up at him feeling my confidence come back a hundred times stronger than it was when I got out of my car. He nods his head and gives me a half smile before placing a kiss to my temple.

The affection is needed. It's wanted. I've been remiss in the past to think I don't want or need to be cared about by someone, by a man. I tried so hard to not miss the comfort of a hug from someone who meant it, other than family and the memory of affection from family. Tommy's entire being vibrates with meaning as he reaches up to brush the hair from my eyes. He's contemplating something, I can see it in the tender creases at the corners of his mouth and his wrinkled brow, but I'd rather not ask.

He'd tell me if he wanted me to know.

He doesn't say a word.

He simply pulls me to his chest, lays his palms against my cheeks, and kisses my mouth with purpose. He steals my breath away little by little and then breathes it back into me, renewed.

"Promise you won't let me ruin you," he whispers against my lips, and I open my eyes just in time to see a passing glint of fear in his.

I don't make promises.

I don't say a word.

I simply fall back into his chest and press my lips to his, treading lightly into the water and trying not to cause a tidal wave.

I offer him the quiet acknowledgement of his fear, the unspoken dread that he tarnishes the good, leaving behind him a wake of broken relationships. It's all I can offer him because I can't fix the past and I can't predict the future, no matter how much I wish I could.

"Whenever y'all are done, we'd like to start baking some pies," Kathryn whispers closely to my ear. Tommy's lips stop moving, my tongue retreats to my own mouth, and she walks away before yelling into the dining room to Mrs. Barbieri. "Jenny! I have to tell you what I just did!"

"I should go to the garage," Tommy says softly, his lips still touching mine. "You should."

"We can finish this conversation later," he says, his cheeks pinked from the cold and embarrassment, and mine probably match. At least, I assume it's embarrassment for him, too.

"We can," I say with finality as I smile and take a step back. Clasping my hands in front of me I turn and walk to the counter.

I try to keep a safe distance and say hello to the sisters. Steph and Stella forget about personal space and sidle up on either side of me as the back door to the house shuts and the three of us stand shoulder-to-shoulder while I regain my composure. I can't believe his mom did that, but at the same time what a way to break the ice. "You've made quite the impression on Mama," Stella says.

"I'm sure I have. She's going to hate me."

The sisters lean back and I feel them look at each other behind me. I bite my lip to keep from saying anything else, then cover my face to hide the lip-biting.

"I don't think you need to worry about that. But, just for clarification's sake, what's going on with you and Tommy?" Stella asks. "I thought you'd mutually friend-zoned one another for the time being. That's the rumor climbing up the family tree, anyway."

"I ...," I sigh, removing my hands from my face. "I have no idea what's going on. I think we're just playing it by ear."

"Yeah. Play it by ear. It worked fabulously for me," Steph says, sarcasm and humor lacing her voice. "It's how I ended up married to Max after dating for about a minute."

Stella joins in, saying, "Same here. Well, not Max, but Brian. I thought we were going to take it slow and it just didn't pan out that way. Fate has her own plans, Jacey." Her arm wraps around my shoulder and, from the other side, Steph wraps hers around my waist. "Tommy's been through a lot, you know that. It might take him some time, so expect your 'playing it by ear' to take longer than ours. Brian was pretty adamant he was going to make me his wife from the minute he stepped back into Brockport. Max had some things to figure out where his past was concerned before he was certain about Steph, but then he moved fast enough to spin our dad's head around."

Steph laughs as she adds, "He's kind of impatient. Tommy, though? T is a patient man and if he cares about you, he's going to make sure it's the real deal. After Sutton left he swore off romance. The only reason he's on a dating site is because our husbands don't want him feeling like a fifth wheel when we all get together."

It's like watching a tennis match as my head turns to give attention to one sister, then the other, as they take turns talking.

"Don't get us wrong," Stella interjects. "He's the life of the party with everyone under the age of two, but with the adults he's sometimes sulky if it's all couples."

They're making me even more confused. Am I supposed to be happy that we're taking things one day at a time? Should I be pressuring him into a more solid commitment?

"Can we just not talk about my love life right now? Not that I don't want to, it's not that at all. I'm just not sure how detailed I want to get about what's going on between us when his mom is in the other room," I say.

Neither sister removes her grasp on me. It feels like they move in closer and I'm curious if they realize how afraid I am of my life getting turned upside down again by a man. If I give him my whole heart, it's because I want him to hold it forever, not just until he loses interest.

"Jenny, do you think she's going to be the next one?" I hear Kathryn's voice, but it's not coming from inside the kitchen and I deduce she must be standing in the doorway behind us that connects the kitchen and dining room.

"Damn it, Kay, don't jinx it," Jenny hisses back.

I snicker, Stella groans, Steph throws her hands up in the air.

"You two are horrible! The magic is broken. We might as well cancel Christmas," Steph says turning toward the matriarchs peeking around the doorframe.

"You're being unreasonable," her mother says.

"It's all in good fun," Kathryn adds. "Besides, she's just what that boy needs. I saw it in the way they looked at each other."

"What look?" I ask cautiously, turning to watch as she strides into the kitchen. She doesn't readily answer, instead she reaches for a mixing bowl and begins throwing ingredients into the bottom. "Mrs. Stratford? What look?"

She drops butter into the bowl and as she measures the vanilla extract, she says, "He looks at you like Brian looks at Stella and their daddy still looks at me. It's a Stratford men thing."

She says it so nonchalantly, like it didn't just fill my entire world with hope. My mouth drops open, just a little, and I attempt to close it before I give too much of myself away. I don't want anyone to know how much I want her to be right about this. Kathryn places both her hands on the counter as she hovers over her bowl and looks me in the eyes.

"Jacelyn, my son has never loved anyone. He's had girlfriends. He's run around like a stray dog at times. My youngest child has never been in love. I have a strong feeling that is changing."

I nod. What else am I supposed to do? How do I respond to that, particularly when Tommy and I are not even dating? We aren't officially a couple and we aren't labeling this thing we're doing.

"Just keep doing what you're doing," Kathryn says as she comes around the end of the counter. I'm not even sure if we know what we're doing. Taking my chin in her hand, her eyes warm me as she speaks and it feels like I've known this woman my entire life. "Thomas needs you. Take the time to know him, learn about him, find out what makes him tick. He's trying so very hard not to let you have his heart, but he's failing horribly at that. Whatever the two of you were talking about on the porch had him all tied up."

Her hand is still at my chin as I say, "I told him I donated a lot of money to a women's shelter." I don't tell her to be boastful, it's not a point of pride for me to share that information. I tell her because I want her to know. It's a piece of information that I need her to have.

"A girl with as big a heart as my boy. It's a Christmas miracle." She pulls me into a hug, the kind that comforts to the core and eases your soul on the hardest days of your life.

That's the kind of hug Kathryn Stratford gives.

Chapter Twenty-four

Tommy

She's standing in the kitchen with me and the evening is finally winding down. It's already nearing midnight, but I really don't want the night to end. "So, what are your plans for tomorrow?"

"Tomorrow is Christmas. What do you think my plans are?" She answers my question with a question and I hear the skepticism in every word she speaks.

I wait for her response, but I'm met with silence.

"I don't know, actually. I assume you and your brother are getting together with family," I say. Leaning against the counter, I cross my arms at my chest and then do the same with my legs at my ankles. I wait for an answer but her constant smile falters. I want to know her plans because she's never talked about family and I don't want to be unkind by asking out of the blue why that is. I don't want to assume she has no one but Fisher. "Bri makes this coffee cake every year for Christmas morning. I really think you'd love it. It's basically dough coated in sugar and cinnamon. He makes Stella and Steph's grandma's apple pie, too. It'll knock your socks off."

Her smile turns down, just slightly, and I imagine she knows what I'm asking without actually forming the questions. I saw Jacey smile all night long, and something I said made it go away.

Mama was treating my maybe-girlfriend as though she was a daughter. I was able to watch her have conversations with my mama as though they're old friends. Or family. Mama approached her conversations with Jacey like she does with Stella, and I don't think Jace understands how intense that was for me to witness. No one does. I've never seen it happen before, not with a woman I care about in this way because there's never been someone who makes me feel the way Jacey does, so I'm really not prepared for how my heart grew three sizes in the span of one evening. I'm unsure how it fits inside my chest right now.

"Why do you assume I have nowhere to go tomorrow?" she finally asks. She's backed herself into the corner cupboards where the counter juts out from the wall and hoists herself up to sit on the countertop. Her hands are clasped between her knees.

"You only talk about your brother when you mention family, with the exception of your grandfather earlier. That's all," I say, quietly. "You haven't even decorated, so you can't be expecting company. Christmas is supposed to be a joyful time and you don't even have a wreath."

The look on her face is pained, but she attempts to hide it. She does a horrible job. "Christmas is just really hard for me, Tommy. I'll get together with Fisher, but we stopped exchanging gifts a long time ago."

My oversized heart twists in my chest and I want to ask all the why's — why is it hard, why no gifts, why no happiness? The questions must have played out on my face because she lets out a small laugh and drops her head back. Staring at the ceiling she says, "My freshman year of college our parents were killed in a car accident. I was home from California for the holiday and they went out for the evening to some benefit in Rochester."

Her eyes glaze over with unshed tears. Her voice softens with the memory.

"It was one of those snows that starts as freezing rain. The temperature kept dropping and my dad lost control going around a tight curve on the way home. The car was wrapped around a tree. There was nothing that could be done."

She gives me a tight, mournful smile that conveys all her sorrows.

"I don't really talk about it. Fish and I have tried to move past it."

"Oh my. I remember that accident," Jenny says from the doorway. Her hands are at her mouth, covering her surprise and her interruption, but she briefly glances at me before she goes on. "Jacey? You were Jacelyn Reilly. I can't believe I didn't put two and two together after all these months. It never even occurred to me after you talked about working at the restaurant. Not that it's a very common name, but it's been a lot of years."

"Reilly?"

She smiles at me again. A sad smile. Jacey has a smile for every occasion, it seems. "I still have my married name. It was too much of a pain in the ass to try to change it back."

Jenny walks across the room and, taking Jacey's face in her hands, says solemnly, "I wasn't trying to eavesdrop, I swear." Jacey gives her a gracious smile, and Jenny smiles right back, adding, "Not that either of you would have thought that, but I just wanted to be clear. It's not like I don't trust two consenting adults alone in my kitchen."

I can feel my ears burn slightly with embarrassment. It's not often Jenny can get to me, but when I'm around Jacey everything is different.

"Do you and Fisher want to come to dinner tomorrow? There's always room for more," Jenny continues.

"That's very kind of you Mrs. Barbieri, but Fish and I actually have a bit of a custom on Christmas," she replies, reaching up to press her reassuring palms against Jenny's hands. She pulls their hands away and holds on just a little bit longer. She may not realize it, but her eyes convey the need for a mother figure in her life. There's a longing for something maternal in the softness of her voice and had I been paying closer attention throughout the evening, I might have noticed it before now. "Some of the staff comes to the restaurant on Christmas morning and we open the dining room for everyone else like us ... everyone who isn't fortunate enough to have a place to go. We do it in their memory. It was my dad's idea, but he didn't have a chance to start the tradition."

Leaning in to hug Jacey, Jenny says, "Your parents would be so proud of you and your brother. I had no idea the two of you were running the restaurant together. The steakhouse was closed for a bit after the accident and we've only been a few times over the years since it reopened."

"They left it to us in their wills. Dad was a good businessman and already had Fisher learning the financial side. Now, everyone gets to look at my beautiful face when they order drinks and get rowdy." Wiping a tear from her cheek, Jacey says, quietly with a laugh, "And here I thought I wouldn't cry this year. I didn't think anyone remembered them."

"They're pretty difficult to forget, sugar. I remember the town planning board meeting where your dad was going over plans for the restaurant. Did you know he wanted to name it 'High Steaks'? He was very good at playing with words. I always remembered that. Your mother wouldn't let him, though. She convinced him to go with Canalside Grill, which was more in line with what the board was going for."

And just like that, Jacey smiles again. A smile that lights up the room.

"Yeah, that sounds like something my dad would do."

Jenny steps back and, holding Jacey at the shoulders, says, "You spent the entire day in my house and I didn't even realize who you were. I feel so horrible. It just never came up, but I am so glad you've been here. We'll get through the holidays and then you and Tommy come over for dinner? I'll make something that doesn't involve turkey or pumpkin pie, yeah?"

Watching them interact I realize just how small this town is. So small that someone new was simply accepted into the fold, into the family. A few different times I came in to reheat or refill coffee mugs and there wasn't a single hiccup in the way all five women maneuvered around the kitchen. It was as if they'd been doing it for years — baking pies and cookies, prepping food for a holiday, clinking glasses, and sipping wine over stories — and maybe that's just a woman thing, but in my absence, they also failed to inquire more about Jacey's past. Why?

Because her past doesn't matter.

If I'm being honest, it's her future I'm concerned with.

"So, tomorrow? You have plans at the restaurant, but if you and Fisher have a chance, we'd love for you to stop by. We'll be at Stella and Brian's house," Jenny continues. "We tend to stay up late playing cards after the kids are asleep, so no silly excuses, you hear me?"

Jacey nods. "Yes, ma'am."

Jenny excuses herself, grabbing the hand towel she originally came in for on her way out, and we're once again left alone in the kitchen. I notice the fresh dampness under Jacey's eyes and wonder when the last time was she allowed herself to get emotional.

"How long has it been since you had a good cry, Miss Jacey?" I ask.

"A real long time. I'll be okay tonight," she responds without looking me in the eyes. One more deep breath and she looks suddenly exhausted.

It's late. It's been a long day and now she's had to add a heavy level of emotions on top of it. I ask if she can give me a ride home since I caught a ride over with Dale and my dad. She raises an eyebrow, gives me a cocky smile and asks, "You want to ride in my— what did you call it? A midget mobile?"

"I'll give it a shot," I say, pushing my hands into my pockets. "Maybe I shouldn't poke fun when I haven't actually given it a fair chance. Plus, my only other rides left hours ago. Stella and Brian took Britt and Emmy home to prepare for Santa's arrival. Max and Steph took Jake home to pretend he cares about the guy coming down the chimney. I mean, really, he's five months old. He honestly doesn't have a clue."

She brushes the hair from her face and looks at me thoughtfully from where she's seated herself on the kitchen counter. The Christmas lights draped across the archway leading to the other room reflect in her eyes and it's magical. The entire day has been nothing short of enchanting and I catch myself moving slowly toward her again, spellbound. Standing before her, I reach to tuck a lock of hair behind her ear and feel the moment her breath catches in her chest because it catches in mine, too. It's sudden and there's an urgency vibrating within me to act without thought, to kiss without abandon, to love her without looking back.

"I'm not sure what I'm doing," I admit quietly, bringing my forehead to rest against hers. "I'm in foreign territory."

"I was told to keep doing whatever it is we're doing. We'll find our way together," she whispers against my lips.

My mouth connects with hers right there in Jenny and Dale's kitchen, as her hands fist my shirt and pull me closer, as my fingers find their way into her hair and my thumbs caress her jaw. Opening her knees, she hooks her feet behind my thighs and allows me room to step into her and I know she feels the same urgency I do.

We pull back at the same time from the kiss. She places her cheek against mine and her palm against my heart as it hammers away in my chest, chiseling her name on its surface.

Jacelyn.

It's imprinted there.

"We should get you home," she says quietly.

"We should," I respond.

We sneak from the kitchen to the mud room for our shoes and jackets. I press my hand to the small of her back as she opens the door. When I turn to pull the door closed behind us, it's hard not to notice the calm smile on Mama's face. She watches us quietly from the kitchen and I want to say something, I want to ask her if I'm doing this right, but without a word more we leave the warmth and head out into the cold and snow.

M.L. Pennock

Chapter Twenty-five

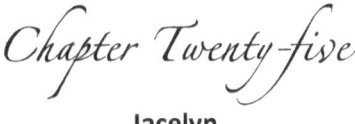

Jacelyn

I hand my keys to Tommy, tell him to be sure he puts the seat back where I like it, and slide in through the passenger door. I'm buckling my belt and he hasn't even opened his door yet. When he finally does, he leans down and gives me a quizzical look.

"What?" I ask.

"Really?" he responds.

"I'm not going to drive and open myself up to you criticizing," I say. I've driven with Fisher in the car before and usually the conversation turns from normal talk to him claiming I'm trying to kill him or cause an accident. I can handle it from my brother because he's always picked on me and I'm fairly certain he's just full of shit.

Tommy slips into his seat and, putting the key in the ignition, says, "I wouldn't criticize you, Jace. I'd rather you drive. You know your car. It's a stranger to me." He glances in my direction as he puts it in reverse and begins backing down the driveway. "But, since you're obviously concerned, I'll drive tonight." He shifts into drive and eases off the brake, pressing slowly on the gas to propel us forward through the freshly fallen snow. "On one condition, though."

"What is that?"

"You stay and try a new recipe with me."

"It's almost tomorrow and you want to bake?"

"I didn't say anything about baking. It's a beverage." In the glow from the dashboard lights, I watch the corner of his mouth lift in a smile, a dimple appearing in his cheek, and my mind wanders just enough to wonder what the future would feel like if it was with him. "I hope you like cayenne pepper," he says, turning into his driveway and pulling to the back of the house.

"A beverage with pepper in it? Okay, I'm intrigued," I say in the sudden quiet of the car.

"I like when you're intrigued," he replies, leaning over the console and placing a kiss to my lips so quickly I question if it was real or my imagination. I decide it was real. If it wasn't I wouldn't feel his absence so fully when he exits his door and comes around to open mine. I wouldn't feel more complete when he reaches for my hand. If it wasn't real, I wouldn't want to feel it again and again and again.

He doesn't let my hand go until we're through the back door of the house, standing in the kitchen, listening to the slow second hand ticking away on the clock above the entrance to his dining room. And when he does let me go, I reach for him like he's a life raft.

Tommy moves behind me and slips my jacket from my shoulders. He disappears to hang it on a hook attached to the back of the laundry room door before making his way around the kitchen, opening the fridge for milk and whipping cream before hunting through the cupboards for a variety of spices.

"Come into my office, Miss Jacey," he says, his drawl a little more pronounced. When I first started getting to know Tommy, I thought it was odd he always called me "Miss Jacey," but as the months have passed I've realized he uses it more as a term of endearment than respect with me. That's not to say he doesn't respect me. I'm certain beyond the shadow of a doubt this man does as no other potential love interest of mine has. There's just something peculiar in the way he hums the M and draws out the remainder of the word before adding my name to it that sets my soul on fire.

I'm left standing at the island in the middle of the room feeling my heart race and he's none the wiser. With his back to me, I quietly take a calming breath. He pulls a saucepan from a cupboard beneath the stovetop and places it on the burner before handing back to me a recipe card with no title on it, just a list of ingredients. "We need to put all the dry ingredients in there and then add the water."

"What are we making, exactly?" I ask, the words sounding more breathless than anticipated, and I step forward to stand beside him.

Handing me a whisk from the drawer between us, he replies as though I asked a silly question. "Mexican hot chocolate." The "duh" is implied at the end of his response. "I've only made this one other time."

"Right. Of course. Because you can't have Christmas Eve without hot chocolate," I say while dumping cocoa powder and sugar in the pan.

My heart is slowly coming back into rhythm when his playfulness, his inner child, stops it altogether.

"I guess ... but I was thinking more about Santa. How rude of us to expect him to stop here and not provide some sort of sustenance for him," he says with a straight face. Then he winks. It makes me tingle where tingling hadn't happened for a long time. "I forgot to buy carrots, so the reindeer are fucked."

"Keep talking like that and you might never get rid of me," I laugh. "Besides, it sounded like Britt was going to leave the reindeer plenty of vegetables and other treats. Pretty sure I overheard him tell Emmy they needed to leave cherry tomatoes and tofu."

He snickers when I mention the tofu. "I might have started that. I convinced him one of the reindeer was on an Asian cuisine kick and he ran with it. I think Stella wanted to disown me when she found out that's why Britt suddenly wanted her to get tofu when she went grocery shopping."

"He's a cute kid. I really like him and his sister," I remark nonchalantly as I whisk the mixture together and wait for it to boil.

"He was so excited tonight hyping up the big guy's descent on the town for his baby sister," he says, animatedly. "That boy has loved Christmas more and more each year since Stella came into his life. She really made their first Christmas together feel like the biggest event of the year," he says. I don't miss the wistful look in his eyes or the way his brows knit together in a crease above the bridge of his nose when I turn slightly to look at him. "It was the first time he had a mom at the holidays and I think she wanted to make up for all the Christmases before."

Now isn't the time to pry into the whys. I know enough of their family history to understand the hurt behind the healing. Instead, I place a reassuring kiss on his cheek while his hand finds the curve of my back like the two were created with one another in mind.

"Emily was special to me," he begins. "She would have been perfect for my brother if it weren't for ..."

"It's okay, Tommy, we don't have to talk about it," I say quietly, a pensive smile forming on my lips. "The past hurts. It's the past for a reason, remember?"

He ducks his head and breathes in deeply. "You're right, it is. Besides, if the past hadn't happened, who knows what the present would be like."

"Exactly. The present." His tongue lazily dampens his bottom lip. I feel my teeth bite into mine. I hear the clock chime midnight as he reaches to turn the knob for the stove burner to 'off.' "The present. Merry Christmas, Tommy."

His fingers trail up my spine to tangle in the short hairs at the nape of my neck. The other glides along my arm until he's cupping my face, then twirling a piece of hair around his index finger. My eyes close at his touch when his thumb slowly caresses my cheek.

"Merry Christmas, Jacelyn," and without another word I feel the softness of his lips against mine. He's gently drawing me in and holding me captive. This isn't a kiss among friends having fun. The energy vibrating off Tommy presses into me, enveloping me until my body hums with want and need as he pushes me back. I take one step, then another, and another until my back's pressed against a wall and my fingernails are tracing the outline of his abs.

The only sounds I hear are the thundering of my heart beating in my ears and his rapid breathing as he breaks the kiss. I don't want to talk. I don't want to ruin whatever this is with words when our bodies can say it so much better. Rising on my toes, I place a trail of kisses to his jaw while my fingertips find the hem of his shirt and slide beneath the fabric. A sigh escapes his lips when my skin touches his; his hips push into me as I slowly scrape my nails up either side of his spine and back down again to dip beneath the waistband of his jeans.

"Table?" he questions.

"Table," I respond as he grabs my hips and slides me the short distance along the wall to the doorway.

He finds the button to my pants as my fingers grip his belt. Together we take six steps through the door until my backside is flush against the dining room table. He fingers the pull tab on my zipper and slowly slips the slider down each and every tantalizing tooth as I stand unmoving with his belt buckle clasped in my hand. Tommy's mouth finds mine again, his hands working their way into my jeans and pushing them down my legs. I'm consumed by the intense feelings he causes within me until he softly bites my lip. It's like someone releasing the pause button. His belt comes off; his jeans pool on the floor with mine. I pull his shirt over his head and place a kiss above his heart as he fumbles with the buttons on my blouse. The fabric sweeps down my arms and is wadded into a ball at the small of my back.

Something shifts. I feel it crackle around me. He stills as I wrap my arms around his waist, placing my ear to his chest as I listen to the quickened thrumming of his heartbeat. I feel his chin come to rest on the top of my head as he pulls me into him tighter.

He sighs. That can't be a good sign, not now that my hands and mouth aren't doing anything that would cause him to do it. "I don't want to have sex with you," he says, quietly, and the breath rushes out of my lungs. "I mean ...

I do want to have sex with you. I'd like very much to do that with you. Again. It's just ..."

I don't breathe. How can I? So, I don't. I hold my breath and pray a little that I'll just pass out because I'm standing in Tommy's house in my underwear, and he's in his underwear, and things were going really well. Until he didn't want to have sex with me. But he does want to? It took all of two seconds for him to confuse my libido.

Placing my hands on his chest, I carefully push away. He releases his arms from my body and they fall to his sides. My eyes follow them and it's really difficult to imagine he doesn't want to have sex with me right this second. I could just unhook my bra and drop my panties and pretend he didn't say anything.

I bend and grab my jeans instead of being risky.

I carefully pull my blouse from his fingers.

I won't force him to want more despite everything telling me he wants so much more than just this.

I look him in the eye and swallow my wants and needs and say, "I think I'm going to go home now," before sidestepping him so I can get dressed in the laundry room.

"Jace, wait," he says as I leave the room. I hear him zipping his jeans as he enters the kitchen behind me and I close the laundry room door. The next time he speaks, his voice is so close. He's on the other side of the door. "Jacey, please, can we talk?"

I want to tell him no, but I won't. He's Tommy and regardless of how much I wish I didn't care about him right now, I know I'll listen to him. I'll let him say what he wants to say and when he's done, I'll go home. Alone. And probably masturbate because I'll be alone and sexually frustrated.

Fastening the bottom four buttons on my shirt, I open the door to his incessant knocking. He doesn't even hide the fact his eyes went directly to the open portion of my blouse. I feel my cheeks flush before I remember I'm upset with him and cross my arms over my breasts.

"What, Tommy?"

He sighs.

"You've done a stellar job confusing the hell out of me over the last several days. One minute you're hot, the next you're ice cold," I say. Flabbergasted, I shout, "You're Elsa. You're the ice queen with a penis!"

He sighs again. I'm starting to get concerned, because in the time I've known him, Tommy has never been so off his game. I've watched him sweet talk women over and over, but this? This is a first.

"If you're not going to talk, I'm going home. I have a busy day tomorrow and you have Christmas with your family." I don't want to argue. I don't ever want to fight with Tommy, so what is he doing potentially picking a fight with me?

"I'm sorry."

I step past him as I say, calmly, "For what?"

"For confusing you. I'm confused. Things are so different with you."

"Tommy, I'm just a girl looking for a guy who might care to stick around long enough to get to know me," I say. I slip my jacket back on and shove my feet into my shoes before turning back to face him. "It's no different with me than it was with Sutton or any other woman you might have had a relationship with before me, if this even is a relationship."

The agitated look on his face tells me I hit a nerve, likely with the mention of Sutton. I can't take it back. There's no point in trying. I meant every word I spoke.

"I wasn't in love with them, though, so it is different," he exclaims and I can see clearly it was said without thinking about the words first. He spoke those words with his heart and his brain is trying to catch up. Shock crosses his features but his recovery time is impeccable. It's just a blip before he's composed again. "I don't want to have sex with you, because I want to make love to you. I want to take my time with you. I've wanted to take my time but every time we're together I want to skip ahead to the next step. I don't think I can take my time anymore because it feels like I'm wasting yours by slowing down. I want you to love me back. Please, Jacelyn, love me back."

Chapter Twenty-six

Tommy

"Please, Jacelyn, love me back."

She could destroy me right now if she wanted to. Those five words are the words that have been echoing in my brain for days. They get louder every time I put the brakes on my emotions.

"Please, Jacey."

I've never asked anyone to reciprocate emotions or feel the way about me that I do about them, but she's not just anyone. I'd like to say I just realized how deep my feelings for her go, but that's not accurate. I don't think I planned to profess my love for her before we were officially dating, though. That definitely wasn't in my carefully constructed timeline. None of this was — we slept together before I took her on a date, she met Mama before we decided if we were a couple, and now this. The order it's supposed to go in is go on a date, have sex, meet Mama, profess my undying love for her, have a lot more sex, get engaged, get married, buy a dog, have three kids over the next six years, and die happy and still as in love with one another as the day we said "I do."

Nothing goes as planned. Why have I not learned that by now?

Dropping my head back I grab my hair and ask her to say something. Anything would do.

"Call me a bastard. Tell me I'm an asshole. Call my mama and tell her she raised a jackass. Anything ... please. Just don't keep standing there looking at me like that and not speaking to me," I say. I hear the pain in my voice. I hear my fear. She might not feel for me the way I feel for her. I'm so scared she won't love me back. What if she was serious about keeping things as friends and decided she was okay with the benefits package but didn't tell me? I can't read her now because she put up all her defenses and they're indomitable.

It would take a Sherman tank to break through.

"You're kind of hanging me out to dry here, Jace. Say something. Please," I whisper, reaching out to gently grasp her upper arms. I brush my thumbs over the fabric of her jacket and wait while the blockade lifts from her eyes.

Her voice is low as she drops her eyes to stare at my bare chest, boring into the space where my heart has stopped beating while I wait for her. "It's late and I need to get up in a few hours to go to the restaurant. I think I should go."

I nod, sadly. "Okay," I say. Placing a finger beneath her chin, she lifts her eyes to mine and it's clear she doesn't want to leave. I'm going to let her go, though. The last thing I want is for her to stay for the wrong reasons.

"You're not a bastard. Or an asshole. I won't call your mama even though right now I do think she raised a jackass," she says slowly as she blinks away the tears forming. "But I need you to be certain. I don't play games with my heart, Thomas, and I've allowed you to pull me in and push me away and pull me in all over again in the span of weeks. I'm not a rubber band. You can't twist me up and expect me not to be damaged and weakened in the untwisting."

I am so in love with her, and I want to tell her again.

I step into her space, leaning my forehead against hers as she closes her eyes and a tear sneaks out. I brush it away with my thumb and lift her lips to mine. One small kiss. Not chaste, but not embroiled with passion, either. It's my promise to her. It's my heart being handed over. It's me telling her I'm certain.

She pulls in a deep breath, steps away, strides to the door, and leaves me standing in the kitchen with the clock ticking loudly above me keeping a tally of the minutes she's gone from my life.

I hear her car start, the sound of the engine echoing against the crisp quiet night, and watch as the headlights back down the driveway until the yard is swathed in black again. I want to go after her, but I want to give her space.

I wander around the kitchen, putting away the ingredients for hot chocolate and dumping down the drain what was in the pot. I quickly wash the dishes left from the day.

Turning out the lights, I walk through the dining room and collect the rest of my clothes. Step by step, I find my way to my bedroom only to once again strip out of my jeans and bite back the need to go after her. Pulling back the comforter, I fall face first into the clean sheets and breathe in deeply. "Why am I such an asshole?" I say as I exhale, the words muffled against the mattress.

Climbing out of a funk has never been my strong suit. I really suck at it and just fake it until I make it back to being happy. The most difficult thing to do is attempt faking happiness around my mama. She can smell my bullshit a mile away. Tonight, she saw me genuinely happy and in less than eight hours she's going to see right through my pretend smile and call me out. The last thing I want to do on Christmas is tell her about this. Not the sexy bits, because she's my mama, but the screwing up part.

I push myself up off the mattress, turn on the bedside light, and pull a notepad and pen from the nightstand. Making lists is something I don't screw up. I start with what I need to do in the morning and work my way through the next several days. I can't fuck shit up if I don't deviate from the list.

Beneath each day of the week heading, I write, "Show J. I love her (more)."

I just need to figure out how. Before I have a chance to brainstorm, I feel my eyelids closing and the pen slipping from my fingers.

~*~*~*~

The phone's shrilly ring yanks me from what might have been the deepest sleep I've achieved in months, a sleep made possible only by complete emotional exhaustion. I grab the handset, wondering why the person on the other end didn't call my cellphone. I'm wondering why I still have a house phone, too, when I hear, "You're late, T."

I scramble out of bed and look at the alarm clock across the room. The alarm clock I never set. "Shit. I'll be there in fifteen minutes," I say to my brother and hang up without waiting for a response.

Every year we wait to do gifts until we're all together. Stockings are the only thing that get opened before the rest of the family arrives, but that doesn't mean I don't make it a rule to be there to see Britton, and now Emmy, open their stockings and see what awesome things they received the night before.

I've never been late.

Usually I just spend the night because at Christmas we're all kids again.

Stripping down to what God gave me, I walk quickly from the bedroom to the bathroom at the other end of the hall. The shower I take is quick enough I question if I got everything clean but assume if I don't smell like gym socks I can pass for clean. Cologne and deodorant were created for a reason, and that reason is for moments like this. Wrapping a towel around my waist and running my hands through my hair, I glance in the mirror.

"You, sir, look like … shit. You look like shit. You should have gone after her last night."

Retraining my focus on leaving the house quickly to get to my brother's, I brush my teeth, rinse, and hurry back to find clothes for the day. Jeans with torn up knees? Sure. White T-shirt? Why not. Green flannel to complete the ensemble? It's festive enough. Picking up a pair of socks as I walk from the room, I jog down the front stairway and sit on the bottom step, pull the socks on, slip my feet into the running shoes I left by the front door, and grab my keys from the entryway table.

Ten minutes have passed since Brian called me, and as I slip a baseball cap on my head and step out into the freezing morning the loneliness begins to settle in around me. Contemplating my bachelor status isn't how I want to spend the holiday. She told me to be certain and if my loneliness is any indication, an oppressiveness that only comes when she leaves, then I'm certain my feelings for her aren't fleeting.

For months I've been talking to her and getting to know her without even trying. I haven't felt the uneasiness with her that I have with women I'm trying to impress because I haven't needed to impress Jacey. It isn't important to make her like some public persona I've created for dating purposes when she wasn't ever supposed to be a prospect. She was the least likely person to fall into the pool of potential women I was to try to woo. Because she's sassy and not blonde and a little bit shorter than I usually like.

Jacelyn has secret strips of pink and purple hidden in the bottom layers of her dark brown hair. They play peek-a-boo when she wears it down, but stand front and center the moment she pulls those locks back into a ponytail. They were new to me the night we spent together and I felt like an explorer making a discovery as I wound the colorful strands around my index finger while she slept peacefully beside me. I didn't comment on the change, I just enjoyed it.

Liking the small stud in her nose is just as out of the ordinary for me, but it adds character to a person who already is bursting with it and I've found myself wondering at times if the scar on her left eyebrow is from another piercing or something else she has yet to share with me.

Her eccentricities are subtle, and maybe that's part of the attraction. Jacelyn hasn't dyed her hair or pierced her skin to make a statement. They're little changes here and there that have been done with purpose.

I pull up in front of my brother's house renewed and hopeful that she'll take me for who I am, too. It's all I can offer.

Chapter Twenty-seven

Jacelyn

"Fisher! I'm missing things! Where are all my ... things. I had more bowls in here. I know I had more bowls," I say. All morning I've been claiming I'm missing utensils and dishes, only for my brother to walk into the kitchen and point to the lost item sitting in plain sight. We only have about two hours before we plan to open the doors and I got no sleep. I couldn't sleep. Not after Tommy and his revelation.

"No, you're not. This is a fully stocked restaurant kitchen. We make meals here every day and always have enough 'things' to create food," he says.

"Are you mocking me?"

"Yes," he deadpans. "You're losing your mind and I don't understand you. What did he do to you last night? You're a train wreck."

I spy the bowl I was missing and grab it with a victorious, "Ah ha! I found you!" and stick my tongue out at him.

"He didn't do anything to me. I mean, he tried, but then it didn't happen and then it just went downhill from there."

So far downhill, so fast. I crack one egg after another into the bowl, whisk them together and add the rest of the previously measured ingredients. It's the third quiche I've made this morning and I'm already tired of eggs. Fisher walks around the end of the prep area and stands a few feet from me at the counter.

Pulling a batch of cinnamon roll dough from a dish and setting it on the floured surface, he says, "What'd he do? Get nervous and forget how to use it?"

My eyes roll without any effort on my part. "You're ridiculous, but no. He didn't forget how to use it. He knows exactly how to use ... it."

"And now I'm thinking about Tom Stratford's penis. This is the worst Christmas ever."

"I can think of worse things to think about at Christmas," I say. The laughter following my words cuts any tension caused by my absentmindedness and the lack of music or caffeine, but my thoughts wander to Tommy and everything that's attached to that one appendage. The smile slides from my face until I feel the muscles relax, only to realize I miss him. Not just the thought of him, but the physical and emotional aspects of him as well. Last night may not have gone exactly as planned, but it went in some direction that won't leave us stagnant. His claim has the potential to propel this non-relationship well into established and public relationship territory. Am I ready for that? I think I might be ready.

Fisher and I work in comfortable silence, together rolling and cutting the cinnamon rolls our dad taught us to make as children. They aren't anything special. No secret ingredients. We only considered it magical because the weekly baking lesson in the family kitchen gave us an additional creative outlet we needed as flour was tossed around, easily coating every inch of floor. So many weekends were spent baking these rolls that Fisher and I have the recipe committed to memory.

"Can I try something different with this batch?" The thought strikes like lightning and I feel warm all over. Fisher looks at me as he spreads the butter, brown sugar, and cinnamon mixture across the flattened dough. I smile and he raises an eyebrow.

"Tommy gave you an idea, didn't he?"

"Maybe. If it tastes delicious I'll give him some credit," I say, realizing my brother is way more in tune to me than I give him credit for.

He groans as I coat the butter with baking cocoa.

"What are you doing? You're not ..."

"I am." I sprinkle a light amount of cayenne pepper across the dough, crossing my fingers behind my back as I do so, because if this is going to taste even a little bit like I hope it will I'm going to need all the luck and good mojo I can get. I only got a little taste last night on the tip of my finger before things got sexy, so I hope my memory serves me well.

"Explain," he says.

"Mexican hot chocolate," I say.

"I see," he says.

"I thought you would," I say.

"This better taste good or you're buying the next hundred pounds of flour."

And I laugh because my brother is both hilarious and probably serious.

~*~*~*~

When we officially open the doors for Christmas breakfast, we're met with the kind faces and warm smiles of those who have nowhere else to go so early in the morning. Some of them, we know, don't have a physical home — their home is simply Brockport. They find shelter in any empty alcove or deep storefront doorway, spending the freezing Western New York winter nights huddled against bitter winds and blowing snow. Some of the store owners are kind enough to offer a sandwich and hot cup of coffee during the day, providing a heavy hunting blanket or pull-out couch on the worst nights, to those who would otherwise freeze to death in the elements. There is no local shelter, but when they give up their pride, the priest at St. Peter's Catholic Church takes them in and gives them a chance to shower, shave, and share a hearty meal with him in return for prayer and the offer of communion.

Not everyone we welcome for the holiday is homeless, though. Most are men and women with no children or extended family and merely want to share the holiday with someone else. This year one couple arrived with care packages for the other guests. Last year, the same couple unloaded the back of their car into our walk-in, filling shelves with extra eggs and milk. Their reasoning was, "Because life can be hard and this year was good to us."

When Fisher and I began this tradition, we just wanted to follow through with Dad's hope to provide at least one meal for the community, to give thanks for the support that had been shown to him over the years. It's turned into so much more.

"Jacelyn, what can I do to help?" My thoughts are interrupted by Will, a middle-aged Army veteran who spends his days doing odd jobs around town. I once asked Will what he does with his evenings, fearful he was one of the lost ones, but his smile broke through as he told me about his volunteer efforts. Five nights a week he travels to the VA Medical Center in Canandaigua to visit and offer support to others who share his history. He says he's lucky to have the opportunity to spend time with his comrades because his volunteering has saved him from himself on more than one occasion, but I think the luck goes both ways.

I offer a smile and hand him a stack of napkins. "Would you mind setting these out? I haven't gotten that far," I say.

The meal has turned into more than just the soup kitchen assembly-line atmosphere we started out with a handful of years ago. I think when Fisher and I moved forward with the idea of Christmas breakfast, we figured all the work would be on us and a few additional staff members if we could afford to have them come in on a holiday since typically we close for Christmas. The first year, the extra hands to help refused to be paid, instead taking a plate each for themselves and sitting to visit with our guests. We took what money they would have been given and put it back into the budget for the following year. Fish and I haven't been doing this very long, but it's been successful and that's what matters. The goal isn't to make money here. The goal is to give back, one meal at a time. I'm amazed, though, each time we open the door, at how the community we're helping shows up ready to help in return. I once said to a guest that they weren't expected to come work for a meal and was shut down when she reminded me that we aren't merely providing food, but fellowship. That's when I stopped feeling like I didn't want help from the friends coming through the door.

I turn to watch as Will carefully places one folded cloth napkin at each place setting. Two tables are set up in the center of the main dining room, each filled with twelve place settings, and I take in the carefully orchestrated commotion unfolding before me. One person fills water glasses, another sets out carafes of orange juice, and yet another places multiple plates of cinnamon rolls on the linen tablecloths so they're within reach of everyone once they take their seats.

This is my family. A roomful of people I wave to as I leave the pharmacy, or chat with in the produce section at Wegmans, has become my family when I felt like Fisher and I had none left. We did this out of loneliness and need. Neither of us ever said it out loud, but we both felt lost. For a while after Mom and Dad passed away the only time I would come home was at Christmas. I would fly in on Christmas Eve and fly out on December 26. This was the only thing I came home for. I came home to find a family where mine had disappeared, save for my brother.

The warmth of someone's arm wraps around my shoulders and I turn slightly to see Genevieve from the corner of my eye. She pulls me close. The town historian tends to grandmother all of us "young folk," and having buried all of mine I welcome the comforts she provides. She has family, a very large one, but since Fisher and I started this tradition she's come to spend the holiday first with us before enjoying the day with her own kin. "Why are you crying, Jacelyn? Today is a happy day," she whispers into my hair.

I reach up to brush the wayward tears from my face. I don't like crying, particularly in public, so I quickly collect myself and feel a smirk start to appear.

"Because they're happy tears, Gen. A lot of feelings are hitting me this year and I'm afraid I'm feeling them all today," I say, leaning into her. "It's nice to spend the holiday with family."

She pulls back slightly and smiles a smile that lifts from her chin to her eyes. "Your brother was so happy when you decided to move home, you know. He talked non-stop for weeks about how you were finally coming back. I think he missed you as much as you missed him. Family is important."

"I'm not talking just about my brother, though," I say matter-of-factly. Scanning the room, I feel Genevieve's eyes follow the same path. "Isn't this what the holiday is supposed to be about? This is family, Gen. This is what makes me whole when I feel like my life is full of holes."

Placing a kiss to my temple, she quietly says, "You are a magical person, Jacey. I don't know how we survived without you."

"I often wonder the same." I squeeze her around the middle and excuse myself to the kitchen. Survival is a funny thing. Some might say in order for them to survive their basic needs must be met — food, water, shelter — which I suppose if you break it right down, of course that's what we all have to have in order to live. But when I talk to Genevieve about surviving I mean it in a different way. I need love, touch, companionship, emotions. I need more than a roof over my head. That's what brought me home. Years of being gone depleted my reserves. I was becoming the empty shell of who I had been. All the art and teaching couldn't fill the gaping voids left from a lack of others who truly cared. I was married, but in the end it wasn't a marriage that was ever built on love. It was convenience and then he conveniently left with whatever he could get his hands on.

The night I talked to Sutton and told her I was moving home she seemed shocked. Her early responses weren't typical for a friend who would welcome me back. More than once through the course of planning my drive east she attempted to talk me out of relocating. I had a collection of texts saying there was nothing here, the town was shrinking, no one ever wanted to come back home, and a slew of other unkind things. She seemed to finally resign herself to the fact I wouldn't be talked out of my decision. I rarely can be, and this time was going to be no different. Looking back, I see why she might not have wanted me to uproot myself from California and why her responses became less and less frequent.

Fisher sees me walk through the kitchen and though I try to ignore the obvious concern in his expression, I can't.

"You okay? I mean, I know this time of year is hard for both of us, but you're not a public weeper."

"I'm not weeping now, nor was I before. I had a momentary lapse of handling my emotions at work. A glitch. Cross my heart, I'm okay," I say while dragging my index finger across my chest in an X pattern. "Besides, it wasn't out of sadness and now I don't want to talk about it because you ruined it."

He mocks disgust before turning toward the window overlooking the back parking lot and saying, "I ruined it?" His tone changes drastically from the normal playfulness I'm accustomed to and his body responds in kind. Fisher doesn't tense up just because. "I don't think I'm going to be the one to ruin your day, Jace. Maybe you should go home, or to Tommy's Christmas thing."

I'm not sure what he's trying to pull, but watching my brother pop his knuckles is enough to get me over to the counter next to him. That's when I get it. I understand why he thinks I should leave.

The tightness in my chest gets tighter with each step she takes toward the rear entrance of the restaurant. I'm choking on the air trapped in my lungs as I watch a casually dressed man come into view, and the thought strikes me that they might be here together, which is silly because she hasn't mentioned a man.

"Maybe you should go see Tommy. Go hang with them for a while," Fisher says. Neither of us take our eyes off the scene in front of us as Sutton turns back and holds her hand out for him. He takes it. She smiles at him. He smiles back as they disappear around the building.

"Don't," Fisher says as I take hurried steps toward the dining room. "Don't make a scene. Whatever you're going to say to her, say it quietly or take it somewhere else. I don't want today to be tainted. Not today," he says sternly.

There isn't a response good enough for me to give him, but I acknowledge his request with a nod before making a beeline for the front of the restaurant. I don't plan to make a scene, but does anyone ever really plan those things? I'll do my best to not ruin the day, but the hundred-pound weight on my chest feels heavier as I hear her voice. As I hear his voice. Cement pools around my feet and I'm stuck just steps from the coat room where they quietly talk.

"I don't understand why you want to do this," he says.

"Because I need to make amends, Silas. You need to try to understand that or you shouldn't have come. There's a long stretch of Thruway calling your name if you want to high-tail it back to Rockland County," she says.

"The Thruway was only a small portion," he says.

"A long stretch of highway, then. Is that better?" she asks.

Eavesdropping makes it possible to hear people say things without them changing their demeanor, either purposely or not. Hearing her laugh, and then the sound of a brief kiss, pulls me out of snooping. I cough. I hear the sharp intake of her breath. He asks if she's ready to do this. Do what, I wonder? She says she is and I hear feet shuffle in my direction. The tips of her shoes peek out of the room and she takes one more deep breath before stepping into my line of sight.

I offer a smile, a small one. She pales. He smiles warmly and says, "You must be Jacelyn." He offers me his hand and I shake it.

"I am. I'm afraid I don't know who you are though," and his smile fades slightly. I turn my attention back to my friend. "Hello, Sutton."

"Hey, Jace," she offers meekly. "I figured this was the best place to find you. Remember, I said I would see you at Christmas? Surprise."

I recall the conversation. It was just one of the phone calls we had that twisted my heart into confusion because she tried to convince me not to move back home but also said we'd get together over the holidays.

"Surprise, indeed. Are you here to eat? Or just to wreak havoc on my emotions?" I bite my lip. My stupid mouth. "I didn't mean that." But I did. "It's just been an emotional day for me already and I wasn't expecting to see you, or you with a man."

I shake my head and excuse myself, turn on my heel, and walk to the bar. It's not private by any means, but I need distance. My phone vibrates in my back pocket. It's persistent. The third time I feel the vibration against my rear end, I look at the screen. Sliding to answer the call, I skip the hello. It feels like we're well beyond formalities at this point.

"Was I sending up bat signals?"

"Fisher called me. I'm coming down there," Tommy responds. "I just wanted to forewarn you. You've had enough surprises for one day."

"I can handle this." I'm unconvincing. My voice wavered.

"She showed up unannounced with some dude. You cannot handle this." He doesn't need to be told he's correct, he knows it, so I stay quiet. His voice softens, "I'll be there in ten minutes. Don't commit a double homicide before I get there. We'll handle it together."

I say nothing and hang up as I sit on a barstool, waiting for the anxiety to dissipate and wondering if ten minutes could pass just a bit quicker. She stands in the doorway, watching me, a softness in her features that makes me wish whatever pushed us apart had never existed. When did that separation begin? How long has this been coming to an end?

"I didn't mean to spring myself on you," she says softly. "If I called to say I was coming home, would you have answered? If I had sent a text message, would you have responded?" She waits. I say nothing. "Jacey, there are a lot of things that have happened since I moved downstate. I didn't talk to anyone about it. Not you, not my mom … no one."

I find my voice and finally look at her. "Who is he?"

"His name is Silas. He's my son's adoptive father." She must see me tense up as I shoot a glance toward the bar entrance at the man standing there, his hands hanging lazily from where he's hooked his thumbs into the front pockets of his pants. "Before you judge me, please understand this isn't something I sought out."

"It never is," I bite back. "You can't ask me not to judge considering the rest of what's come to light recently. You don't get that luxury."

The flame rising from my neck to my ears is so hot, I welcome the cool rush of air as the front door swings open and shut.

"Give me the abridged version," I say stonily. "At least give me that much."

She composes herself, sits down on a stool opposite me, and with her back to the door doesn't see Tommy walk in. I see him, though, and the small smile that plays on his lips before he mouths the words, "I'm right here."

"I did an open adoption, Jacey. That meant I was able to meet the people who wanted my baby before just sending him off to live and grow up without me. It means I get to be there as much as his adoptive family is willing to let me be. Silas and his wife were the perfect people to raise Chandler and I knew it the moment we met. What I didn't know was how much I would love Chandler's new family," she says. I feel like I know where this story is going, but make the snap decision to do as she asked and attempt to reserve judgment. At the very least, Sutton seems genuine and happy, so I give her the benefit of the doubt. "The thing is, they love me, too."

She struggles to find her words as I watch over her shoulder at Tommy, a look of confusion on his face, as he tries to make sense of something Silas has said. He isn't at all quiet when his eyebrows rise in astonishment and he says, "They share you?"

I turn my attention back to Sutton, who hangs her head, and mumbles, "So much for letting me ease into it."

"Share?" I ask.

"They sort of have an open marriage."

"You mean she allows him to cheat as long as she knows who it's with?" I'm not a stupid person, but I'm honestly curious. I was pretty certain she was going to tell me something along the lines of he was leaving his wife for her. Open marriage wasn't even on my radar. I'm well aware they're all consenting adults, but it's shocking that Sutton would want to be part of something like this. She can be possessive and triangles aren't like her.

"It's not cheating. It's an agreement between us all." Her voice wavers at the end of her statement, but I hear her plead with me to understand. "Things have been rocky between the two of them."

"You don't like to share your food. How is sharing a man working out for you? Is there a contract? Did you have to sign something? This is beyond my comprehension," I say, erupting in nervous laughter. I can't turn it off. "This is absurd, Sutton. You couldn't even tell me you were going to give birth and give your baby up for adoption, but you can walk in here with the man who adopted him and tell me you're in a relationship with him and his wife. It's bullshit. Utter bullshit. Our friendship has meant nothing to you if you can keep things like this from me. We talk, or at least used to talk, about everything."

Or did we talk about everything? Two steps forward, one step back seems to be my friendship with Sutton and it's become more apparent the more mature I become. Sitting with her, I'm realizing I may have outgrown the longest friendship I ever had. Maybe we've outgrown each other. I want to be sad about it, but I can't force a feeling if I'm not experiencing it.

I catch her eyes rolling just slightly as she haughtily replies, "Don't whine, Jacey. Our friendship has meant the world to me. There are just some things I didn't want to share with you because I didn't think you'd ever understand."

"Like dating a married couple? I'm still very much a small-town girl despite the years I spent out west, Sutton, so no I don't think I'd ever understand that. Hell, I can't successfully date one person without screwing it up let alone two. Especially not two people who are married to each other!"

Tommy shoots me a glare. I didn't mean I can't successfully date him, but I don't say it because the conversation isn't about us right now. I'm not ready to have that talk today.

"I'm not in a relationship with his wife," Sutton quickly interjects. I'm not sure if that makes this better or worse. "We've become friends, yes, but I'm only dating Silas. It's not even really dating. It's more like friends with benefits right now."

Friends with benefits is language I can grasp, and my attention snaps to Tommy again. She sees me looking at him, not that I hid where my gaze wandered, and I need for her to not question me about it.

"When you put it that way it doesn't sound horrible, but the fact he's married bugs me, Sutton. I'm in no way going to try to tell you how to live your life, but as someone who has known you for a majority of it, be careful,"

I say. This may be the end of an era, but that doesn't mean I wish her ill will. It simply means I know when enough is enough.

She purses her lips and studies me momentarily. Leaning toward me, she quietly asks, "Is there something going on between you and Tommy?"

I want to tell her about us, I want to share with her the emotions he makes me feel, but now it doesn't feel right. She no longer gets that part of me. Besides, it feels like she's searching for gossip, or at least for the spotlight to be shone somewhere other than on her. I don't blame her, but at the same time I don't want to know more about her relationship so she doesn't have to be concerned about me attempting to get more details. Spotlight officially turned off.

"He's a good friend and someone Fisher's done business with. That's all you need to know," I say, a tight smile crossing my lips as I stand up from my seat at the bar. She gives me a look, one that tells me she's thinking about trying to pry. I won't give her that. "It was good to see you, Sutton. I hope you've been able to find what you were looking for. Merry Christmas to you and your family."

As I walk from the bar back through the dining room, I feel lighter.

 Chapter Twenty-eight

Sutton

I'm stuck. I can't make my legs move as she walks from the room and slings her arm through Tommy's. It's a casual gesture, and while it could be one among friends, there's something intimate about it.

That kind of intimacy is one I have yet to find with anyone. I don't think I've allowed myself to be emotionally intimate even with Silas. We've been intimate, but there's a huge difference between sexual intimacy and emotional intimacy. We're not there yet. Watching Tommy and Jacelyn, they have both. It's in their body language. It's in the way her shoulders relax the minute he touches her.

Silas rests his hand on my lower back and I shudder at the sudden invasion of my personal space.

"I didn't mean to startle you," Silas says. There are questions hanging in the air between us as I tilt my head to smile at him.

"You didn't," I lie. "Are you ready to go? I think it's time to head back."

He thinks I mean to the hotel. I mean to Nyack.

"Sure, if you are," he says, raising an eyebrow as he studies me. "Did you get what you needed? Amends and whatever?"

"I got exactly what I deserved," I say, sadly, and find the will to move, taking long strides to the coat room.

Silas stands behind me, holding my jacket out, and I slip my arms in. We walk to the car in silence.

Dead silence.

He starts the car as I climb in the passenger seat and pull the seatbelt across me.

Silence.

It's like the day of my first ultrasound all over again and I feel like I can't be with Silas, just like I couldn't be with Tommy. I can't have this baby in my life now, just like I couldn't have him in my life then. But I do have him in my life and I have Silas, and I honestly don't want to give up either. I want the deeper emotional connection with him. Just once, I want to have that with someone.

Silas puts the car in drive and pulls from the back lot to the highway. I stare out the window as the loss begins creeping in, the void and emptiness of no longer having Jacey to turn to. I haven't confided in her in a long time. I could have if I wanted to; I just didn't. Now, I simply can't. She's not open to that relationship with me anymore. I wouldn't want to be my friend either if I were in her shoes.

"What did you mean? You said you got exactly what you deserved. What do you think you deserved?" he asks.

I take a moment to find my voice, because it's lost inside somewhere and I'm not sure why. I've never lacked for words. Looking at my lap and my intertwined fingers, I say, "I deserved to lose her. After all I've done and not done, I deserve that."

"What do you mean you lost her? She was right there. I mean, she seemed pretty upset at first, but by the time you were done talking it looked like everything was okay," he says.

I rest my sights on his profile, his beautiful dark hair that curls just below his ear and the sharp jawline that made my breath hitch the first time I met him. When he smiles, the beginnings of crow's feet appear at the edges of his eyes … and I love them.

"What you saw was my best friend breaking up with me. She was being nice about it, but she was dismissing us. I don't blame her. We've become two very different people," I say as I continue studying his features. "It's the way things are. You grow together and then, sometimes, you grow up and grow apart. I never thought it would happen with me and Jacey, but I also never thought I would get pregnant, go through an adoption, and start fooling around with the man who adopted my baby."

Silas brakes and brings the car to a stop at a red light, cocks his head slightly, and waits a beat to speak. "Is that what this is to you? We're just fooling around?"

I smile disingenuously. "It doesn't feel like dating, Silas. It's not a monogamous relationship where we come home to each other every night. You split your time between me and Daphne, but she gets you at home every night," I say quietly. This conversation has happened before. I knew what I was getting into. I agreed to have him part-time. "I'm not angry about it."

The light turns green and I feel the car slowly accelerate. "If we were just 'fooling around,' I probably wouldn't have driven nearly six hours on Christmas so you could talk to your best friend in person. Why did you want me to come with you, Sutton?" His tone has a harshness to it, a defensiveness I haven't heard before.

I don't have an answer for him. Not a good one. Not one where I can tell him I've thought a thousand times in the last few months how having a nice little family and not having to share him would make me feel complete. It's not the right time to share that with him.

"Can we not do this right now?"

He signals and turns into the hotel parking lot, parks the car, opens my door, and waits for me to exit. My legs feel leaden, but I make them move the rest of me through the parking lot, to the room, and to the bed where I collapse. He stands at the entrance to the room, sadly staring at me.

"Let's just not do this, okay, Silas?" I pull a pillow to my chest as I lay with my eyes closed and listen to him move around the room. "It's Christmas and I don't want to argue."

"I'm not planning to argue with you," he says. I feel the weight of his body as he lays down on the bed beside me. I feel his fingertips as he moves the hair from my cheek and tucks it behind my ear. "I'm going to tell you, though, that I don't feel like we're just friends with benefits or fooling around. I wouldn't be leaving my wife if that was the case. There are emotions involved, and I think that's why you wanted me to come here with you."

I slowly open one eye.

"I'm here for moral support," he says.

I close my eyes again.

"I don't think I want to talk about this anymore," I say.

"Is an open adoption what you really wanted for him? Are you sure this is the best thing for you?"

That's a question I would have expected before we finalized the adoption, not eight months after. "That's kind of a low blow right now, don't you think? Yes, this is what I wanted for him," I say, wishing he didn't see my vulnerability. "There are days when I'm not sure it's best for me. Today is one of those days. Not having my best friend to talk to makes it worse."

He and Daphne know I've battled with my decisions and continuously remind me I made the best choice I could for Chandler. I don't regret those decisions, or the relationship I've built with all of them, but I also don't admit to anyone just how much I feel like I'm on the losing end. Each time Silas leaves my bed, I lose a little more as he goes back to a family and I go to sleep alone.

"When you said you wanted to be with me … why me? You and Daphne have this great relationship and what looked like a pretty solid marriage until I came along," I say.

His laughter surprises me.

"Great relationship, yes. Solid marriage, not so much. We've known each other for so long it's just … routine. A routine," he says, reaching out to rub my arm. I watch as he struggles for the next words. He squints his eyes and says, "It's a ruse, Sutton. Daphne and I are married on paper. She's my wife and we share a last name and an apartment, but, to use your word, I'm in a monogamous relationship with you."

My confusion is apparent and I question him. I put him in front of the firing squad and aim.

"We did the pact thing in college — if she wasn't married by the time she was thirty and I wasn't married either we'd marry each other. It sounds ridiculous, but she's my best friend, so it seemed natural to move in that direction. No one else lived up to what I had with Daphne and the day she turned thirty, we went out for drinks and I told her it was time to make good on our pact," he says, laughing. I'm not sure I see the humor. "We knew we both wanted kids and we tried for a while without any luck. We gave it almost two years. You know all this."

Silas looks at me, a serious expression on his face.

"We've had an open marriage since the day we signed the license. It gave us an out if 'the one' came along. I was fine being with her and only her. Things have changed. A lot of things have changed. We were in the process of deciding if we wanted to continue pursuing adoption or give up all together when you popped into our lives," he says. "We opted to move forward with an open adoption, and then take things one day at a time."

There's a "but" coming and I can feel it as Silas props himself up on his elbow.

"But …" I prompt him, because the anticipation is horrifying.

"But neither of us wanted to close the door on the other if true love came knocking. She realized the more you came around, the more time we spent with you, that there were qualities about you that I was falling for," he says sheepishly. "Our marriage was never meant to last. It was an effort to not grow old and lonely because everyone else we knew was getting married and having kids. Daphne could see the end coming for us. I think she saw the beginning of you and I coming as well. You were already such a huge part of our life. She wanted me to see what, if anything, could happen if I pursued a relationship with you. The reason I go home every night I'm with you is so I can be there to help with the baby during the night and during the morning rush. Sutton, Daph and I are getting divorced. That's the truth. I'm moving into an apartment halfway between you and her. I was going to wait to tell you until we could all have dinner together."

I'm not sure how I'm supposed to feel. Happy I won't be dating a married guy should probably be one of my emotions. Then again, I'm sad to learn my friends are getting divorced and there's definitely shock being felt.

"What does this mean for us, Silas?" I ask, hoping he'll tell me how I should feel about everything. I need him to spell it out for me. It's not even noon and I'm already exhausted from the day. It's all been too much.

Silas reaches for my hand as I push myself off the bed. I don't let him take it. Gathering my hair in my hands, I pull it back into a ponytail in hopes it will make the sensation of vomit rising to the back of my throat go away. At the very least, if I do get sick I'm prepared for it.

"What am I supposed to feel?" He stares at me as I toss the question into the air. A hand on one hip, I point my other hand at him, and make accusations. "This isn't a lie is it? You're not bullshitting me because I'm having a hard time being with you but not being with you, are you? It's not nice to play games like that. I would know. I've played them before!"

He shakes his head as he pushes himself to sit on the edge of the bed, taking my outstretched hand in his. "No. No bullshitting," he says. "I want you in my life, but, considering all of the circumstances surrounding our being together, and where Chandler is concerned, it would be nice if we can take our time. Maybe we can start over. I can ask you out on a date instead of us just jumping into bed together."

"Monogamous."

"Just you and me."

"You're going to have to woo me. Flowers once in a while would be really nice after all this."

"Got it. Flowers. I've added it to the mental check list."

I wish my life wasn't so screwed up. Then again, if it wasn't, I probably wouldn't have wound up where I am.

M.L. Pennock

Chapter Twenty-nine

Tommy

No one is immune to Jacey's cheerfulness. As she moves around the dining room, visiting with people who came out to spend Christmas morning with her and Fisher, there isn't a sign of regret present for the ties she cut in the other room.

Jacelyn's smile spreads a warmth through me I tend to feel only when I'm looking at her. As I sit with a cup of coffee and a cinnamon roll in front of me, I catch her eye. She mouths, "Hi, handsome," to me from across the room with a little wave. Playfully, I turn and look behind me, then turn back, point to myself, and feign shock. She laughs, and my heart explodes.

"I'm in love with you," I mouth back to her.

"No, you aren't," she says out loud, but laughs again before retreating to the kitchen.

Oh, but I am, Miss Jacey.

Fisher settles his tall frame into a chair next to me, a mug of coffee in one hand and a plate of bacon in the other. Just bacon. I stare at the plate. "Is that your breakfast?" He drops his gaze to the table and shrugs.

"Apparently Jace's amazing new cinnamon rolls actually are amazing, so I didn't even get one. Go figure," he whines.

"Aw, poor Fish didn't get a special breakfast roll. Here, you can have mine," I say and push the plate toward him, but he shakes his head.

"Nah, you can have it. You're the one who gave her the idea for the filling so you should at least try it," he says.

I'm not sure how I gave Jacelyn the idea for anything when I've been nothing but hot and then cold with her. Tepid. I've been tepid and it's been a horribly strange mix of comfortable and wanting to step out of my comfort zone.

Just to appease him, I cut the roll in half in case Fisher changes his mind and then cut a piece to eat. It's in my mouth and I can taste something familiar, but can't put my finger on it, and Fisher is watching me curiously.

Then I taste the sting of cayenne pepper and laugh. "Wow," I say, more to myself than to Fisher, but I see him nod his head. "When did she make these?"

"About six this morning. I don't think she slept after you fucked with her head. She was all wound up and losing things in the kitchen that were right in front of her and then out of nowhere she starts throwing cayenne pepper and cocoa powder down on my dough like she discovered a number after infinity," he says dramatically. He's spun up about something or it's Irish coffee in his mug instead of just black. I'm highly amused by him this morning. "There is no number after infinity, Tommy! She was giddy."

I don't deny that I messed with her emotionally. I did and I have enough guilt eating away at me as it is, so I resist the temptation to have a man-to-man conversation with her brother about what's going on. He doesn't need to be in the middle of it and I hope he doesn't intend to insert himself. This might be one of those things Jacey and I need to figure out on our own. We won't know until we actually take time to talk to one another.

"And you, my friend, are grumpy," I counter. "What is with you?" I have a strong feeling I know what's with him and it starts with a capital S. With her being friends with Jacey I'm sure there's history there with Fisher as well, I just don't know how much or exactly what sort of history it is. He groans beside me. I take another bite of my breakfast, which is a fantastic substitute for Brian's coffee cake. I'm hoping there's some of that left over for me when I get back to my brother's house, though, because it's not Christmas without it. But if Fish leaves the other half of this cinnamon roll, it's going with me.

Before I can get too distracted by food, Fisher shifts in his chair so he can speak quietly. "They've been friends, like best friends, since they were kids. If she worked things out with Sutton, she'd be here having breakfast and visiting with Jacey. She's not, which means that entire era of 'them' is done, right?" he asks, rhetorically. Leaning closer to me, he adds, "Jacelyn's way too calm about this. Look at her. She's on cloud nine. It makes no sense."

I take his lack of argument into deep consideration before speaking. Isn't it okay for his sister to be content with leaving her friendship behind?

"What if she really is at ease about it all? Are you going to watch over her like a hawk until the end of time worrying she's going to crack and break into a million pieces because she and her friend grew apart? People grow and change, Fisher. Just because men usually do it without a bunch of fanfare doesn't mean women can't satisfactorily end a relationship or friendship in the same manner," I say.

He looks at me in disbelief and I feel like shrinking in my seat just to get away from the glare. Did I say something wrong or does he believe me even less than I believe myself? Instead of withering, I sit up straight like my mama always told me to.

"Too many big words, T. Too many," he says, then grabs his coffee and bacon plate, stands and walks to the other end of the table.

I gather my dishes and my thoughts. Heading toward the kitchen, I stop along the way to pick up empty plates and cups that were forgotten in the midst of new and old friends visiting with one another. I push through the door and stop short when I see Jacelyn standing at the sink, her cheeks pink and splotchy. Lifting a bubble-coated hand from the water and swiping a sleeve across her eyes, she manages a sad smile in my direction.

"Hey," she says.

I say nothing, but walk to her, set the dishes on the counter beside the sink, and pull her to me. She wraps her arms around my waist and holds on tight.

"I wasn't crying," she says and I kiss the top of her head.

"I know," I say, agreeing not to acknowledge her breakdown.

"I'm okay with her having her life and me having mine. It's been that way for a while," she says. She sighs deeply. She's accepting change and resigning herself to one less person to rely on. Her fingers find their way beneath my flannel shirt and trail up and down my spine, dishwater and a tingling sensation left in their wake, as we stand silently holding onto one another as a chapter in both our lives comes to a close. Day by day, I allowed the feeling of losing Sutton to dwindle and disappear. But my time with Sutton is a blip in history compared to Jacelyn's. She takes another deep breath, and then, "It's the finality of it that feels strange. I broke up with my best friend, Tommy, and it feels … good. It feels good to have had that conversation, have that goodbye. I'm almost more upset I feel good about it than that it's happened at all."

She lifts her head and looks me in the eye, a question bouncing around on her lips. She purses them slightly, trying to keep from saying what's on her mind now, but she can't help it. "An open marriage, though? Say nothing about her having that kind of relationship with the guy who adopted her baby. Who cares who it is, it's the fact he's married that I'm having trouble with. I mean, to each their own, but I don't think that's something I could or would ever be comfortable with."

I give her a crooked smile and hug her to me a little more tightly.

"It's weird, right? Sharing your husband?"

"I've never had a husband, so I can't say for certain," I tease. "However, I don't know as though I would want my wife, if I had a wife, to consider sharing me. I'm sure it works for some couples, but I like to think of myself as a one-woman kind of guy. Sometimes I even have trouble handling one woman, so two would be out of the question."

She presses her cheek to my chest. I feel her relax against me.

"You can barely handle yourself, say nothing about handling a woman, Tommy."

"I could handle you," I say. Pausing, I add, under my breath, "If I could stop screwing it up, anyway."

"You're really good at screwing it up," she says. Her fingers continue making small circles on my back, the tickling sensation doing things to my lower half I can't seem to control and I shift uncomfortably. She snickers. "Seriously?"

"I'd apologize, but I was hoping you'd take it as a compliment not just a physiological reaction," I say.

"Big words so early in the morning," she says, echoing her brother's sentiments. "I do take it as a compliment, though. It's nice to know even after walking out on you last night I can still get a reaction from you."

I hold myself to her longer, hoping she doesn't let go and wondering how I should respond to that. "You were right to walk out," I finally say. "I've kind of been a dick." She doesn't dispute the fact, so I go on. "Jace, it's been a really long time since I've had any sort of romantic relationship that didn't end badly. I tend to feel too quickly and get hurt too easily, so I've made a point to not fall in love with anyone. It was easy, until you came along."

She makes no attempt to step out of my arms, but the slow circles continue to be drawn on my back.

"You're the first one to take your time with me. There was no pretense that our friendship would stop being just a friendship and there was no expectation of going from acquaintances to bed partners," I say. Kissing the top of her head again, I add, "With you, it feels natural, which is why I've had a difficult time getting my head on straight. It's always felt forced. But with you? I learn more about you every time we talk and it doesn't feel like we're rushing to know everything about one another just so we can justify having really good sex."

She laughs and lifts her face so I can see her eyes. "It is pretty good, isn't it?"

There's a mischievous glint in her eye as she bites and tugs the edge of her lip into her mouth. Pulling away from her just enough to place my hands on either side of her neck, I caress her jaw and lower my mouth to hers. She releases her lip and I feel the rush of a kiss that tastes like perfection. She fits me, every bit of me.

~*~*~*~

"Wow."

"You don't have more to say than that? Come on, Brian, you're rarely at a loss for words," I say. I stayed at the restaurant to help clean up and in the process convinced Jacey and Fisher to come back with me for dinner. While Jace and her brother are busy playing Chutes and Ladders with my nephew, I've been trying to bring Brian up to speed on Sutton.

"Sure, I have a lot I could say," he responds. "I'm trying to figure out the mechanics of a relationship like that, though. And the baby? How does it all work?"

I shake my head but don't tell him I refuse to give it more thought than it's worth. Sutton made her decision to leave me, leave Brockport, and leave everything behind. Her life is her life and I'm not part of that any longer. Her leaving me opened doors that would have otherwise stayed closed and locked.

"What's Jacelyn think?" he questions, nodding toward the other room.

"That's not really something I can answer, but she seems to be in the 'to each their own' camp," I say, glancing through the open kitchen doorway and catching her watching me. She gives a small smile before giving Britt her undivided attention once again. "I don't know how she does it. It's like she grabbed hold of all her anger, shook the hell out of it, and then shoved it to the curb. I think the closure from seeing Sutton was what she needed. The rest of it? So be it. Enough about that. What are the plans for New Year's Eve?"

I need to change subjects. There's no reason to focus on Sutton when we're supposed to be celebrating the holiday and being together as a family. With less than a week until the new year, nothing has been planned for a big gathering like we've had in the past. I'd like to say I'm surprised, but with the family baby boom, no one really has their minds on champagne toasts and staying out past midnight. I'm not even sure Steph and Stella would be able to stay awake that late.

"Stell wants to get a sitter and go out for a little while at least. Max and Steph said they'd go out for a drink, but not stay out all night. Greg and Caryn are going to some event in Rochester and staying the night out there," Brian says. He tips a bottle of beer to his lips and rolls his eyes slightly, saying under his breath, "You're single and lonely."

The sting he hoped to deliver with his words doesn't even register because I'm not lonely. Taking another peek at Jacey, I'm not so sure I'm single, either.

"Not so, brother, not so," I say. Leaning against the cupboards, I grasp the counter and tap my index finger.

"To which accusation?"

"Definitely the lonely part, possibly the single part," I respond. "I acted stupid last night, but I think she might forgive me. Jace and I talked about it a little today, but not like we need to. Plus, it's not like we've had much time alone what with surprise visits and family gatherings."

Stella wanders into the kitchen with Emmy attached to her hip and grabs a pie from the counter. "Boys. Dessert. Grab plates." She gives directions like a drill sergeant, but we don't waste time carrying plates, silverware, and more desserts to the dining room. It seems like everything baked yesterday at Dale and Jenny's is on the table today.

"Are you boys taking your ladies out for New Year's Eve?" Mama asks. I shoot her a look, curious if she heard me and Brian talking or if she's just utilizing her motherly instincts, and notice her rubbing a spot on her chest.

Brian shares with her the same thing he told me, leaving out the part about my relationship status or level of loneliness.

"You know, your dad and I were planning on staying in New York until next weekend. If you'd all like, Jenny and I would keep the kids while you go out," she says, pausing to take a bite of apple pie. "Then you don't have to worry about paying a teenager and we can just camp out with the kids at their house. Remember when you boys were little? We set the clock forward so it was midnight at your normal bedtime and made party hats. Jenny, we need to do that with the kids!"

"Way ahead of you. I have construction paper and sparkling grape juice in the cupboard already," Jenny says. "What do you say, guys, let you go out and act like twenty-somethings for the night?"

Steph and Max jump at the offer, but plan to pick Jake up before going home for the night. I could be mistaken, but I think Stella started making a mental list of what to pack for Emmy and Britt to take for their sleepover before the offer was finalized.

Sitting next to Jacelyn, I knock my knee into hers under the table. "What are you doing for New Year's?" I ask softly as everyone else begins discussing plans. "Would you like to join us for a few hours of debauchery and alcohol induced laughter?"

Lifting a glass of wine to her lips, Jacey turns her head to look at me. There is joy in her eyes, contentment in her smile, and playfulness on her tongue. "Wild horses couldn't keep me away."

I smile back and over Jacelyn's shoulder I see Mama, a pleased look on her face. When she notices me watching her, she winks.

~*~*~*~

The night began winding down when the wine started running out. There wasn't a whole lot to begin with, but we made it last longer than Christmases past.

"You should let him take you home. I need to go back to the restaurant and pull some things from the freezer for tomorrow. You don't need to come with me to do that," Fisher says. "What you do need is sleep."

Jacelyn softly responds, "I can take myself home. It's not that bad out and it's not that far. I've walked longer distances in worse weather."

I take that as my cue to stop listening and take a little action. Walking toward the front door, I grab my boots and apologize for interrupting a family conversation. Fisher cocks an eyebrow at me before saying, "You can take her home, right? She won't listen to me that it's too cold to walk back to her place."

Slipping my feet in, I pull the laces of each boot tight. "Fish, I grew up down south and even I don't think it's that cold. I can walk back with her if she wants to walk, though." I smile at Jacey and grab my jacket from the hook, then reach for her coat and hold it out for her. "Mama! I'm heading out. Y'all have a good night!"

A chorus of "good night" echoes through the house because everyone answers when I call out. Fisher wishes Jacey and me a merry Christmas and offers me his thanks for walking with her as he follows us out the door and turns the opposite direction to his car.

We walk in silence for the first half block. Then we each try to start talking at the same time. So, we both be quiet again, in anticipation of the other starting a conversation. Her breath comes out in tiny puffs. She chances a glance at me and catches me doing the same to her. She smiles and tucks her chin into the collar of her coat, then lifts her scarf up higher to keep the chill out.

"So ..." I start. Then my hand finds hers and her gloved fingers tangle with mine. That's when I feel them. The butterflies.

And I'm certain.

This girl is my one.

Chapter Thirty

Jacelyn

A week ago, I was standing in Tommy's kitchen telling him, in no uncertain terms, to get his shit together. I told him to be certain, and then walked out and left him standing in his kitchen with an erection.

Then he walked me home on Christmas and I felt like a high school kid finding out the boy she likes, likes her back. He took my hand as if it was the most natural thing to do.

I felt them. The butterflies. But, what if he didn't feel them, too?

I dare not ask, because how childish of me. A thirty-year-old man does not feel butterflies. Does he? Even if he did, he didn't act on them. He walked me to the door of my building, not up the stairs to my actual door. He kissed my cheek, but didn't try to touch my lips. He asked me if I had a nice Christmas and I replied I had. He smiled, said goodnight, and walked away with his hands in his jacket pockets and a satisfied bounce in his step.

He hasn't talked to me since and despite all the text messages I've started to write, I haven't talked to him either. That doesn't mean he hasn't been in contact. Flowers were delivered to the restaurant the next day. The day after that, a sweater I had been eyeing online and had brazenly sent him a screenshot of weeks ago showed up on my doorstep. A new set of paintbrushes came after that. Each day it's been something different, usually a small gesture. Size doesn't matter because even the smallest gesture from him has spoken volumes. There's never been a man in my life to go out of his way like this. Ever. It's overwhelming and romantic. I'm not used to romance.

Now, here I am, on New Year's Eve wearing actual lip stick and eyeliner and a dress, but the rest of me isn't ready. The butterflies are back every time I think about him. Is this a date? I don't know if this counts as a date. The last several days have felt like a courtship, not a lead-in to group activities, but we're going out as a group. I'm not entirely sure if Tommy is bringing me along as a friend or if we're going as a couple since nowhere in the gifts he's sent me has there been a note saying, "Will you go steady with me?" like kids used to do in middle school. Do kids still do that?

There's a knock at the door and I hastily walk to and open it. I fling it open with a whoosh that swirls the skirt of my dress around my knees and gives me a dramatic flair. He takes in the sight and lets out a low whistle.

"You look gorgeous," he says. "But I think you need more clothes on your body. You can't go out wearing that. Guys are going to look at you and I can't have that."

By the way, Fisher was invited, too, and that is throwing me way off. My brother is wearing his protective sibling hat tonight as he pushes through the door and goes to my bedroom.

"Come on in, Fish. Make yourself at home and, please, go through my things," I mutter in his absence as I lean against the open door.

He yells from the other room, "Here! Put this on!" as he comes back out to the living room holding an old, men's dress shirt I use as a spare smock while I'm painting.

"No." I'm going to stand my ground. He can't dictate what I'm wearing. He's never tried to before and I don't know why he would now. "It's New Year's Eve, I'm going to wear this dress and feel pretty."

"You leave nothing to his imagination," he refutes.

"He's seen me naked, there's not much more he could imagine," I say.

"Men forget things so easily," he replies.

"Are you calling me forgettable? That's super nice of you. Why are you here? We were supposed to meet downstairs at the coffeehouse," I say. I'm trying to tamp down the frustration, but it is what it is.

He drops his arms, tosses the shirt over a chair, and looks slightly defeated. "I just don't want you to think it's more than it is yet and him to stomp all over your heart. The last guy did a number on you and if Tommy does anything remotely like that ... I just don't want you to get hurt and run away. Again."

"Again? I've never run away because of a guy," I say, confused.

"You have! When we were kids you used to get mad about boys and take off. It was scary and I don't want to have to worry and wonder where you've gone if he breaks your heart," he yells.

"I don't think that's going to happen," I say, my voice and features softening to his concern. This is my home. It has always been my home and I've grown a lot since any of the other times I've apparently taken off, presumably because of a guy. I didn't realize my brother thought I was flippant enough to run away simply because of a man. While he takes the time to dwell on my years in junior high and high school, and my alleged "running away," he doesn't understand I was usually just going somewhere to clear my head. Sure, sometimes that meant I was gone all day and well into the night, but I tended to go sit at the lake and sketch. Before I could drive, I'd ride my bike until I found somewhere quiet and secluded to do the same.

"Don't think what's going to happen?" Tommy's voice catches me off guard. When I turn my head, he's leaning against the doorframe, his hands in the pockets of his slacks, wearing a stark white dress shirt beneath his black Pea coat. He looks from me to Fisher before standing upright and taking his hands from his pockets. A worried look darkens his eyes. "Should I come back?"

I shoot Fisher a wilting glare before turning back to Tommy. "Nope, you're fine. Fisher was just acting like a brother is all."

"I have a feeling acting like a brother between a brother and a sister is different than if it was with another brother," Tommy speculates.

He has no idea.

"It is," Fisher and I say in unison.

I stare at my brother, narrowing my eyes and twisting my mouth as thoughts run through my head about his fear that I'll take off. It's possible he thinks I left California because of a guy, but he'd be thinking of the wrong guy. I left because of him, not my ex-husband. Fisher needed me to come home and I knew it. I think I had needed to come home for a while, for myself more than anything. I waited to make sure the decision was mine, though, and not a knee-jerk response to his concerns the restaurant was going to go under. The trip back started around the time Tommy stepped in to help him with marketing. Over the years since our parents died Fisher had stopped spending money on decent advertising and the business was taking a huge hit because of it. Sometimes I think he has the business sense of a wet bar rag; other times, he's a freaking genius.

Regardless of what he might believe, moving back has been the best move I've ever made and I'm not leaving any time soon.

"I'm going to go downstairs and see if everyone else is ready," Fish says, interrupting my thoughts. He moves slowly through the room and, as he walks through the door, Tommy puts his hand on my brother's shoulder. He leans in and says something I can't hear. Fisher nods his head and I hear him say, "I know."

What is it you know, Fish?

Tommy gives me a sad smile and shrugs before finally crossing the threshold. He puts his right hand back into his pants pocket, and then, taking my right hand with his left, he sets a small burgundy box in my palm.

"What's this?" I say skeptically. Tonight is about going out and having fun, not gifts. "You've done too much this week already. Whatever this is, I can't accept it."

He gives me half a smile, but says nothing as he lifts back the top of the box. He gently tugs the chain loose and, turning me around, hangs the necklace around my throat. I walk to the mirror and finger the delicate, rose gold painter's palette and hand stamped "J" charm.

"Why are you doing this?" I ask him quietly as he comes to stand behind me.

"Because, I love you," he replies. There was no pause. He didn't stop to think before he spoke. I could feel the words coming straight from his heart.

"You don't know what love is, Tommy," I say, adamant in my own way that he needs to be certain. If making sure he's sure means me wallowing in this grey area a little longer, making excuses as to why I can't just hand him my heart on a silver platter, I will.

"You're right," he says, placing his hands on my shoulders. "I may not know what love is, but neither do you it seems. I sure know what it isn't, though, and this between us doesn't feel anything like that. What's between us feels natural. From day one it's been extraordinary, even when I didn't know I needed more than what I had. Every day with you is more, Jacey. And the days without you? Those are just more days I need you. If that isn't what love is supposed to be like ... what's the point?"

I don't say a word. How can I? I keep asking him to be sure, but what if it's me that needs to be absolutely certain? What if it's me who isn't ready yet? "I love you" — that isn't a phrase I throw around. Not anymore. I've stopped saying those words to just anyone, because they are some of the most important words I can say to another person. I'm not going to waste them if I'm not ready to share myself fully with someone. Those words are said when I know I can give the kind of commitment I expect in return, and I keep fighting the possibility that Tommy is capable of the commitment. I'm too afraid of being hurt. Aren't we all? Falling in love opens people up to the prospect of falling out of love, and that is a painful reality. This feeling I have for him is a wickedly sharp double-edged sword. I know it's more than just affection. I can be affectionate without being in love. This is so much more than that and yet, here I am, trying to fight it. Constantly, I'm trying to fight it.

His thumbs gently massage the back of my neck and I feel his energy seeping into me. Whenever he's around me I can feel the vibrations, and it's like his soul is humming a gloriously happy tune.

"I care about you, but it's more than that," he says, close to my ear. His breath is warm against my skin and I want to feel it everywhere. He places a tender kiss to that most sensitive place where my neck meets my shoulder. "Life is too short to not say 'I love you' to the people you care about, Jacelyn. I'm going to love you until the day I die whether you want me to or not."

My mouth betrays me and I smile as I take in the words, a vow, a declaration of his commitment. I want him to love me. I want so badly for him to love me forever because I've never had a forever. No one has offered me their forever in exchange for mine. Others have taken and taken and taken from me, but Tommy Stratford is the first to offer to give and give … and give.

"I don't need you to say it back. Not yet, not if you're not ready, but part of me is pretty sure that's how you feel, too, Jacey," he says. "Every day I've spent away from you this week, purposely avoiding reasons to make a phone call or send a text message, meeting clients at a different location, has been me making sure this isn't fleeting. It was painful. The only reason I slept at all this week is because I had tonight to look forward to."

My eyes meet his in the mirror.

"I've been falling in love with you more every day since the day I first laid eyes on you," he says after a moment of silence. "I'm certain."

"I —," I open my mouth to say it back. I want to say it back. The sudden need to tell him I love him back fights to climb out of me as his cell phone begins ringing in his coat pocket. His eyes search mine, questioning, curious what I was going to say. Instead, I say, "You should answer that. It could be important."

And he does. And his jaw goes slack. And I hear him say, "Mama doesn't get indigestion, Brian. Are they taking her to the hospital?"

And I wait for more of his side of the conversation as an invisible hand grips tighter and tighter around my throat and I'm thrown back to the night State Troopers called me asking if my parents were my parents. There's one thing I can do, and that's take action. It's a small action, but I take it. I face Tommy and, grabbing his hand and my coat, pull him out of my apartment.

"We're on our way, Bri. Just … just call an ambulance. We'll be there in five minutes," he says, gripping my fingers tighter as we reach the bottom of the stairs as Fisher opens the door to the sidewalk.

"I was just coming to get you. Tommy, your mom —," he tries to say but I interrupt.

"We're on our way there. Get in the car," I command. As I start the car I left parked on Main Street and put it in drive, I ask my brother, "I thought Brian was at the coffeehouse?"

Tommy fiddles with the buttons on his coat, but shifts uncomfortably in his seat as the glare of flashing red lights comes over the knoll behind us.

"They forgot to leave Emmy's blanket, so he ran over with it, and then called Stella because Kathryn was having some chest pain," Fisher says.

"Mama's never had issues with her heart. The woman is the healthiest person I've ever known," Tommy says. He scrubs the palm of his hand against the scruff on his jaw. "I don't think there's even heart disease on her side of the family."

We pull into Jenny and Dale's driveway, the ambulance following us into the dooryard, and before I've put the car in "park," Tommy has unbuckled, opened the door, and begun jogging to the door.

"Fish?"

"Yeah, Jace?"

"Everything's going to be okay, right?"

My brother's hand grips my shoulder. "That's the plan. Let's go."

Chapter Thirty-one

Tommy

I walk into the house to find Mama sitting at the kitchen table like nothing has happened. The only indication she might need medical attention is her pale complexion. She gives me a sad look as I take long strides to get to her. She's silently chastising me like she did when I was a little boy and I try to not let it affect me.

"Tommy, I am fine," she says, emphasizing each word. "Why would you have Brian call an ambulance?"

"Just a feeling. I go with my gut, Mama." I look from my father to my brother to Dale to Jenny. Jenny will be honest with me. "What happened?"

"She got winded, Tommy, that's all. We were playing with the kids and she got winded," Jenny says. "It's happened once or twice before."

Before I have a chance to say anything else, I hear the door open and Jacey's voice instructing paramedics where to go. Then there are questions from them as they begin checking Mama's blood pressure and pupils.

"She's never complained of pain," I say, hearing my voice rise with each additional word as I frantically try to remember her saying anything to be about her health. "Has she, Dad?"

He looks at me sheepishly.

"Once in a while she will, but it's usually when she's doing something strenuous. Son, I think we may be worrying about nothing," he says. The look on his face contradicts everything that came out of his mouth. "You know your Mama. She's a strong woman."

"Mrs. Stratford? Are you having pain now?"

The question gets my attention and Dad pushes past me to walk over to where Mama is sitting.

"Katie?" he questions, using the nickname only he has ever called Mama. He uses it in serious situations.

"It's nothing, Ben, just a little uncomfortable," she says, gripping her abdomen and sucking in a painful breath. One of the paramedics gets up and leaves quickly while the one remaining in the kitchen with us begins telling Mama he feels it would be best to take her to the hospital to get checked out. "But, I don't want to go. I'm fine," she says on another sharp intake of breath.

"Mama, you're not fine. We'll go and just have them check you over. Please," Brian says, his concern suddenly as present as mine.

"Boys. I swear I'll be fine. I just need to go sit down and watch a movie with all those babies in there," she says. As she attempts to stand, she cries out painfully. She presses her hand to her chest once more before there's a flurry of activity in the kitchen. A gurney is pulled through the door, Mama is settled onto it, strapped in place, and rushed out. Jacelyn takes my hand and pulls me toward the door because I can't seem to make my feet move. Then we're pulling out into the road to follow the ambulance toward the center of town. Dad rides with Mama, Jacey drives me, Fisher takes Brian's keys and drives him.

The ride in Jacelyn's car is quiet. It's heavy with the burden of not knowing what's happening in the vehicle in front of us. She reaches through the dark to take my hand again and I'm comforted by her presence but the fear of "what if" grips even more tightly.

"They're not running the lights or siren," I say.

"That's probably a good sign, right?" she asks. "They aren't going too much over the speed limit, either."

I notice how quiet the street is. In a couple of hours, they'll be busy with people heading to the bars and out for dinner reservations. We had hoped to miss all the craziness by going to dinner early, having a few drinks, and then heading back to Brian and Stella's to play cards.

"I'm sorry we won't make it out for dinner," I say.

"I don't care about dinner. I care about you and I care about your mom," she says, squeezing my hand. "Let's worry about her. We can eat dinner another night."

I nod my head, unsure if she sees it. The text message notification sounds from my phone and I check to see Steph's name on the screen.

Steph: What's going on? Is she okay? Mom won't tell me anything other than Kathryn is on the way to the hospital.

Jacey releases my hand as she begins turning a corner and I take the opportunity to message Stephanie back.

Me: We're following the ambulance. Mama's having chest and abdominal pain, blood pressure was elevated, we'll know more once we get there.

Steph: Keep me updated.

I don't respond as the car comes to a stop in the parking lot facing the emergency entrance. Brian and Fisher pull into the spot beside us and the four of us sit and watch as the ambulance brakes and the doors open. Brian and I open our doors and get out of the cars, leaving Jacey and Fisher behind. My brother and I look at each other and then begin walking toward the emergency department as our dad hops out of the back of the ambulance, his age showing in his landing. Dad and Brian follow the medical team toward the sliding doors, but a wave of emotion makes me pause. I remind myself to stay composed, to keep my fears in check until we know what's going on.

Jacey and Fisher are holding back, taking their time walking across the parking lot and I can see the pained look on her face as they move closer. She's a strong woman, like my mama, but strength only carries a person so far, and when reliving her own tragedies her strength wavers. I see it and I feel like a voyeur — I'm looking in on a scene that isn't meant to be watched as Fisher wraps his arm around her shoulder and her arm loops around his waist. It's not that I feel like watching the interaction is morally wrong, but rather there's a slight pang of jealousy that I can't give her what she needs right this second. I wish I was able to comfort her, and I will in time, but right now is not my turn to take her burdens from her.

Her fingers brush away a lock of hair that's blown in her face and I step toward the door before either can see me. Brian is waiting for me inside the entrance, his hands in his pockets and his jaw set tight as he watches Jacey and Fisher.

"She okay?"

"I don't know. I think this is dredging up some memories. She was quiet on the drive over," I say, and I sigh heavily as I'm snapped back to reality. "Do we know what's going on yet with Mama?"

He leads me back to a curtained area where she's been wheeled and the three of us — the "Stratford Trio" as Mama always refers to us — congregate around the end of the bed she's been moved to and together we wait. She stares at us and none of us talk until she breaks the silence.

"If they don't find anything wrong with me, you're paying the ambulance fee, Thomas," she says sternly. Then she motions to me and Brian, patting the thin padding that passes for a mattress, and says, "Come here, boys."

And we do, because what Mama says, goes.

"Have you had any more pain?" I ask as I sit beside her.

"No pain, but I'm uncomfortable," she replies. "It's gone on for a while, a few months at least, but it usually goes away once I've sat and rested."

She hasn't gone to her doctor, because it goes away. Mama isn't the alarmist type. If she has a little pain that can be explained away, she explains it away. If she takes a pain reliever and it does the trick, she's happy. Mama has always put her worry for herself on the backburner and focused on everyone else. That's just how she is.

But now? Mama is in the emergency room and a nurse is pushing her down a hallway in a wheelchair to run tests and the good Lord only knows what else while we wait. It's the first time I can recall seeing my mother in such a vulnerable position.

"I'm not a patient man," my father says finally as he leads us out to a waiting area. "Maybe I should have gone back with her."

"Dad, she's in good hands," Brian says. I catch his eye as he nods and I turn to see Jacelyn sitting alone in the corner. "Let's go grab some coffee. They've got to have a cafeteria around here somewhere."

They leave me standing there in an eerily quiet waiting area with the girl of my dreams and I'm not sure if I need her to comfort me or if I need to comfort her, so I decide if we're going to make this work, we'll comfort one another. I take my time walking to the other side of the room, my hands in my pockets and my coat draped over my forearm. She's standing by the time I reach her and without a word she wraps her arms around my waist. I pull my hands from my pockets, tossing my coat to the chair behind her, and hug her back. I hug her like I can't survive without her touch and it feels like heaven to be held by her and to hold onto her.

"How is she?" she asks, her voice muffled by my chest.

I kiss the top of her head and say, "So far, so good. She still had some discomfort so they're running tests now to find out why. Are you okay? I'll understand if you don't want to stay. I imagine Stella and Steph are at their parent's house if you want to go —"

"Shut up, Tommy. You're not getting rid of me," she says, squeezing her arms a little tighter. I smile, more to myself than anything, because it feels like I just won the World Series, but jumping up and down would be in poor taste. It's not a declaration of her love, but it's something, and I'll take something over nothing any day of the week. "I'll stay as long as you need me."

I release my grip and slide my hands up her arms until my thumbs reach her jaw and I lift her lips to mine. One small kiss is all I ask of her.

"What if I need you forever?" The words slip past my tongue before I can stop them. I'm not sorry. I'm learning to live fearlessly when it comes to Jacelyn.

"Then I'll stay forever."

Her words slay me and the only healing salve is another tender kiss. She nips my bottom lip with her teeth. I treasure the initial touch for what it is — sweet and innocent — and for what it promises to be, which is far less innocent.

"This might not be the best time to mention this," she says, pausing just long enough for my heart to stutter in fear she's going to curb stomp it, "but, you do realize we aren't technically dating, right? You've never actually asked me to go steady."

I pull back and blink. "I've professed my undying love for you. That's not me asking to be exclusive?" I question, coating the words thickly in sarcasm.

"I wouldn't say it was undying love, but yeah … you may have mentioned that word. Doesn't exactly mean I'm your girlfriend, though," she responds, matching my mocking tone with her own. "A girl can only know it's serious if you pass her a note in class and turn beet red while she's opening the paper. Or at least I assume that's what it's like. I was never cool enough to get a note like that."

Lowering myself down on one knee, I take her hand in mine. Looking up at her, I realize I can't wait until the day I do this for real.

"Miss Jacey, will you please be my plus-one for all future engagements? Will you be my automatic date for all affairs my presence is requested at? Will you —"

"Oh, shit," Brian says behind me as he and Dad walk back through the waiting room. "We were gone for ten minutes and you're proposing to the poor girl."

"Jesus, Tom. Could you at least wait until your mother is out of the hospital? Do you really think now is the time?" Dad says, but he chuckles. "You boys. Never ones to wait for nothing."

Amusement lights up her eyes, and I repeat, "Will you?"

Jacey, not letting on that what they've walked in on isn't what they think it is, smiles back down at me and says, "Yes." Then she winks.

I stand and kiss her once more before facing my father and brother. Brian is furiously texting someone. Dad, with one hand in the pocket of a pair of well-worn jeans and the other holding a cup of hospital grade coffee, shakes his head slightly before gracefully retreating.

"Who are you texting?" I ask, cautiously.

Brian holds up a finger signaling me to wait a minute.

Then my phone chimes, followed closely by Jacey's phone. It does it again. When it happens a third time, I cuss at my brother.

"Yup. I did," he says in response to the question I didn't ask. I don't have to because I'm well aware the message he was busy sending was to Stella.

Jacey's phone starts ringing.

"Brian, he didn't propose. He was asking me to be his girlfriend. It was a step we skipped," she says, then walks toward the exit while answering her phone. As she reaches the door I hear, "No, Fish, he did not ask me."

"You assumed and went so far as to tell her brother?" I question. I can feel my anger mounting.

Brian's eyes widen and he says, "That wasn't me. I texted Stella and Steph, not Fisher. I was excited for you. I'm sorry."

He means well and I know that. As sincere as the apology is, though, it isn't necessary. I wish I had been brave enough to propose to the girl I wasn't yet "officially" dating, but maybe this is one thing we should do in order.

I head toward the door, Brian following close behind me, and before we reach the threshold we see Jacelyn and Fisher through the glass enclosure. With his hands in his hair, Fisher looks frantically at his sister before saying something else to her.

"I thought he took Jacey's car and headed back to his place," I say, as I hear Fisher raise his voice loud enough to hear through the glass. "Wait, did he just say what I think he said?"

"It was muffled, but definitely sounded like it to me," Brian says. "Why would Fisher say you can't marry Jacey?"

Chapter Thirty-two

Jacelyn

"He didn't propose to me, Fisher. Get a handle on yourself."

He's losing it after seeing Tommy kneeling in front of me and it would be funny if it wasn't also very sad. What would be so bad about someone asking me to marry them? Just because the last one didn't have a fairytale ending is no reason to lose his shit and tell me I can't have a happily ever after.

"He can't marry you, Jacey. He can't. Not until you get your life together," he says.

"Get my life together? What are you talking about?" I thought I had a pretty decent grip on my life. We're running the restaurant together and that's basically my life. I have it under control.

"You have so much more potential. I thought you wanted to teach and open a studio and ... paint things," he exclaims. "You should talk to Brian about the space you're living above. He's mentioned trying to find someone to lease it. He talks about it at the business association meetings. That could be your business. Open one of those paint night places like they have in the city. Do anything. Anything other than be at the restaurant all day every day. The only reason you're not there seven days a week is because I forced you to choose a day off."

All I hear is, "I don't want you around." I know that's not what he said, but it feels like that's what he means. When I moved home, my dreams of continuing with my artwork evaporated and he knows that. The whole point of coming back was to help him, be here for him, work with him. It was all about Fisher and I don't regret that decision. I needed to focus on him.

"You don't like working with me?" I ask finally, trying to slow the smoldering hurt and burning anger that wants to consume me.

He frowns, pulling his hands from his hair, and says, "I love working with you. I've missed hanging out with you all these years." I hear the implied "but," and impatiently keep my mouth shut while I wait for it. "But, you need to do things for you, too. It can't be all about me. I'm not selfish enough to keep you from your happiness."

"You sure about that? Because it sounded like you wanted to keep me from being happy when you told me I couldn't marry Tommy, not that I am or want to, and that to me sounds like selfishness." My defensiveness might as well have been a fist to his face as I watch his reaction.

"Jacelyn, do you hear yourself?" Fisher speaks quietly to me now in an attempt to calm my anger. "You're going to twist my words into something they aren't, and why? Because you want to be right? Or is it because you're afraid I am?"

I don't want to listen to him. I don't want to try to be something I'm not, and after too many years of being told my art would never be good enough, that my vision was too small, that the children I was teaching painted better with Crayola finger paints that I did ... why would I want to continue? I can work at the restaurant and not worry about that part of my life. I can pretend it never existed if I never talk about it. Tommy is the only one other than Fisher who has ever shown an interest outside of college professors, but I'm afraid to tell him how I've been cut down by others in the art world. What if he stops seeing in me what I already can't see in myself?

Fisher takes a deep breath before placing his hands on my shoulders. "I want you to be happy. I think you're content right now, but you have the ability to be happier. Let me help you."

I consider his words.

"What if I'm too afraid to try anymore?"

"You're home now. There's no reason to be afraid," he says. "You have family here. We support one another."

"This feels more like bullying than support," I say, crossing my arms over my chest to block out the cold.

"Bullying. Support. A gentle shove in the right direction. Aren't they all the same when we break it down?"

I glare at him. "No. Not really. But if this is meant as support, I'll take it as such. Just ... try not to piss me off in the meantime. And don't tell me who I can and cannot marry," I say as I take a step toward the building. "I do what I want."

He laughs heartily and says, "You always have. I expect nothing different." Reaching out to grab my arm, my big brother pulls me into a bearhug, kisses my temple and says, "I love you, Jacelyn. Don't ever think anything different."

I breathe him in deeply, wrap my arms around him, and hug him like I haven't in years. I need him more now than I thought I did, and I want him to know that. "I love you too, Fish."

~*~*~*~

I find myself seated alone once more in the emergency room waiting area. I could text Tommy and ask if there's an update on his mom, but the possibility of hearing bad news keeps my fingers firmly planted on social media apps and the pen I grip a little too tightly as I attempt to complete last Sunday's crossword puzzle.

I wait for what could be forever, when in all likelihood it's only been an hour or two, before a tall gentleman emerges from the emergency department and shuffles warily toward me. I keep my head down as he settles himself into the uncomfortable chair beside me.

"Pen, huh?" Ben asks curiously. "Tommy used to do his homework in pen. Drove his mother crazy. His teachers threw fits about it, sent notes home about how he should use pencil in case he makes a mistake."

I tilt my head so I can see him out of the corner of my eye and smile. I can see Tommy being like that as a kid.

"Know what that boy used to tell us?" he asks, rhetorically. "He would tell us, 'Mama, Dad, just stop. I don't make mistakes.' And you know what? He tended not to. Smart as a whip and stubborn as a bull, that one. But he knows what he wants. I got to give him that."

The smile on my face grows. I don't respond because this isn't a conversation that requires pithy responses. This is a man simply telling me about his son and I get the impression he doesn't have the chance to share his knowledge often.

"His brother, though, he's always led with his heart. That's how both my boys ended up back here, you know? New York was just a memory for us for the longest time. Friendships had faded and rekindled and faded and rekindled again throughout the years, but I think Brian always planned to come back and stay. The kid was head over heels for Stella from the time they were in elementary school. Tommy, on the other hand, was so set on being a big shot businessman that he got so caught up in what he thought he needed to become that he failed to remember where he came from." He pauses and takes a deep breath, mulling over his words as he twists a toothpick around between his lips. "When Brian came home to visit a few years ago, Katie convinced him to bring his brother back up here. Tom was driving us both crazy because he went from having a vision to not being able to get a job. Something about the market being saturated. So, she worked her magic and sent Tommy on his way when Brian came back up here. We miss the boys like crazy, but this is what Tommy needed. He needed his brother to kick him in the ass and put him to work. He's been through some tough times since coming back, but he's no worse for the wear."

Ben pauses once more before adding, "Then, he introduces us to you."

That's it. He doesn't continue and I feel my nerves begin to fray around the edges. "He introduces us to you." That could mean practically anything, but, as I bite the tip of the pen to keep my frown from showing, he says it again.

He leans forward in his chair, places his elbows on his knees and clasps his hands together, looks at me with surprise on his face and with more emphasis, says, "He introduced us to you. Jacelyn, my son doesn't make mistakes. Not when it counts. I need you to know that."

"I ..." I don't know how to respond, but I'm going to try. "I make mistakes. I made mistakes in the past, and a lot of them. It feels like I made a lot, anyway, and each one was one more reason to move back home."

This isn't how I thought I was going to keep the conversation going, and judging by the look on Ben's face, he didn't expect me to admit there are transgressions in my past. No one is perfect, though, and if I'm going to date his son he's going to have to be understanding of that.

"We're all a little broken, Jacelyn. Just because I say Tommy doesn't make mistakes doesn't mean he's perfect. Whatever you believe are the mistakes you've made are likely the pieces of you that make him love you more," Ben says. "Because he does love you. He was raised in a house full of it and you've somehow captured his attention enough that he wants to share some with you. Tommy likes to see the good in people when they refuse to see it in themselves. Where you might see faults, he sees strengths. If you tell him you feel like you're a failure, he's going to tell you all the reasons you're a success. I've never seen him so ..." I give him a moment as he snaps his fingers trying to think of the word he's looking for. "So captivated by a woman. I've hardly seen the two of you together, but that man is crazy about you."

"What if I have trouble believing him? What if he tries to tell me about all the good in me and I just don't have it in me to believe him?"

"He won't stop until you see your own worth," he says. "Know why?"

I shake my head and he leans in closer to me as we both take notice of Tommy and Brian walking down the hall toward the waiting room. I have trouble containing my smile as Ben says quietly to me, "Because he's tenacious and refuses to make mistakes. I'm happy for the two of you. I may not have congratulated you properly, and for that I apologize. But, like I said, my boy doesn't make mistakes."

I open my mouth to correct him, and then close it. Tommy refuses to make mistakes. Tommy also spent an entire week forcing himself to have no contact with me because he wanted me to know he was certain. As much as I could try to deny it and refuse to say the words he wants to — needs to — hear, I can't keep them from him.

But instead, as he reaches us and sets himself down in the chair on my other side and lays his hand on my thigh, I say, "How is she?"

"Dad didn't tell you?" he asks.

"We were talking about other things, Tommy. Just answer the girl," Ben says.

Tommy raises an eyebrow at me before responding. "She'll be okay for the most part. They've diagnosed her with angina and are keeping her overnight for observation," he says. "With the way the discomfort hung on tonight they're being cautious because it could be a sign of something else going on."

Brian clears his throat and tips his head toward Ben. Exhaustion hangs on him now where moments ago was happiness and I reach out to place my hand on his shoulder. It isn't much by way of comfort, so I offer to run errands for items for Kathryn's overnight stay. This isn't my place. I shouldn't be here. This is a time for family and I'm not that.

"Is there anything you need? I can run to the house and get toothbrushes and other necessities for Kathryn if you'd like me to," I offer. "I can grab some decent coffee while I'm out."

Before I finish my sentence, Brian hands me a set of keys. "Didn't your brother take your car?" I nod, having forgotten Fisher was borrowing Betsy. Brian looks at his watch and says, "Take the Tahoe and get coffee from the coffeehouse. Greg and Caryn weren't leaving for Rochester until later and should still be there. We were closing early, but not for another hour or so."

Tommy calmly stands and reaches for my hand, pulling me up from my chair, and announces he'll ride with me. I begin to object and his dad reaches out and pokes my other arm.

"Go," he says, gruffly.

M.L. Pennock

Chapter Thirty-three

Tommy

We walk hand-in-hand in silence through the parking lot to my brother's SUV. As we near the parking space, Jacey presses the keys into my palm. I look down at her and nod my head, understanding how she feels about being the driver. Earlier she had no issue, but earlier I was too busy worrying about what was going on with Mama to drive safely. Jacey took control without even questioning what I needed from her and I'm so grateful to her for that.

For a beat, I worried about her sitting alone after what I assume was a heated conversation with Fisher. When my dad left to get some fresh air, which is merely his way of saying he needed a break from the emotional rollercoaster we all climbed aboard, I was content knowing Jacey would likely be sitting out there. Even if they weren't talking, her presence is comforting. At least it is to me. I hope it was for Dad, too.

When Brian and I left Mama so the nursing staff could begin admitting her to the medical floor, we just happened to interrupt another heavy conversation. I'm not sure what it was about and I won't pry. It was between Dad and Jacelyn. If she wants me to know, she'll tell me.

One thing I am well aware of, because it's been said to me countless times throughout the years, is "other things" is code for "we were talking about you."

"I don't really like hospitals," I say as we both close our doors and reach for our seatbelts.

"Neither do I," she says. "I don't think they're places often equated with happiness, unless you're in the Labor and Delivery department."

"And sometimes even over there it's not all sunshine and rainbows," I say. I look across the cab at her, her features outlined by the glow from the dashboard lights. "Sorry. Not trying to be a pessimist."

She smiles briefly and I put the Tahoe into gear.

"I think, considering the circumstances and everything you and your family have been through this evening, you're allowed to be a little pessimistic," she says. "It took me what seems like years to think positively about anything."

As I pull out onto West Avenue and head back toward the center of town, I chance a glance at her, wondering if there's more coming.

"I still have trouble finding the silver lining about a lot of things, usually when those things involve me and decisions I have to make, but I'm trying," she elaborates. At the stop light, I watch her worry her bottom lip and twist her fingers together, winding them around the strap on her purse. "Decisions are hard, Tommy. I don't usually jump into things, I don't take things lightly."

The light turns green and I slowly accelerate through the intersection, the streets beginning to get busy for the New Year celebrations.

"Fisher likes to remind me that I've always needed to write out pro-con lists for everything, from buying a new shirt to rearranging furniture. It's a little absurd. It wasn't always like that. There was a time in my life when, the second you told me you were interested in me, I would have jumped into your awaiting arms and enjoyed it without considering the consequences," she says. "I used to be carefree."

"What happened?" I ask, cautiously.

"My parents died. I realized I married a guy simply because he liked my art. I was giving everyone a piece of me and keeping none for myself. There was a lot of soul searching, a lot of me pulling back from friends, to try to figure out where I was going. Now I'm here, the place that was supposed to be my safe haven, and I'm still a little lost. I thought I was finding my place and then Fisher goes and drops me on my ass tonight," she says, moving her hands wildly as she talks. "My point is — I think I had a point — is you're going through something that you haven't been faced with in the past and it will take its toll on you. It's normal. Allow yourself to be a pessimist for a while."

I mull over her words as we ride comfortably in the quiet the rest of the way to the coffeehouse. I pull into the back lot so we can go through the kitchen instead of the front door. Having worked at my brother's café for a couple years and helping out when my own business is in a lull, I've gotten to know a lot of the regulars. We're more likely to get in and out quickly if no one sees me. I shut off the engine and neither of us makes a move to get out of the truck.

"I don't like being a pessimist," I finally say. "And I wish I knew you before you forgot how to be carefree. I want you to try to find that girl inside you somewhere. I've seen glimpses of her, but I'd like to meet the whole person."

She smiles sweetly, though a bit sad, and reaches up to place her palm against my cheek.

"I'll try," she says, and I turn my head to place a kiss to the center of her hand.

"You'll try. I'll take it for now. Let's get the coffee so we can run to Jenny and Dale's for toothbrushes and clothes for them," I say as we climb out of the SUV and meet one another in front of the truck. I don't want to confess to Jacey my own fears. I don't want to say out loud that I believe they admitted Mama because the doctors saw something more going on in all those tests but couldn't confirm it yet. It's that gut feeling again. "I don't think Dad's planning on leaving the hospital tonight. It's good he'll be right there with her, but I worry about him. In all their years together, I think tonight was the first time I've seen him truly scared, like their mortality stood up and stared him right in the face. I've never seen him like that."

She doesn't respond as I take her hand and we walk to the building, but I notice her looking at the door to the shop beside the coffeehouse.

"Brian's been trying to get that rented out. So far, he's had a few calls, but no real interest," I say. "Hey, what did you mean about Fisher earlier?"

"If we're going to have a real relationship now instead of all that back and forth, 'I like you, you like me, let's go to bed' stuff, you need to promise right now that you'll always be honest with me. I don't do liars, in any context," she says, again talking animatedly with her hands and arms flying about. I place my hands against her arms and tell her honesty is the only thing I know. "Okay. Fisher wants me to stop working so much at the restaurant and open … something. He wants me to rent that space from Brian and turn it into a studio or a gallery or a do-it-yourself art store."

Her face is a mix of fear, anxiousness, and excitement. This is the carefree Jacey that's hiding. I'm getting another glimpse and I love her even more for it.

"Yes," I say, hardly able to contain my grin. "Absolutely."

"Yeah? It's not stupid?" she questions, pulling her lip in again and moistening it against the chilly air. "I haven't seen inside to even know what would go into turning it into a gallery or anything like that, but … it's not stupid?"

Instead of answering her immediately, I step more into her space and place my forehead against hers. "It's the least stupid idea I've heard in a very long time. Brian is going to love it." I place a kiss against her lips and slowly back her against the brick wall of the building, nipping the skin a bit with each step. "We should celebrate. There are a lot of things to celebrate tonight," I say, my mouth against her.

She smiles into me and playfully pushes me away. "Slow down, Southern Comfort. We were sent on a mission. Coffee. Toothbrushes. Change of clothes. No celebrating anything until we know your mama is coming home tomorrow," Jacey says. "But once we know she's got a clean bill of health, all bets are off."

~*~*~*~

I knock gently as I enter Jenny and Dale's house through the mudroom. The light above the stove is on, as well as the Christmas lights outlining the archway to the dining room, but I don't hear anything as Jacey and I slip into the kitchen.

"They might be in the living room with the kids," I say, stepping in that direction.

Jacey follows behind and we make our way quietly through the dining room to the large family room. The first thing I see is my mama's best friend sound asleep in a recliner with Emmy tucked up in the crook of her arm, passed out with her blanket held tight to her little body. Jenny fell asleep with the phone in her hand, likely waiting to hear from one of us to give an update on Mama. While the girls sleep, Dale is propped up on the large couch, Britt leaning back against him and his eyes glued to the television.

"Hey, Bud," I whisper from the doorway.

"Uncle T!" He jumps off the couch and runs the short distance toward me, throwing his arms around my waist. "How's Grandma? Is she feeling better? When is she coming back?"

I pat Britt's back and hug him tight to me. When did my nephew get so big? I don't remember him being so tall and I see him every day. I missed so much being caught up in my own world — being caught up in Sutton — that he's grown and matured without me noticing.

I raise my hand and give a brief wave to Dale as he stands from the couch and walks toward us. He cautiously looks at Jenny before touching my shoulder and motioning back toward the kitchen. "Let's not wake them," he says.

"She's going to stay the night so the doctors can make sure everything is okay," I say once we're out of the living room. "They say it's angina, but keeping her for observation. Hopefully, she'll be able to come home tomorrow. She'll be alright, Britt. You think Grandma would let something like this keep her down?"

My attempt to allay his concerns doesn't work. He seems way more mature than I ever was at seven. He looks at Jacey before looking back to me and saying, "But they took her in an ambulance. That's serious."

"I know, and that's why they're going to have her stay for the night. Jacey and I are going to take a change of clothes back for her. As far as I know they aren't restricting visitors. I'll come get you first thing in the morning and you can go check on her yourself. How does that sound?" I ask and he begins nodding his head before I finish my question. Mama has always been a bright spot for Britton. She helped Brian with the daily tasks of raising the boy the first five years of his life, so aside from being his grandmother she was also his caregiver and go-to person at home when Brian was working. "Can you help me get a few things for Grandma and Grandpa? I need their toothbrushes. Can you go grab them while I finish talking to Dale?"

As Britt leaves the room, Dale asks, "Tommy, are you sure she's going to be okay? She's told Jenny a few times she had this chest pain, and tonight has really gotten her worried. They're sure it's angina?"

I tell him that's what we're being told, but I don't know for certain. I say they're keeping her and running more tests, so maybe we'll know more in the morning. It seems like such a small task, but I need to grab some clothes for Mama and Dad and get back to the hospital, I think, as Britt returns with the toothbrushes in one hand and a duffle bag in the other.

"I packed a bag for Grandma," he says, handing the canvas satchel to me, as though he isn't aware he made the task of coming here tonight easier for me. He shrugs his shoulders and adds, "The clean laundry was on the bed. Promise you'll take me in the morning?"

I swallow the thickness in my throat, the emotion welling up as I see Britt transforming into more of a young man than a little boy through this experience. Someday when he's a man, this day will be a memory he recalls when he least expects it, brought on by a smell or a sound. "I promise. I'll be here before breakfast." I set the bag down and, pulling my nephew to me, I hope he remembers today only as the day he helped pack a bag for his grandma.

~*~*~*~

By the time Jacey and I make it back to the hospital, Stella has joined Brian and Dad, and Mama is resting comfortably in a room. I set the duffle bag in the chair beside the door as I enter and walk directly to her bed. Mama looks years older in the span of a few hours, and it's more than I can bear. I hear Jacey offer Brian and Dad each a lukewarm coffee from the coffeehouse and Stella suggests the group move out to the waiting area.

Mama has been the cornerstone of our family since the day she and Dad exchanged vows and to see her in the hospital isn't something I think I could ever get used to. It scares me a little bit to think about it. Not that it's a sight anyone should have to become accustomed to, but when your mama is the strongest person you've ever met? Witnessing her confronting her own weaknesses is enough to bring a grown man to his knees.

And that's just what I've been reduced to. A grown man on my knees beside her bed.

The door is pulled shut behind my family as they leave and Mama folds her hand over mine.

"Stop thinking like that, Thomas," she says, squeezing my fingers.

"I wasn't thinking anything."

"Bullshit," she says, cracking a tired smile. "I'm not going anywhere."

"What's going on, Mama? We talk at least once a week. You never mentioned you were having problems," I say. "Are they sure it's just angina?"

She breathes in deeply. "They've got some more tests to run, but there might be a need for surgery. A bypass of one thing or another. They say the angina is just a symptom, so they're looking for the cause. I don't smoke, we eat healthy, I swim and go for walks. Tommy, I am a healthy woman, but for some reason my heart is acting like an unruly child."

Leave it to Mama to liken a body part to bratty kids. She used to say the same thing about my cowlick. She still can't help herself from touching the crown of my head when I'm not wearing a hat, as though she's trying to tame the hairs that, these days, I keep a little longer specifically because of that pronounced swirl.

I lay my head on my arm and watch Mama as she considers her next words. I'm briefly taken back in time to my childhood when I would sit like this and watch her bake. I'd wait quietly for her to tell me it was my turn to help. My best memories have been made with her. I love my dad, but my mom? She's my hero. She's the one who could get through when no one else could.

"We'll decide tomorrow if angioplasty is the route they want to take or if they're going to go harvesting veins from somewhere else to add new highways. Or maybe they'll just send me home and refer me to someone in Tennessee." Her eyes glimmer with unshed tears, but she laughs. She finds the humor in things I never would. "I'm scared Tommy. Your father eats bacon every day and is healthy as a horse. Not that I want Ben to trade places with me, but me? I eat oatmeal in the morning and spinach and tomato salads for lunch. I indulge at the holidays, but that's not enough to cause this."

Twisting my hand to twine my fingers with hers, I say, "Mama, we'll worry about it when it needs to be worried about. If they do one procedure or another up here, you're with family. You and Dad will stay at the house with me. If they refer you to Nashville, I'll come home. Steph can handle the business if I need to leave for a bit."

"You're such a good man, Tommy. I will be fine. I know it. I need to be. You still owe me grandbabies."

I lift my head and turn to see where she's looking, because it isn't at me.

"I forgot to grab my purse. I didn't mean to interrupt, I thought I was being quiet," Jacey says, flustered. She's adorable when she's nervous. "I need a candy bar. Do you want anything? I'm going to get you something. I need to go."

She slips back out and I hear her groan loudly as the door closes. I shake my head as Mama and I both laugh.

"Go. Go be with her, Tommy. I am fine right here. I'm being taken care of. You need to be with her. It's New Year's Eve. Go kiss at midnight. Make love in the backseat of a car. Drink champagne on Main Street. Just. Go." She smiles broadly, lifts my hand to her mouth and kisses it, then opens her arms as I stand and bend to hug her. "I'm not porcelain. Give me a real hug."

"I love you, Mama. I'll be back in the morning. I promised Britt I'd bring him up," I say, squeezing her one more time before releasing her and walking toward the door.

I stop when she says, "I love you, too, baby. Bring me some decent coffee when you come back, would you?"

"You got it," I say, returning the smile she offers.

Chapter Thirty-four

Jacelyn

When I was a little girl I thought I wanted to be a famous painter. There was a world map tacked up on my bedroom wall with push pins scattered across the entire thing. Each pin marked a place I wanted to paint. I had plans to travel through Portugal and Spain. I had an entire trip to Ireland mapped out and was ready to leave home to backpack across the Emerald Isle when I turned eighteen. I wanted to paint everything in Tuscany, Italy — the coastline, the vineyards, the sunflowers, the rolling hills.

Those dreams were brushed aside for more realistic ones the older I got. Go to college, work my way through my MFA, and then teach. Those were my goals. I'd focus on my own art in my downtime. And I did do all of that when I was still in California. I worked in a tiny gallery in downtown Los Angeles and on the weekend, I taught the basics of painting to some skilled and not-so-skilled kids who occasionally tried to eat the art.

Maybe I should reconsider telling anyone I taught the Mommy and Me art class at the community center. The kids were cute, the moms were interesting, and it gave me a chance to do two things I love. Art and teach. It quelled the looming feeling that my ovaries were withering away with each birthday I celebrated.

"Whatcha thinking about?"

My shriveling baby-maker, I almost say before mentally slapping myself. That's the last conversation I need to have with my landlord, who also happens to be my boyfriend's brother which would make it immensely more awkward.

"Life. Dreams. Not achieving the things I thought I would by the time I'm thirty," I respond. "You know, the usual."

He leans against the wall across from the chairs in the waiting room, one hand in his pants pocket and the other rubbing his right temple. "The usual sucks, Jacey. Life gets in the way of those dreams, but only if you let it."

Now isn't the time to talk to him about the space under my apartment. I don't want to be seen as the woman who took advantage of this man's fragile emotional state and I won't give anyone the opportunity to think that about me.

"What's your dream?"

I lean forward and cross my right leg over my left. My face scrunches up as I consider how much to tell him.

"I wanted to open my own paint studio," I say. It's generic enough. "But, I have the restaurant to think about."

"Right. The restaurant." He crosses his arms and stares at me. "The restaurant was doing well before you came back, you know? I know Fisher had run into some trouble, but he got turned back around. Last I knew, things were better than they'd been in years."

"But it's safe."

He scoffs. "Of course, it's safe. You were practically raised there, weren't you?" I nod. "It would be like Britt going off to college, getting a degree, and then coming home to work at the coffeehouse. You deserve to write your own story, Jacey."

I bite my lip, pondering his point before diving in. "Fish said you're looking for someone to rent the storefront below the apartment. Would you be willing to lease to me? If I were in the market for a place to lease, that is. Because I might be."

Before Brian can answer me, I see Tommy walking back down the hall toward the nurse's station and waiting area. I clear my throat, then say, "I'm sorry I interrupted your visit. I was trying to be quick." I attempt an apology along with changing the subject. Brian's eyebrow raises up as he looks at me curiously and pushes off the wall. It's obviously not a secret I'm keeping from Tommy — I might not have the courage to talk to Brian about renting the storefront if it wasn't for his younger brother — but I want to get details discussed with Brian before making it public knowledge. If I tell Tommy now that I mentioned it to Brian, he'll likely mention it to Steph because they own a marketing company and he knows I'm going to need all the help I can get. I want to have a chance to really consider all the —

"Your girlfriend wants my storefront."

"Nice. It'll be a great space for her, right?"

"I'm sitting right here. Did you think maybe I would want to tell him, Brian?" I shake my head at the absurdity. First, he breaks the "proposal" news to everyone and now this. "You're oh-for-two tonight, buddy."

I stand and walk to the brothers, noticing the slight redness along the bottom lids of Tommy's eyes. His stance is identical to Brian's. Feet apart, arms crossed, closed off. I commit the scene to memory. I feel the sadness radiating off Tommy; the concern is burning a permanent crease in Brian's forehead.

"Where's Dad and Stella?" Tommy questions and Brian lets him know they went to find a vending machine as Ben walks back into the room. He positions himself on the other side of Brian, and stands in the exact same manner as his sons. Tommy nods. "She's resting. They're really talking surgery?"

"At least it's not an emergency. She's got a couple blockages in her heart causing trouble, so how I understand it is they want to go in and open those up to get the blood flowing through again. The cardiologist here is coming in to talk to us in the morning. You boys should head on home and get some rest," he says, as his sons begin to protest saying they don't want to leave him and their mama. "We'll be fine. Not going to get into any trouble here when they're checking on you every half hour. Take your ladies home and we'll see you in the morning."

Ben unfolds his arms and pulls Brian and Tommy to him in a hug that resembles a sports huddle. I hear him talking quietly to his boys, but can't make out the words until he very clearly says, "Amen," and the boys pull the huddle tighter.

"I'll bring coffee in the morning," Tommy says.

"I'll be up early to bake before the coffeehouse opens, so I'll bring breakfast. Any special requests, let me know before seven," Brian adds.

Stella hooks her arm through mine and pulls me toward the group, and then I'm wrapped into a hug with her and Ben.

"If there's anything you need us to do for you, Kathryn, or the boys, you have my number," Stella whispers to her father-in-law. "If anything changes in the night, call my phone."

Ben tips his chin down to look her in the eye, then he looks at me, "You women. You remind me an awful lot of my Katie. My boys are lucky, lucky men. I promise, Stella, I will call you if anything changes. Take them home. They need to sleep as much as the rest of us."

With one more, quick hug, Ben releases us. Tommy reaches for my hand, Brian intertwines his fingers with Stella's, and together the four of us head toward a bank of elevators along the east wall. The doors open, we step in, turn, and wait in silence as we're carried two floors down to the lobby. Before the doors open to let us out, Tommy says, "I have tequila at my house."

"I guess we're going to Tommy's then," Brian responds.

"Let's go ring in the new year and pray the excitement is over for tonight," Stella says, grasping Brian's hand and pulling him from the elevator, leaving me and Tommy alone.

My hand hasn't left his and he gives a gentle squeeze. "You want to come have a drink with us?"

"Are you asking me on a date?"

"Not formally. This is just drinks. I might have a block of cheese in the fridge. We can make it fancy if you want," he says, hinting at his less serious side. He leans in to kiss my forehead. "Thank you."

I smile.

He smiles.

I'm in love with him and it happened when I wasn't even paying attention.

"I love you back," I say. Finally. It seems like it's taken too long to say it and yet, if I cared about the opinions of others on the matter, I'm sure some would believe not enough time has passed for me to feel this way at all.

Chapter Thirty-five

Tommy

"What do you want to call it?"

Brian loves being a business owner. Having been raised by two blue collar working class parents gave him the drive to do … more. It took me a lot longer to figure it out. Brian had his entire life planned out from the time we were kids. I was a college graduate before I had half a clue what I wanted to be when I grew up. It hasn't been easy, particularly because there have been times it feels like I'm living in his shadow. I love and look up to my brother, but a few years ago it was hard to figure my shit out while he was opening a business and buying buildings and generally being this awesome guy. It wasn't until after moving to Brockport that I figured out how to be an adult and started using my degree and my brain again and, along with Stephanie, opened Mile 63 Marketing.

Our parents deserve most of the credit, though, because they truly shaped who we became as adults by working hard day in and day out. They took pride in what they did and set these great examples of how to be a successful person, no matter what success we were attempting to achieve. My brother and I simply handle our professional lives differently. For instance, I'm typically fine leaving work at the office in town. When it does come home with me, it does not leech out into the rest of the house. That stopped for the most part when Steph moved out. Brian, on the other hand, takes the chance to talk shop whenever he can.

Before my thoughts can swirl out of control, I go about making myself busy finding snacks while Brian dives into the innerworkings of Jacey's brain.

Jacelyn taps her finger on the rim of an empty shot glass. "I was thinking TopCoat. It's paint related and just artsy enough to work for the location, but not so much that it's going to scare away the older folks," she says. Reaching for the bottle of liquor, she adds, "Who knows, maybe it'll intrigue them enough to come in and check it out?"

"Grab that," I say and nod at the bottle in her hand.

"It's in my hand already," she says lifting the bottle higher and cocking an eyebrow. "Should I grab it harder?"

"Maybe you should …" I say as I shuffle toward her, slowly pushing her closer to the dining room when she lets out a laugh. Never will I tire of making her smile. Behind us Stella and Brian make gagging noises. "Alright, alright, you two talk about business and Stella and I will sit here and look intrigued. Better?"

"Much," Brian replies.

I pull a chair out for Jacey and then sit in the one beside her as Brian and Stella sit across from us. It feels comfortable, like we've done this a thousand times. Only we haven't. This is the first and I want it to be the beginning of a lifetime.

Tipping my shot glass back and forth on the table, I'm vaguely aware of the conversation beside me. It's not that I don't have an interest, there are just so many more things in my head right now. The evening was exhausting and it's catching up now that I've put a couple ounces of alcohol into my bloodstream. I'd like to know more about what's going on with Mama, but short of begging nurses for information they don't have yet, I won't know until morning. If it weren't for Brian being able to talk about Jacey's plans, he would be at home thinking the same things. There are too many questions that need answers. Should we be concerned about a hereditary link? Is this a fluke? What could go wrong with the procedure she has tomorrow? Should I just start packing to move back to Tennessee?

I hear my name, but it sounds distant, and I look up at Stella at the exact moment her foot connects with my shin when she kicks me under the table.

"Kitchen? We're out of crackers." She stands and shoots a worried look down at me. Jacey and Brian have stopped talking, both looking at me, and Jacelyn's hand rests comfortably on my left thigh. She puts pressure on my leg, squeezing the muscle beneath the fabric, as though to reassure me. Of what, I don't know.

"I'm coming. I'll help you search. It's kind of barren in there right now," I say, moving my arm to Jacey's back and leaning toward her as I stand. I kiss her temple and say, "I love the plans so far," but she gives me an odd look as I move away from the table.

Walking through the door, there's a weight bearing down on me. A weight so heavy it could crush me if I let it, and Stella can see. Stella always sees.

"It's okay, Tommy. She'll be okay," she says. I'm a tall man, but right now I feel so small as my sister-in-law pulls me into her arms. I feel every emotion seep out of every pore until there is nothing left of me. I'm a puddle and she shushes me, attempting to console me because each fear that I've carefully lifted and set aside all night is toppling me. It's crushing me and I can't stop it, so I let the weight push me into Stella and allow her to bear the brunt of my sobbing. Because when there's something wrong with your mama and you can't handle it anymore, it doesn't matter how tall you are or how grown you may be, you cry like a baby. You just do. So, I am.

I don't know how long we stood like that, her rubbing my back and telling me it would all be okay and me not believing a damn word of it.

"But what if she's not?" I barely am able to get the words out because the last thing I ever want is for them to become the truth. "What if something goes wrong tomorrow? I should go back to the hospital and sit with her tonight so Dad can get some rest."

She pushes me to arm's length so she can look at me, really look at me, and says, "You. Will. Not. Ben is there and she is under great care. You are where you need to be right now, Tommy. You and Brian are both where you need to be." Her attention shifts to something behind me and she says, "Can you just take him upstairs and tie him to the bed so he doesn't go back to the hospital until morning? You don't have to do anything fun, just make sure he can't leave the house."

Jacelyn's arm encircles my waist and her other hand rests easily at the crook of my elbow. "I can do that," she says, looking up at me with weary eyes. She swallows and whatever sadness may have been showing itself is blinked away as she turns her attention back to Stella. "It's really late and I think we could all use some rest. Should we make a plan for morning?"

Stella says she and Brian can meet us at the coffeehouse. Jacelyn says that will work. I'm too tired and numb to contribute, but I know I promised Britton I would take him with me in the morning. I don't break promises. Stella gives me a hug, tells me again everything is going to be all right, and she and Jacey walk back toward the dining room. Knowing Stella, she's going to gather up the dishes we've used and put them in the sink, but when I turn toward the doorway my brother steps through instead of his wife.

His hands are shoved into his pants pockets and his shoulders are slumped down. We're practically mirror images of one another — exhausted, scared, poorly attempting to hide our fears — if not for the fact I'm slightly taller and broader.

"Stella keeps telling me she's going to be okay. I don't know if I believe her yet," I say.

"You know Stell. She seems to know more than the rest of us. Her intuition is typically on point," he says. "I'm hopeful she's right. She has to be."

My brother is bound to break. His façade is wearing as thin as mine and as he looks at me looking at him, the tears well in his eyes.

"Right? She has to be?" he questions.

It takes two steps for me to get to him and hug him. I haven't hugged my brother like this since he told me he was moving up north, when I felt like he was abandoning me. All I wanted to do was hold onto my best friend until I could come to terms with not seeing him every day. Turns out, he didn't abandon me at all. He just gave me the room to grow up.

"Yeah, Bri. She has to be."

~*~*~*~

The light over the stove is left on, but every other switch and lamp on our way from the kitchen to the bedroom is turned off as we pass by. At the top of the stairs, I carefully reach for her hand in the dark and lead her to the room at the end of the hall.

There are no expectations. None, except for sleep.

"You don't need to tie me to the bed," I say. "I promise I won't leave in the middle of the night."

She sets her palm on my chest and stands on her toes to kiss my cheek. "I know you won't," she says with quiet confidence.

Without hesitation, Jacey begins undressing me. She removes my shirt and my undershirt, placing her lips against my skin. It's the spark that sets the rest of my body ablaze. I drop my head and bury my nose in her hair, breathing in the citrusy scent of her shampoo, as my hands find the curve of her hips. They glide up the fabric of her dress until I reach her waist and grip tightly, wondering if she knows what she does to me. Her fingers dip below the waist of pants, stroking my lower back. She knows exactly what she's doing, I tell myself, and her fingers trail along the path of my belt sitting low on my hips until she finds the buckle.

It feels like a million years are passing as she slides the belt from the clasp and pulls it, ever so slowly, through each loop until I feel it freed from the last one and it hits the floor. I'm helpless and give her all control. She doesn't need to restrain me and take it. I want her to have it and, with my face again pressed against the top of her head, I tell her. I ask her to take the lead because I need her to.

And she does. Grasping the button and pulling the zipper and gripping me tightly, she does. Each movement I make is a reaction to one she makes, and I don't make a move otherwise unless she asks me to.

"Unzip my dress," she says, her teeth nipping my jaw.

I trail my fingers up either side of her spine until I reach the tab and tug. Each time her teeth pinch my skin, I tug. When she lets out a low moan, I tug. As she presses herself against me, I tug until I feel the resistance and can tug no more.

She shrugs her arms from the bodice and the skirt falls in waves at her feet. I watch her reach behind to unhook the navy blue lace contraption she hid beneath and wait for it to release the rest of her. She holds it to her chest instead of allowing that, too, to sink to the floor. She leans in to bite my chest gently as my hands move along her biceps, reaching for the straps slipping off her shoulders.

"Let me," I say, my voice full of want, as she tilts her face up to look at me in the shadows. Her lips part slightly and her hair falls back. My mouth connects to the exposed skin on her neck as my fingers pull the lingerie from her body. I can't keep my hands to myself as she releases a breathy sigh coupled with another moan and I allow the pads of my thumbs to rub along the tips of nipples I can't wait to get my mouth on.

"Please," she says, pressing her hips against mine again, eliciting a sharp intake of breath from me.

I feel everything more strongly with Jacelyn. Every nip of her teeth, each stroke of her hand, and kiss from her lips, I feel it to my very core. In turn, every time I touch her it's grounding. She could pass by me on the street and I brush her hand, and I'd know she's the one.

She's the one.

She's home to me.

"Make love to me," she whispers.

"You're my everything," I whisper back before pressing my mouth to hers and sliding my hands south to push a pair of lacy blue matching panties from her body and watch them join the rest of our clothes on the floor.

"I. Love. You," she says, punctuating each word. She makes me feel how much she means it and for a fleeting moment I wonder how long she's known. "I love you back, Tommy."

I place my hands against her jaw and kiss deeply as I walk her back toward my bed.

"You're not saying that just so you can get in my pants, are you?" I tease, biting her bottom lip. "Because, if you are, it'll probably work."

She smiles against my mouth. "Never. I only tell the truth," she replies, turning me and gently pushing me onto the bed. She crawls up my body, her hair coaxing goosebumps from my skin as she straddles my hips and leans into me again. Bare skin brushes bare skin and I'm met with slick warmth as her lips find mine again.

My hips lift against hers and I know we shouldn't take chances. We shouldn't and I quietly tell her to reach into the nightstand. I won't destroy her future. I want to build one with her before precautions can get tossed aside. I hear the packet tear open and feel her hands in the dark as she places the condom over the head of my penis and firmly rolls it down the shaft, massaging all of me in the process. A low, guttural moan escapes my throat and she takes my nipple in her mouth, biting me cautiously as she replaces her hand with her body.

She moves slowly, rocking against me and taking her time as the pressure between us builds. Her head falls back and I feel the ends of her hair brush against my fingertips as they encircle her waist and crawl up her back. I wrap it around my hand and tug. She moans at the unexpected action. I do it again and feel her body react, gripping me tighter. I'm not ready to give in to the orgasm, but every time she moves I'm one second closer. I tell her, and she says, "Good."

Her hair falls from my fingers as she lays her body down against me. Kisses and nips and a solid slap on the ass and I can't hold on. She follows close behind, her body shuddering as I hold her in my arms. We stay like that until I slip away from her and in that moment, she sighs. I told her weeks ago I wanted to make love to her. I want to make love to her for the rest of my life and it's a want I truly couldn't fathom until I admitted my feelings for Jacelyn and tested myself when she asked me to be certain. Something finally clicked.

Her cheek is pressed against my chest, which barely contains my racing heart. It's hers now. My heart belongs to her. Jacelyn is the best thing to walk into my life and I want to give her all of me. I don't tell her just how much. I don't want to take the chance of moving even faster than we already have.

She lifts her head and pushes up on her knees to reach my lips. She kisses them one more time before crawling over me and pulling back the covers. I stand and pull the sheet over her naked body, then slide the quilt over her. Her eyes are already closed and I place my lips against her forehead.

"I love you, Jace," I whisper, not sure if she can even hear me with how quickly she's already fallen asleep.

Grabbing my boxers from the floor I quietly leave the bedroom, stop by the bathroom to clean myself up, and then go down the front stairway to the first floor. I drink milk straight from the jug and then put it back in the fridge. Jacey loves me back, and it feels amazing to have that emotion reciprocated because I didn't think I would find someone like her. I wasn't looking for her, but there she was — in the coffeehouse, in the restaurant, showing up in the produce section at the grocery store, and walking past the park when I was playing catch with Britt. She was everywhere and it took me months to realize she has become a constant in my life. My memories are saturated with images of her, and when she isn't part of one, I wish I could insert her into it. I can't rewrite history. We both have heartaches and sore spots, but there's a future for us. We have the chance to make our own history.

I climb the stairs back up to the bedroom and slide into bed beside her. She's facing away from me, one arm under the pillow she lays on while the other is bent so her chin is against the back of her hand. There's a calm and peace about her and I wish I could feel it, too. I curl into her back with my hand resting on her hip, and listen to her inhalations and exhalations until my breathing synchs with hers and my eyes feel heavy. They just aren't heavy enough to win the battle against my brain, which won't turn off.

The clock tells me it's after two in the morning, and I'll suffer the consequences of not resting. Old fears hover and I wonder if she'll disappear if I close my eyes too long. Or will she still be here in the morning? Will she be here forever?

"What if I need you forever?"

"Then I'll stay forever."

Our conversation at the hospital hits me. It stops the pessimism in its tracks.

"Why did it take so long for me to find you?" I ask, brushing the hair from her cheek while I watch her sleep, hoping it will come for me soon as well.

~*~*~*~

I wake with a start and panic.

The bed is empty.

The room is still dark and the bed is empty.

I toss the covers aside and slip from the mattress, in a few steps I'm at the door. In seconds, I'm down the stairs that lead to the kitchen. Hanging onto the doorframe, I stop.

Jacelyn is seated on the counter, a jar of peanut butter in one hand and a spoon in the other. She's swathed in moonlight, a halo illuminating her from behind and framing her in softness, as she sits cross-legged wearing my shirt. I wonder if she can hear my heart pounding in my chest.

"You're getting germs in my peanut butter," I say, shattering the silence.

She isn't startled. She heard me come down from the bedroom.

She stares at me from across the room as she dips the spoon in, pulls it out, and sticks it back in her mouth. I stare right back at her for a beat before unhinging my fingers from the molding and walking through the room to where she sits. That's when I see the tears. I feel my forehead wrinkle and she rolls her eyes.

"A lot on my mind," she says.

I reach for the spoon in her hand and the jar of peanut butter, climb up onto the counter beside her, and take a scoop for myself.

"Germs?" she questions.

"I think we're safe. We've shared a lot of germs in the last several months," I say, bumping her arm with my elbow. "What could be taking up space in your mind that causes a four-in-the-morning peanut butter binge?"

I pass the spoon back and hold the jar out for her. The name falls off her lips.

"Sutton." Her face twists as though saying her name out loud causes physical pain and I understand the tears. The years of friendship that couldn't stand the test of time are going to leave a scar. "I just ... I'm in love with you, and I can't even share that with her. She was supposed to be the one person I could turn to always. First, I couldn't tell her I had feelings for you months ago because I found out she was your ex-girlfriend, and you didn't know I knew or that I knew her, then everything else over the last couple weeks happened. The entire situation is more than I can handle. I wish I could let it go and just be. I just want to be."

Then I suggest something that shocks us both. Call her, I hear myself say.

"Call her and tell her. Heck, I should call her and thank her. Her hurting both of us? It gave us a chance," I say matter-of-factly. "The way it happened, it sucks. She lied, she broke your heart, she walked out on me, but I don't really believe in coincidence, Jace. Call her, tell her, thank her, then give it to God to handle the rest of it. She doesn't deserve an apology from us for admitting our feelings to one another, but if this is something you need to share with her, share it. Tell her you love me. Tell her I'm your plus-one. Tell her you'll stay forever because I need you forever."

She tips her head, rests it against my arm, and nods.

"I don't think I'm sad enough to share it with her, though. It's the idea of having someone to talk to who knows all of my history that I miss more than anything. I don't want her commentary. I'm beyond apologizing for who I love and I'm not looking for her approval," she says. "The only approval I'm looking for is your mama's. Your dad already gave me his."

I smile broadly. So that's what they were talking about in the waiting room. It makes sense why Dad reacted the way he did when I questioned him about not telling Jacey what was going on with Mama.

"Apparently, according to Ben, Tommy Stratford sometimes acts irrationally but he doesn't make mistakes," she says, sleepily. "He does crossword puzzles and math problems in pen and is crazy in love with me."

Chuckling lightly, I place a kiss to the top of her head. "I totally make mistakes. The rest of it is pretty accurate."

"I tried to tell him we all make mistakes, but he just reassured me that you're amazing," she says, turning her head to look at me, "which I kind of already knew."

The moon ducks behind an errant cloud and the kitchen darkens. I reach for her hand, rubbing my thumb in lazy circles over the nubs of her knuckles. "You're beautiful. Every part of you, Jacelyn."

"Beauty is only skin deep. Sometimes, it's there to cover the scars. Time leaves a lot of wounds for some people, Tommy," she responds, quietly.

"You radiate kindness, and that is gorgeous," I tell her. "I love you, scars and all."

She looks at me, wariness playing in her eyes, and as the room lightens again from the passing cloud, she says, "Will you still love me if I can't give you babies some day?" Her voice hitches, and the hand I'm not holding flies to her mouth as though in an attempt to cover the words and keep them in as they slip past her beautiful lips.

Babies? I ask and she responds with a nod. Babies. Why wouldn't she be able to have babies with me?

"It's late. Maybe we shouldn't talk about this. It's too soon to talk about a future. We just started dating," she tells me and I shake my head.

"No," I say. "Why would you be worried about babies?"

She says she worries about a lot of things, this just happens to be one of them.

"We can talk about it another time. We're both so tired and your mama ...," she tries to brush it aside.

"Mama's a strong lady, Jace. What's going on? Why the worry about babies right now? We have plenty of time to worry about all of that." I won't let it go. She heard Mama say I owe her grandbabies. Is that what started her thinking about this? She pulls her hand from mine and pushes it up into her hair, twisting her fingers among the locks, as she bites her bottom lip and pulls it into her mouth.

"You want kids. I see it every time you're around your niece and nephew, the yearning for your own. You don't hide it, nor should you, so it makes it difficult to ignore when I know there's a very real possibility I might never have any of my own. Or be able to have them with someone else."

I'm confused. I tell her so. "Yeah, Jace, I love Emmy and Britt and take every chance I can to spend time with them. You're not wrong about me wanting my own. What makes you think you might not be able to have your own?"

There were a lot of issues when she was a teenager, she says. Recurring infections had a field day in her body.

"Are you going to get science-y on me?'

"Science-y isn't even a word, Tommy," she says, rolling her eyes in my general direction. "I won't get science-y. You're a smart man and I'm sure in all your years of maleness you've heard of Pelvic Inflammatory Disease. It left my fallopian tubes pretty damaged." She holds her hand up as my mouth opens to ask an extremely difficult question. "Before you can even say it, no, it wasn't from anything sexually transmitted and if that had been the case I would have been upfront with you. I was just cursed with a lot of bad luck in the bacteria department."

"And the scarring is something that could hinder our chances of sperm meeting egg and miniature versions of you being created?"

She offers me a sad laugh. "Yes, it's possible we wouldn't be able to conceive. At least not without help." She turns and looks at me, narrowing her eyes slightly. Lowering her voice, she says, "Why are we talking about this right now?"

I lower my voice to match hers and say, "Because you're my girlfriend and maybe someday I'd like to make little people with you. It's possible this information would be useful in our future."

"I'm broken."

"You're perfect," I declare.

"I'm overly emotional."

"I have broad shoulders," I say.

"You're a pain in the ass."

"You wouldn't have me any other way," I say, leaning in to kiss her on the mouth.

"You make it hard to breathe."

"I'll breathe for us both," I say, connecting my lips to hers.

M.L. Pennock

Chapter Thirty-six

Jacelyn

He takes my hand and helps me down from the counter. My legs wobble as my feet touch the floor, the feeling in them coming back as pins and needles after sitting crisscross applesauce for so long.

It was never my intention to talk about the possibility of infertility this early in my relationship with Tommy. Having children never even was a topic my ex-husband and I discussed because at the time I was content with the idea of not having a family. I could teach and have an endless rotation of kids to adore. He didn't want kids, so it was a fine plan.

I had no desire to look into options for treating the scar tissue blocking my fallopian tubes until I moved back home and walked into the coffeehouse, which sounds insane. I walked in to get coffee and walked out with a caramel macchiato and the urge to go forth and procreate. Seeing Tommy with his brother's kids, spending time with Stephanie and Jake, walking past the park and seeing children play on the playground — it's all done something to jumpstart my biological clock.

Sutton doesn't even know about all the reproductive system issues I've had. In all our years of friendship, the conversations about growing up and having kids all were started and ended with the idea that it would be nice to have those things someday. I knew we didn't share the same desires to settle down and have families, at least not at the time those conversations happened, so it was easier to let them go by the wayside. The shallowness of our many talks over the years feels ever present as adulthood has crept into my life. I wish there had been more depth, but I can't change the past.

I climb into bed from Tommy's side and he follows behind me. The room is less dark as the sun slowly begins its ascent and the shadows begin to disappear.

"We need to get up in a couple hours," Tommy says, as he places a kiss below my ear. "Unless you want me to let you sleep while I go to the hospital."

Do I want to sleep? I'd love to sleep, but I'd rather give it up to be there for him and his family.

"I want to go with you," I say. "We'll get Britt and then grab coffee and breakfast before going over."

We lay in silence and despite the quiet, I know he isn't sleeping. His breathing hasn't evened out and his grip around my waist hasn't loosened.

"Tommy?" I whisper. "Are we moving too fast?"

"Only as fast as either of us wants to. Do you think we are?"

I bite my lip to curb the smile.

"I don't think so. We could move faster if we wanted to, I suppose."

"I was going to put an ad in the paper for a roommate. You should apply. I'll have to vet your references, but something tells me we'd get along famously," he teases, his fingers dancing along my ribcage. The tickling sensation pulls a laugh from me as I squirm in his arms, rolling over to face him.

"I didn't know you were looking for a roommate," I say, honestly.

"It gets lonely being here on my own sometimes." He brushes the end of his nose against mine and it's intimate in the most profound way. "I realized how quiet it was after Stephanie moved out. It was nice to have organization, but then ... it just felt lonely. I was either making sure I worked late at the office or the coffeehouse, or I was calling Mama at all hours of the night."

Brushing his cheek with my thumb, I cup the side of his face. My fingers touch the hair that's grown just long enough that it's starting to curl behind his ear. Living alone is lonely. There's no one to talk to or argue with or make love to. It's easy to come and go without expectations when you only need to rely on yourself, but it also lacks a certain amount of excitement.

"Do you know any other man in his thirties who calls his mother at midnight to ask for advice on dress clothes and baking?"

"It is lonely," I say, brushing my lips across his. "And no. Not a straight man, anyway."

"I had a feeling that was going to come out that way." He returns my kiss. "But I guarantee you that isn't the case. I just get tired of talking to myself."

He leans his forehead against mine and I wonder what he's thinking about.

"Are you serious about looking for a roommate?"

"I might be. I haven't actually placed the ad yet," he says. "I don't really want to now."

It doesn't take a genius to read between the lines. Do we really want to move faster? Should we be talking about all of this? Babies and moving in. It's a lot of ground to cover in the first full day of couplehood and part of me fears it's because of the stress of seeing his mama ill. The other part of me is certain this is how it will always be with me and Tommy, and I cherish every single thing about it.

"I'll have to take this new information into consideration," I say, kissing him quickly before turning over and curving my body into his. "My apartment is pretty amazing. It's practically prime real estate. I'm not sure I'd want to break my lease or if the landlord would let me sublet."

~*~*~*~

The shrill sound of an alarm ringing wakes me from a dead sleep, but Tommy's leg is wrapped around mine and his arm draped across my chest makes it nearly impossible to maneuver out of his hold. I try anyway. Instead of waking up, he tightens his grip and moves in closer to snuggle.

"Tommy? The alarm," I say, only for him to nod and give me a "mmhmm" in his sleep. I elbow him gently — sort of — and tell him again the alarm is going off.

He opens his eyes and looks at me, and for a moment I'm his whole world.

"The alarm?" I say, questioning his lack of motivation for getting out of bed. I mention the need to shower and pick up Britt before heading to the hospital, and realization dawns as he reaches for the snooze button.

"I wish it had been a dream," he says. His forehead wrinkles and his eyebrows draw closer together, scrutinizing the situation. "Only part of it."

Tommy props himself up on his elbow and looks down at me, bringing his hand to my face and brushing the hair off my cheek.

"We should get up now," I say.

"One of us is already up."

I narrow my eyes, not understanding his meaning until I feel him.

"We don't have time for that," I say, laughing at his forwardness. "Later. I promise."

Pulling his face closer to mine, I kiss him good morning and hope whatever happens today doesn't end in sadness or uncertainty. We pull away from one another, each freeing ourselves from sheets and blankets in an attempt to get the day underway. He quickly turns the alarm off as it begins to sound again.

"Shower. Britt. Coffee. Hospital," he says, as though he's reading an agenda from a piece of paper while he checks his phone. "Scratch that. Coffee, then Britt. Brian messaged and said he has him at the coffeeshop with him, but is waiting for us before going up to the hospital."

I say okay and walk toward the bathroom wearing only Tommy's shirt. Standing in front of the mirror, I look at myself and Tommy in the reflection.

"The last twelve hours are kind of blurry. We didn't go get me clothes last night, did we?"

"Uh … nope."

"I can't go to the hospital wearing the same clothes I wore yesterday," I say, and he raises an eyebrow at me as if to ask why not. "No."

"Shower, throw on some of my sweats and, when we get to the coffeehouse, run up and grab clean clothes. Problem solved," he says, stripping out of his boxers and stepping into the shower as I watch him in the mirror.

As simple as that. Wear his sweats. It's no big deal, I think, removing his shirt and tossing it on top of his discarded underwear. I step into the warm spray and wash quickly as he rinses the soap from his hair and body. He steps out of the shower, wrapping a towel around his waist, and draping one over the curtain rod for me. The chill of the curtain being pulled back momentarily hits me causing goosebumps to prickle my skin.

He pokes his head around the drape and looks at the exposed parts of me. "Sorry. I'm not used to sharing the shower. I didn't take time to enjoy the view."

"I'm cold. Close the curtain! You can enjoy the view later when I have layers on," I say, laughing, as he pulls the curtain closed again and walks from the room.

"Are you shaving before we go?" I ask as I turn the water off and squeeze the excess from my hair. I secretly hope he says no. While cleanshaven Tommy is professional, scruffy Tommy is sexy. I'll take either, but if I had to choose —

"Nope. It takes too long and we need to leave," he replies as he walks into the bathroom and hangs his towel on the back of the door. For a man who looks and smells as good as Tommy, he doesn't have a lengthy beauty regimen. I don't know what I expected, but five-minute showers and generic bar soap weren't it. He's already pulled on a pair of loose fitting jeans that ride low on his hips and he slips a black, long sleeve thermal shirt over his head as I watch. It's so simple, yet I think my lungs forgot how to breathe. He finishes pushing his arms through and pulls the shirt down his chest. He's done all of those things and I haven't moved. I'm stuck staring at him and he notices. How could he not when it's just the two of us?

"What?" he asks.

"I just … I think I'm starting to realize how very fortunate I am," I say, pulling my towel tighter around me and stepping from the shower.

"In what way?" he questions. "You're dripping," he remarks. Then he does something I don't think anyone has ever done for me outside of a stylist at a salon. He pulls a clean towel from the cupboard and wraps it around the end of my hair, squeezing it dry, and then carefully begins combing it. He makes eye contact with me in the mirror and says, "It's been a long time since I had someone to take care of."

I question him with a single look and he knows right where my head was about to go. He laughs, "No, not her. Britt's mom. After the cancer came back and Emily left him and Brian, I used to take trips to see her, help her mom out when Hospice wasn't there. Brian doesn't know all the details, just that we kept in touch."

I've heard bits and pieces about Emily, the important parts I suppose, but hearing about her from Tommy is different. He had a connection with her that I don't think others realize he had. "Did you love her?" I ask, afraid of the answer. I don't know why, it just feels like he's going to tell me he gave her part of his heart.

"In a way. She gave us Britton and I think it was a blessing for our family. We just didn't realize that with the blessing came sorrow, and I had to bottle it up for years because she asked me to keep her secret. I loved her because she was family, and she taught me how selfless a person could be when it really mattered," he says. "I'll grab clothes out for you and leave them on the bed."

I nod, because I have no words, and he kisses the back of my head before walking to the bedroom. He leaves me speechless and breathless and amazed by his character. I wonder if anyone who has ever had the chance to be in a relationship with Tommy has seen the type of man he truly is, or if he's kept it hidden.

I'm more than fortunate, I realize. If I hadn't walked into the coffeehouse that day, I may not have noticed him later at the restaurant. If that one moment when I met Tommy didn't exist, I might not either. I'm not giving him credit for saving my life, but I am giving him credit for allowing me to see, somehow, that I had purpose.

Before Fisher's near breakdown about the restaurant being in jeopardy, before my ex-husband draining the bank account, before the lies Sutton told, I was at the bottom. That loneliness? That feeling of being completely closed off from others? It hits hard, sometimes coming from out of nowhere and when it is least expected. If it weren't for Fisher giving me a reason to come home, I might not be here at all. I was done with living. The clothes I gave away? Originally the plan was to give them because I didn't think I was going to need them anymore. The money I donated? I couldn't take it with me if I left the world, so I wanted to give the world to someone else.

Everyone makes mistakes, but mine would have been fatal.

Coming home gave me life.

Chapter Thirty-seven

Tommy

It has never been about sex with Jacey. The first time our flirting went that far was a surprise to us both, I think. The feelings for her were there already and going to bed was a bonus that merely strengthened my emotions. This morning, though, something changed between us as we were standing in my bathroom. I don't know the specifics, but I'm well aware of the way the energy shifted. Jacey looked at me like she was seeing me for the first time and there was an avalanche of feelings — the intense need to take care of her wrapped itself around me and won't let go.

I hear her in the bedroom above me as I wait for her in the kitchen. Standing at the cupboards where I found her sitting early this morning, I lean against the marble countertop with one arm crossed over the other as I chew on my thumbnail. This old house creaks and groans when the wind blows, so following her movements through its rooms is easy. I listen as her footfalls land lightly first on one side of the room and then venture around to the other, and I shake my head as I realize she's making the bed. It's something so normal, so simple, and yet I'm fighting against a lump in my throat as she descends the stairs to the kitchen. That avalanche of emotion cascades through me again as my eyes find hers.

"I was serious. Move in with me?" I say. I don't take the time to think about the words. With Jacey, it's all action. She makes it easy to forget about the consequences of loving her. She makes it possible to love without worrying about the hurt that so often comes with it when it's not real.

She stops on the last step, but doesn't speak. She looks at me, but it feels more like she's looking at all the pieces of me I've kept hidden from others. Her lips part slightly, and then … nothing. I shouldn't have asked. I should have waited. I should have —

"Okay."

I breathe.

"Okay?"

"Tentative okay. Let's talk to Brian about the apartment first. If he's not set on keeping it as an apartment, maybe I can continue renting it as an office and private studio area. It would make work easier if I'm going to open the business right below it," she says. There is no questioning my intentions or asking my opinion. She shrugs her shoulders, takes the last step into the kitchen, and walks toward me. "I slept on it. I realized it was an opportunity I didn't want to pass up."

I reach for her and she steps into me, wrapping her arms around my chest and pulling me closer. She hugs me as though she's afraid to let go, but I'm hanging onto her just as tightly.

Minutes tick by and my phone rings. I answer, still tangled in her embrace, and Brian asks if we're on our way. I tell him we'll be there in five. I kiss Jacey's forehead and, as though we've done this countless times, we quietly gather our jackets, put on our shoes, and leave the house at half past seven.

~*~*~*~

Mama isn't in her room when we arrive shortly after eight.

"Maybe she and Dad went for a walk around the floor. She probably started feeling cooped up. It's possible they're running more tests this morning like she said they wanted to," Brian says.

"Something doesn't feel right, though," I respond. Britt's face falls, and I place my hands on his shoulders. "Why don't you, Stella, and Jacey sit and have something to eat and your dad and I'll be right back. We'll find out where she is."

He nods, a tight smile on his lips, and climbs up on the hospital bed. I motion toward the door with my head and Brian follows me out to the hallway.

"What are you thinking?" Brian asks, falling in step with me.

"I don't know," I say. My gut tells me something happened in the night, and as I make a beeline for the nurse's station, I'm almost certain the feeling is going to be confirmed. The nurse behind the desk sees me coming and gives a warm smile before I can open my mouth. "Kathryn Stratford was admitted last night with angina and kept for observation. She's not in her room. Was she taken for tests?"

The nurses' smile slips. "Uh, she's ... Are you family?" she fumbles with the medical chart in her hand before looking at a large white board on the wall behind her. We tell her we're Kathryn's sons and her shoulders visibly relax as she tells us, "She's in surgery."

"Surgery?" Brian asks. He looks at his watch. "How long ago was she taken in?"

I grab my phone from my back pocket and as I'm about to press the call button, Dad walks through the door in the waiting area with a cup from the cafeteria.

"I hope you boys brought me good coffee. This tastes like someone ran water through Tommy's gym socks," he says. "Morning, Felicia."

"Good morning, Mr. Stratford," the nurse responds, as my father turns and walks past us on his way back to Mama's room. I turn my head and follow his retreating form before giving my attention back to the nurse. Felicia looks at me and Brian again, and says, "Your mother had an episode in the night. The plan was to do an angioplasty, but depending on what they found there was a possibility of bypass surgery. We'll know more when the surgical team can update us."

"So, nobody knows what's going on, is what you're saying?" Brian says, flustered.

Felicia holds her composure, "The surgeon does. I just haven't been given an update."

I thank her and ask her to let us know if or when she hears something. Pushing my hands into my pockets, I turn and bump my elbow into Brian's arm so he'll come with me back to Mama's room. Dad gives us the least scary run down of what occurred on account of Britt being in the room with us, but when I see Stella wrap her arm around his shoulders it's apparent even he heard through the G-rated version.

"The surgeon told me there was a likelihood of them doing a bypass and to not get concerned if the procedure took longer than a couple hours," Dad says. "I'm glad I stayed the night here. You boys know your mama. She would have brushed it off otherwise. But it was worse than the pain she'd had yesterday at Dale and Jenny's."

He's calm, though. Mama's chest could be sliced open right this second and he's acting like it's an ordinary day. With one exception. His hand trembles just enough for me to notice as he lifts the cup to his mouth, dribbling a tiny amount of coffee down his stubbled chin. He wipes it away. Nearly forty years of marriage didn't prepare him for this. There is no way to prepare for something you don't expect.

"They said if they needed to do the bypass, she was in a good place for it. The surgeon here has started using some fancy new technology, so they'll only have to make a few little cuts and go in with robots to fix her up," he says. Staring into his cup, he says, "Robots. Doing surgery on my Katie."

His fear is palpable and, while I know the idea of Mama needing her heart fixed is part of it, I imagine a lot of it has to do with the suddenness of it all. One day they're joyfully spending time with friends, visiting and celebrating the holidays, and the next they're here being asked to fill out health care proxies and HIPPA forms.

"It sounds like they're trying to do what they can to make it easier on Mama," Stella says. "I've done stories about this procedure. It's new to the hospital, so they wanted an article for the paper. It's completely endoscopic so they can go in and graft the artery to bypass the blocked artery without making that huge incision everyone associates with heart surgery. The healing process is much quicker from what I understand."

When she finishes talking, we're all staring at her. Some of us give her a raised eyebrow. Dad looks at her with his mouth agape.

"What?"

"Nothin'. Just, your brain has so much in there I don't know how you keep it all straight," Dad says to her as Felicia pops into the room. "So, this robot surgery is supposed to help her recover better?"

Felicia smiles at Dad's description and steps into the circle we've formed in Mama's room. "It's a lot better than the old way. I just heard from the operating room. Mrs. Stratford is out of surgery and in recovery. It'll be an hour or so before she comes back to the room, so if you want to go grab more coffee you have time," she says, offering a smile to Britt. "And what about you? I've got crayons and coloring books at the nurse's station if you want to come take a look."

Britt looks from Brian to Stella, waiting for one of them to tell him he can go. Stella nods and reminds him to use his manners and, as he walks past his dad, Brian tousles his hair and kisses the top of his head.

"If you bring crayons and a coloring book back, I'll color with you, bud," he says. Britt turns and wraps his arms around Brian's waist and it's then that I see the energy drain from my brother's body. Britton isn't paying attention, so for thirty seconds Brian can let his fearless front fall, but when my nephew pulls away my brother regains his composure. "Pick out a good one, okay?"

I know he's had seven years to practice and figure out how to be a dad, but I wonder if I would have been even minimally prepared for fatherhood. I question it and, even when it happens for real, I'll probably still question my readiness and my ability to be a parent. Brian's told me before that nothing truly prepares you for parenthood, but when I watch him with his kids it feels like he simply knows how to do all of it, from changing diapers to handling bullies. I can't even handle myself some days and that's likely where a lot of my fear comes from.

I feel eyes on me and catch Jacey watching me watching them. While the rest of the room talks about going for coffee and waiting for Mama to come back upstairs, her eyes don't leave mine and I wonder if she's reading my mind. I wonder if I'm as transparent as I feel.

Jacey turns her attention back to the rest of the family and says she and Stella could go get coffee and stop by Dale and Jenny's to update them.

"I need to check on Emmy anyway," Stella adds. "This will give you guys time to talk. Do you want us to take Britt?"

"He's probably going to want to be here when Mama comes back," Brian says

She knows the kind of relationship Britt has with his grandma and there's a possibility he might feel like he isn't wanted here if she asks him to go with her. She gets it, but she was willing to offer. Stella gives an understanding nod as she stands from the bed and steps toward my brother, kissing him quickly, before turning to my father. "Is there anything specific you want to eat? You can't survive on coffee the entire time she's here."

"Sure, I can," Dad declares. "But maybe can you pick me up a turkey sandwich?"

"A turkey sandwich. Got it." She pats his arm and then asks Jacelyn if she's ready to go out for a bit.

Jacey turns her attention to me before responding. Without taking her eyes off mine, she says she's ready and stands, grabbing her purse and jacket. As she walks past me, she grabs my arm and gives it a gentle squeeze before tipping her head for me to kiss her lips. "I'll be fine," I say, taking mental note of the questioning look she gives me. "Cross my heart." She mouths the words "I love you" and before I can say it back she and Stella are stepping through the door.

I lift my coffee to my mouth and refuse to make eye contact with Dad and Brian. They're both watching me. I can see them from the corner of my eye.

"So …" I say after a few quiet minutes.

"Yup," Dad responds.

"Recovery?" Brian offers. "Do you think you'll stay at Dale and Jenny's until Mama can travel?"

"Not sure. I'll have to talk to them and your mama about it," Dad says. "I guess it'll depend on how soon before we'll have to travel back up here for the wedding. Y'all set a date?"

We never told him I wasn't proposing to her last night. I've hardly had time to talk to him at all, and I shoot a look at Brian. I guess in a way I thought he would have cleared that up for me, but now am proven wrong and shouldn't have just assumed.

"We're not engaged, Dad. That was a misunderstanding," I say, though it feels so very wrong to say it.

"You love the girl?" he asks, and I nod. "So where is the misunderstanding? When I realized how much I was in love with your mother and that I didn't want anyone else but her to spend the rest of my life with, I gave her my heart and a ring. It's not that difficult, Tommy."

I look at Brian, hoping he'll give me a little guidance here, but he literally turns his back and walks away with a shit-eating grin on his face. "Asshole," I say as he pulls the door closed behind him.

"Don't call your brother names. He got the same talk about Stella." I open my mouth to say something when he puts his hand up to stop me. "Don't you dare say a word to Dale about that. He'd give me hell if he knew my little chat with your brother is the reason they got married so quickly after reuniting."

My face betrays me, my shock transitioning quickly to amusement.

"You do realize Jacey and I have only been officially dating for," I stop to look at my watch, "approximately twelve hours, right? I'd say it might be a little early to be buying rings."

"But not too soon to tell the girl you're in love with her?"

Every excuse I could give him falls flat before it leaves my mouth. I suppose the truth works best in these situations.

"I felt it. I needed her to know. For an entire week, I stayed away from her just to be sure that me saying it wasn't just me being lonely," I say, though a bit sheepishly. Admitting I've been lonely isn't exactly manly.

"And?"

"It was torture. Every minute I forced myself not to go see her or text her or call her was a lesson in patience."

"Good. It means you learned something. Now ask the girl to marry you," he says.

"I want to, it just takes time. Why are you so insistent?" I laugh despite the lack of humor in the conversation. My dad has the ability to get right to the point and doesn't mess around doing it.

"Thomas, tomorrow isn't guaranteed," he says, exasperated. He places one hand on his hip and, after placing his cup on the hospital table, reaches up to scratch his forehead with the other. "It's not. Do the things that will make you feel whole and real and do it with every fiber of your being, and if that thing is marrying Jacelyn ... do it. Don't wait for tomorrow."

There it is.

I watch my father as his face slowly becomes streaked with tears he's skillfully held back for God only knows how long. His reason for the sudden push is completely valid. I get it.

"Okay, Dad," I say, my tone sobering. "Okay. I'd like to make it somewhat special, though. Can I have a little time to plan out this proposal? Maybe at least wait for Mama to be out of recovery and discharged from this place."

That's when I laugh, heartily even, because I watch my father roll his eyes at me, like I'm taking too damn long to get things done.

"You have always had to have a plan. Such a perfectionist," he says, grabbing my shoulders and pulling me into a quick, tight hug. "You do it your way, but don't wait too long. We like her. She brings out all the good things in you, T. For quite a while you weren't yourself. Then you started talking about this woman from the coffeehouse and the restaurant and it was like hearing you come back to life."

Was it really that noticeable when the hold Sutton had over me was released? I had relapses out of pure loneliness, but did I change so much that even Mama and Dad noticed through phone calls?

Jacelyn isn't like anyone I've ever dated. I knew there was something more about her even before the friendship that preceded our official declaration of coupledom. She isn't helpless. Jacelyn has never made me feel like she needs a man who can give her everything she wants. Since our first real conversation after meeting in the coffeehouse, I've known she strives for and prefers to be self-sufficient. I don't know all of her stories yet, but I know she's worked hard to be a survivor. I'm lucky she moved back and walked into the Jumping Bean the morning I was covering for Greg. I can't even pinpoint what it was about her that triggered the feelings that coursed through my body. All I know for certain is, that morning I realized there's more to her. So. Much. More.

"She made me feel like I had a purpose."

M.L. Pennock

Chapter Thirty-eight

Jacelyn

"Mama's back from recovery and getting situated in her room. Brian said he's been coloring in the waiting room with Britt because Dad and Tommy were having a little one-on-one father-son talk about … life," Stella says after walking back into the kitchen at the coffeehouse.

"Life. That's a good thing to talk about. It's good for them to talk about … life." What the hell does that mean? "Are we good on coffee or should we grab some for the nurses, too?"

"Greg's on it. He's filling up extra cups for us to take. I've got the sandwich for Ben and extras for the guys. There's a container of cookies from my mom. I grabbed a couple books in case Mama wants to read when we leave and let her rest," she says, ticking each item off on her fingers. "I think that's everything, but he's swamped. I asked Steph to come down and help out for a bit. Greg's working at breaking in the two people Bri just hired, and he really needs a little break."

Brian recently hired a few of the local college kids to help out at the café in an effort to force Tommy back onto his side of building and focus on Mile 63 Marketing. I know he works hard, but Stella was afraid his focus was wavering. Brian was getting busy and Tommy wanted to make sure his brother was able to spend time with his family without compromising his business. It's heroic in a sense, but I understand Brian's reason for squelching it, or attempting to.

Greg walks through the café doors into the kitchen and waits for me to open the door as he helps us get our orders to the car out back. The new guys are supposed to handle anyone out front, but one of them pokes his head out the door and asks Greg where the napkins are. Greg's a nice guy, though, and instead of showing his frustration, he politely tells the kid where the spare supplies are kept. I admire his ability to handle the change in staffing for the day, though. Working at the restaurant as a teenager I saw how my dad treated anyone new, and seeing that interaction reminded me how much my father always made everyone feel like family. I can feel the emotions flooding in, so I get in the car and wait for Stella as she finishes talking to Greg and updating him on what we know about Mama's surgery, which at this point isn't much.

We parked right behind my building and I stare at the blackened windows of the back entrance to what will be my business someday soon. I sent Fisher a quick text on our way from the hospital to tell him what was going on with Kathryn and to break the news to him that I actually took his advice and talked to Brian about the vacant storefront. He probably knew I would, but without the push from him and me mentioning it to Tommy I likely would never have had the courage to bring it up to Brian. Putting myself out there is scary. Working at the restaurant is comfortable. It's something I've always known, so to go back to thinking about my own studio after abandoning the idea long ago is foreign. I'm not uncomfortable with the concept, just fearful. Of what? I have no idea. The unknown, maybe. I've been facing the unknown since I got in my car and drove across the country, and I survived that and embraced it even though it was a new experience. Opening my own business is different. This is opening myself up to the community that raised me and showing them my insides.

"What are you so deep in thought about?"

Stella's voice surprises me. I hadn't even heard her get in the car. I blink at her, but it feels like my eyes close and open ten times slower than normal, and say, "I need to get in there and see what I have to work with for space."

She laughs and smiles as she starts the car. "Don't worry, I'm sure you'll get dragged over there when we leave the hospital. Brian could hardly sleep last night between not knowing what's going on with Mama and excitement over you being interested in the storefront. He's had a few people express interest, but in the end, nothing came of the inquiries." She stares out the windshield as we wait at a stop light. "I told him he just needed to be patient. I'm so glad he didn't say yes to the guy who wanted to open a taxidermy shop."

"A taxidermist? You're kidding, right?"

"I wish. The very nice gentleman who approached Bri said the actual preserving happens at a shop he has set up in his barn, but he wanted the exposure on Main Street because then he could display his work more prominently," she says. She's dead serious, too. Not so much as a giggle from Stella about this. "It just didn't really flow with the vibe Brian was going for."

I never really felt like there was a vibe to any part of town — laundromat, village hall, fire department, a dress shop, the newspaper, a travel agency, a bank, and restaurants — the entire place is a mish-mash of normal little things you would expect to find in a small town.

"What kind of vibe is he hoping to create? Because right now it's just like every other tiny town I've ever been to. You grew up here, too. It hasn't changed much in thirty years."

"He wants Brockport to embrace the arts," she says. "It does. A lot. We love the arts. It's just most of it seems to be on campus and he really wants to see it spread into downtown more and get the community involved. I think he might have wet his pants in excitement when he found out about your background."

I can't help myself. I need to ask. "Was I set up?"

"In what sense?"

"In the sense that my brother was trying to push me out of the restaurant and into opening a studio space business thing. Did Brian and Fisher plan this?"

She turns the car off after coming to a stop in a parking space at the hospital and looks at me. "Doubtful. It is possible Fisher got the idea after Brian brought up trying to rent the space out at the business association meetings, but other than that? I don't think they intentionally worked to get you to agree to rent it."

I bite my thumbnail. "Fisher's a smart person. He has a habit of knowing what I need and when I need it. You're probably right." I think my past has made me paranoid.

"If you're worried that's what happened," she says to me sincerely, "ask Brian. He's not going to keep something like that from you, especially not if I'm standing right there."

Settled. I'll ask him, I tell her. I text Tommy that we're on our way up as we gather our things from the car and walk toward the building, carefully balancing takeout trays filled with hot coffee, cookies, and sandwiches. As we step off the elevator, Tommy meets me and takes the tray, places a quick kiss to my cheek, greets Stella, and motions toward Mama's room.

"She's resting, but said she's in the mood for some visitors," he says. Laughing, he adds somewhat loudly, "For someone who just went through heart surgery she's in pretty good spirits. No hollering about all of us doting on her. I'm afraid she might get used to it."

He winks at me as he pushes the door open for us to enter.

"Don't think I didn't hear that, Thomas," Mama says. "Give me a few days and I'll be back to my old self."

Ben catches my eye and he gives me a look, one that says he won't let her get away with too much. I smile at him and suddenly, it doesn't matter who talked to whom or if my business decision was influenced by someone else's conversation. I'm fairly certain I'm exactly where I was meant to be and it feels like home. It's the kind of home I forgot I was allowed to have because it isn't made of bricks and sticks and mortar; it's comprised of laughter and love and kindness, and those were things I stopped thinking I needed. Those weren't crucial for survival. Closing myself off from all of those things has done me no favors. Reopening the doors and inviting new people in has been rejuvenating. It's reigniting a flame that I snuffed out when I decided to let other people decide my worth. I'm worth more than I give myself credit for. I don't have to prove myself to anyone but me, and it's about damn time I take back my professional life, even if it means needing a nudge from Fisher ... and Tommy and Brian.

A hand at my elbow causes my attention to shift from the family before me to the woman beside me. Stella cocks an eyebrow at me as if to ask if I'm doing okay. It feels like every time I turn around someone is asking if I'm okay, but there's Mama laying in a bed having just had her heart operated on. I don't think I'm the one anyone should be worrying about, but still Stella silently questions.

"I'm fine," I say quietly, and she gives me an unconvinced look.

"Of course, you're fine," she says, moving us back toward the door. "But are you okay?"

"There's a difference?" I ask.

"'I'm fine' is something you say when you don't want to talk about something. That's the kind of thing I say to Brian when I'm rage cleaning and he tries to ask me what's wrong and I'm not ready to talk about it," she says. I nod and purse my lips together, understanding what she means. "Being okay is different. Somehow. It feels different."

I smile at her, "Stella, I'm okay. There are just a lot of emotions I'm juggling right now."

"Makes sense. A lot has happened."

"More than you're aware of at this point," I respond, then bite my lip because it's one of those comments that always leads to more questions. She gives me look that asks "Are you going to elaborate?" and I roll my eyes. "Sleeping arrangements have been discussed. Mine. Where I sleep regularly."

Her eyes grow wide. "Already? He moves fast."

"You and Steph said he was patient, so I figured the moving in together talk was still a ways out. Not so. And now I'm not sure if I just take all my clothes over there or wait and gradually take them because we haven't had a chance to really thoroughly discuss it and it's so much all at once," I say quickly and then suck in a deep breath. "So many changes."

As Stella and I talk quietly, my back more to the room than not, I don't notice the stopped conversations behind me, but I feel the penetrating gazes from the other four adults as I turn back toward the room. Tommy wears a pleased smile, his parents don't look surprised at all, and Brian starts to say something but stops himself. Britt, on the other hand, sits unfazed and continues coloring in a chair next to Mama's bed, his eyes glued to the pages in the book.

"Are you and Uncle Tommy getting married now?" he asks, changing one crayon out for another color. "Can I finally call you Aunt Jacey?"

All the heads turn and look at the sandy-haired boy in the corner. He wants to call me his aunt? I've never been an aunt to anyone, not even just in name, and I feel the tightness in my chest that seems to follow every emotional encounter I've had since the day I met Tommy Stratford.

"Finally? Britt, we've only been seeing each other for like a day," Tommy responds, and I'm thankful he did because I wasn't sure how to, or if I even could.

"Maybe, but you wanted her to be your girlfriend a lot longer than that. You always act funny around her," the child replies, and I don't think anyone misses the know-it-all tone in his voice. He's very matter-of-fact about it all and doesn't bother to look up at us while he speaks his piece. As if an older, wiser man, he sighs deeply and places his hands in his lap over his coloring page. Looking dead in Tommy's eyes, he says, "You act like Dad acts around Mom, so you should probably just marry her and let me call her Aunt Jacey."

I attempt to hold back a laugh. It doesn't work, so I just say what I'm thinking, something somewhat out of the ordinary for me when in the company of my elders. "It's so easy when you're little. When did we all lose that kind of innocence?"

"Around the time puberty hit," Mama remarks. She reaches over and strokes Britt's hair. "Sweetie, can you go ask the nurse for some ice? I'd like some for my water."

As Britt exits the room, Brian and Tommy fidget. I glance at Stella, who shrugs, and then look at Ben. He's sitting straight up in his chair as though he's waiting for a show to start. I'm not sure if I should be nervous or amused at how all the men in this family respond to the matriarch, but I am impressed.

"Is there something you boys need to discuss? In the hallway perhaps?" she speaks directly to her sons.

"Yes ma'am," Brian says, and as he steps toward the door he grabs Tommy's arm to drag him out of the room.

"Stella?"

"Right, I'm going. I'll let my mom and dad know you've come through surgery well and they can visit this afternoon?"

Mama nods, then turns her focus to me. I'm supposed to feel nervous, I think, and it's to the point I can feel my hands shaking even as I push them into the pockets of my paint-spattered jeans. I know from my time with her over Christmas that Tommy's mama is a really wonderful woman, but that doesn't mean I'm not a little scared of her, too.

"Ben and I were talking last night after y'all left, before all of this," she begins, motioning to her chest before lacing her fingers together on her lap. "Tommy told me when we had a moment alone that if I ended up needing to stay up north for a surgery and recovery, which obviously happened, that we could stay at the house with him."

I open my mouth to agree with her, that they should stay with him if that's what they think is best, but she quiets my thoughts when she continues, saying, "Jenny and Dale already have us set up at their house and plan to keep putting up with us for the time being, so I don't want Thomas getting a burr up his ass about us not staying with him. We're just fine where we've been for the last couple weeks."

My shoulders relax a bit as I try to understand what might be the underlying message. I can't imagine she made everyone leave the room simply to share with me their plans for where they intend to stay while she recuperates.

"It seems, though, we're going to be here for a bit longer than planned. We just want to make sure you don't mind us meddling. We're probably going to meddle. I can't even say I'll try not to. It's just in my nature and I think you kind of saw that when we got together to bake."

Ben scratches his temple. "That's the truth," he says. "She likes knowing everyone's ins and outs and deep thoughts. While she takes it easy and pries into your life, though, Dale and I'd like to help you at that new store you're planning to open. Talked to him about it this morning and he's on board. Brian took me in there the other week and it's going to take some elbow grease to get it ready. It's going to need to be painted and it'll give me something to do."

He wants to do what? It's possible there are people who simply do nice things because they are kind humans, it's just such a rare occurrence to come in contact with them these days. Yet, here are two people who want to help just because it needs to be done. I hadn't even started thinking about what kind of work might need to be done in the store, and now I have someone offering to go in and do it without me asking. The tops of my ears grow warm, a giveaway to my nerves slowly fraying, and I reach up to touch the back of my neck and fiddle with my hair.

I'm so grateful for the offer, and plan to accept, but instead, "Here I thought I was going to get lectured for how quickly Tommy and I are moving with our relationship," comes out of my mouth. That's the kind of thing I would like to believe my mom and dad would want to have a private conversation with my significant someone about. But if she wants to delve into the who and what that I am, it might be worthwhile to stop trying to censor myself. I seem to lack the ability to use my filter when I'm around this family anyway, so what's the point in stressing out about policing my every thought?

I hear myself nervously laugh. Then I chide myself for not thanking them and ball my hands into fists, pressing my fingernails into my palms.

Ben and Kathryn exchange silent words, I can see them talking in the way they look at one another before they turn their attention back to me. "Jacey, the men in this family aren't exactly known for taking their time. Patient men? Yes. The ability to wait when they really want something? Not so much," Mama says to me. Scrunching her eyebrows together in a concerning manner, she adds, "You tell my boy to slow down if you need time to breathe. He loves you. He'll listen."

It's like she was listening to our conversation in bed early this morning.

"What if I don't want to slow down?" I ask, cautiously.

"Then move at the speed you're most comfortable with. He will follow your lead."

I pull my bottom lip between my teeth and nod my head.

"I guess I should take my toothbrush over and let him know which side of the closet I'd like," I say.

A broad smile lights up Mama's face. That approval I was wondering about before? I know I have it. Her smile shows me she's given it to me in spades.

"Welcome to the family, sweetheart."

I feel that tightness in my chest again. I know without a doubt, I'm home.

M.L. Pennock

Chapter Thirty-nine

Tommy

Mama kicking us out of her room was predictable. She saw Brian's reaction to overhearing Jacey talk about moving into the house — it was a little bit of shock and a lot of "what the fuck," probably because she hasn't had a chance to have that talk with him yet about possibly keeping the apartment as office space. I figured Mama telling us we needed to have a talk was her way of easing a potential sour situation.

"She's moving in with you? But, the apartment? She loves her apartment."

"I know she does," I nod. "Which is why she was hoping to talk to you about using it as a private office and studio. She said something of subletting or breaking the lease, but I'm not asking her to uproot all of her things and move to the house today."

I want her to take her time and bring over the things she wants to when she wants to, and if Brian says yes to the office idea, that gives her a chance to ease in and decide what furniture needs to come and what can stay.

"An office makes sense," he says. "She's really moving in? Already?"

I cross my arms and lean my shoulder against the wall, looking at him intently. I don't think he was paying attention to his son a few minutes ago.

"Your kid and our father want me to propose to her immediately. Maybe you missed that whole exchange? Dad practically cornered me this morning and you high-tailed it right on out of there. I don't think moving in should be the concern."

Brian laughs and then stops. I hear a door close and my attention is instantly diverted. Stella pops into the hallway with us, but Jacelyn isn't with her. It should make me leery of the conversation happening behind that closed door considering who she's alone with.

"Should I go in there?" I ask Stella, pointing to the entrance.

"Nope."

"Do you know what they're talking about?" Brian asks.

"Not a clue. Probably living arrangements and marriage. You know, if I had to take a stab at it." She places her hands on her hips and stares us down. "What is it with this family? There is never a courtship. Why are there no courtships? What ever happened to showering women with flowers and going to the movies and doing all of that romantic shit?"

I'm not quite sure what's going on, but I don't think it has anything to do with me and Jacey. Brian is considerably pale after Stella's short outburst, so it's safe to assume he did — or didn't do — something. I look from one to the other and wait for someone to tell me what's going on.

"Do y'all need a moment?"

"No," they respond in unison, and it's definitely apparent they don't want to talk about whatever it is that's going on. I see Stella's glare soften.

"We've just been busy. I need a date night," she says, sadly. "The holidays are so hectic."

"Then I'll watch the kids and you two go have dinner. Pick a night and I'll be there. Now, can we focus on me and Jacey and that closed door?" I say. "You both know Mama and Dad love to get their fingers into people's business. I should probably go in there."

I move away from the wall, but they each place a hand on my chest and shake their heads.

"Not a good idea. We should just let them have their chat and when Jacey comes out you can ask her all the intricate details," Brian says.

They walk away and leave me standing in the hall while they check on Britt. The two people in my life who I know are good for words of wisdom and all they can tell me is I should let the situation play out.

I stare at the solid wood hospital door for what feels like an eternity before it slowly opens and Jacelyn emerges looking unscathed. There's a feeling of relief that hits me square in the chest and a nervous flutter a bit lower. She's the kind of woman who makes me feel tingly just by walking in the room, but when her eyes find mine I'm a goner. She makes a beeline for me, stretching up on her tiptoes to wrap her arms tightly around my neck in the hug to end all other hugs, and I stand there for a beat soaking it in before enveloping her in my embrace. Neither of us pull back and I make a memory while holding her in the hospital hallway.

"I need to go get my toothbrush," she says, close to my ear. Her breath caresses my neck, tickling the skin, and I pull her closer to me.

"Just your toothbrush?" It's a specific thing to need. Very specific and I assume it has some meaning behind it, but right now I'm just happy she came out of Mama's room with a smile on her face.

"Until you move things in your closet, that's going to have to do," she says. Lowering herself from her toes, she bites her lower lip and reaches back to twist her hair between her fingers. "I have a dresser I can bring over for T-shirts and jeans, but I would like somewhere to hang my flannel shirts and fancy dresses. It just depends on how much moving you want to do today versus what might be able to wait until we both have a chance to acclimate."

When she pulled away, my hands slipped to her waist. At the mention of moving a dresser, my fingers tighten the fabric already gathered in my hand.

"Acclimate."

"Get used to sharing a bathroom," she says.

"How long do you think that will take us?" I smile at her, amused that this is what she came out wanting to talk about. Not a single mention of my parents accosting her and wanting her life story.

"A day or two. Three if I catch you leaving the seat up," she smiles back at me.

I reach up from her waist and cup her face, leaning in to kiss that sweet mouth of hers.

"You're sure you want to start today? We can wait if you want to," I say, hovering just a breath away from her lips. I don't say it because I don't want her to move in immediately. I say it because I want her to want to move in immediately. Letting her control the situation is important to me. The last thing I want to do is have Jacey feel like I'm in the driver's seat all the time.

Without intentionally trying to compare the two, it is glaringly obvious the difference between Jacey and Sutton. It is every time I let myself think about how different Jacey is from anyone else I've dated. Again, I'm finding myself thankful Sutton left me. She just sort of did what she wanted when she wanted. There was such a lack of communication that when I would question something, she was quick to get defensive and I was just as fast to apologize for everything. Jacelyn, though? She's exactly the kind of woman I need in my life. She talks to me. There are actual conversations we have that don't end in an argument.

"Positive. What are you thinking about?"

"How absolutely amazing you are," I say.

My lips brush against hers once more and we begin to make a plan for the rest of the day. Speaking quietly in the hallway, Jacey decides what clothes have to be moved today and what can be left behind.

"I can wait on a dresser and live out of a laundry basket for the time being," she says.

I almost tell her she can have one of the drawers in my dresser but stop myself. This situation requires more than a drawer. Noticing Brian walking back down the hall, I lift my arm to get his full attention. "Come here," I say, and he gives me a "what's up" look. "Can I borrow the Tahoe?"

"For ...?" he questions, but pulls his keys from his pocket and hands them to me.

"I have a dresser to move. I'm going to let Mama know we're heading out and then we're grabbing lunch if you and Stella and the kids want to join us," I say as I start across the hall to Mama's room. "Oh, and then after lunch, I need your help."

"With what?" he asks, like he doesn't already know.

"Moving a dresser," I say, and disappear through the door without looking back at my brother.

Mama is resting when I close the door quietly behind me. Dad's sitting in the chair beside her reading a book Stella brought with her. I glance at the cover and Dad catches me eyeing it.

"Romance? Since when do you read romance novels?"

"You could learn a thing or two reading one of these manuals," he says, closing the book around his thumb to keep his page. "I think the nice guy finishes last in this one."

"I bet he does," I laugh. Mama stirs slightly in her sleep and I lower my voice, sharing with him that Jacey and I are going to go grab something to eat and then start moving some of her things to the house. I told Mama they could stay with me, though, and I feel a little guilty for upending those plans, despite Dad telling me they planned to stay put where they've been. "You're sure Jenny and Dale are okay with y'all staying there longer? I doubt Jace would mind you and Mama staying at the house with us."

"Tommy, you don't want your Mama and me in that house the first week you're living with a woman. I ain't stupid." The smirk on my father's face causes a heat to climb up my neck and face as I realize what he's saying. I honestly hadn't even thought about how much of that would be happening while we "get acclimated" to living together. My dad chuckles and rubs his hand along the two days' worth of scruff on his chin. "You didn't consider it, did you?"

"The thought hadn't really crossed my mind, but ... thank you. For giving Jacey and me the privacy we may need."

"'May need?' Son, who are you kidding? I'm old, not dead. I remember what it was like being young and in love," he says. Standing from his seat, he presses his index finger to my chest and looks me straight in the eye as he continues, "She's a good woman, Tommy, and I'm happy you've found someone who makes you feel whole."

I throw my arms around him and he laughs. "You will never cease to amaze me. Let me know when you need my help moving some things. I'll be starting work on her store this week, so use me while you can."

I wasn't aware he was planning to help with preparing Jacey's storefront for business, but if it was a decision he came to recently I can understand why the need for a private conversation with her earlier. He's got woodworking skills like Brian and an eye for detail, so I imagine he's already got a vision for TopCoat if he's had a chance to look at the space.

"I'll let you know. I've got Bri on the hook to help with some furniture today," I tell him as I walk back toward the door. "Dale know you're going to be working in town?"

"Who do you think's going to help me?" he asks, rhetorically. "You boys have your own businesses to run and I'm not going to pull you away from them or family time in the evening. Dale and I are retired. This will keep us out of your Mama's and Jenny's hairs."

We exchange a smile as I step back into the hallway and before closing the door behind me, I watch him sit back down in his chair, propping one ankle over the opposite knee. He opens his book back to the place he left off and I watch his head move slightly as he scans the sentences on the page. For just a moment, I find it odd he referred to a novel as a manual, until I realize I, too, often read books with the hope I'll learn something from the words trapped between the covers and it becomes very clear that my father is one of the humblest men I know.

M.L. Pennock

Chapter Forty

Jacelyn

Unlocking the door to my apartment, I smile.

I don't smile because I'm moving. I smile because of why I'm moving. So much has changed since coming back home. I've had to take some bad in order to get to a lot of really good, and in eight very short months, I have changed in ways that a year ago I couldn't have comprehended. I've felt the differences and seen my own growth, and even if home is nothing like it was when I left, it is still home. It has a smell for every season and conjures up memories I thought were long ago buried. If I had come back sooner, I don't think it would be like this. The person I am today wouldn't exist.

Tommy walks past me carrying a box I never bothered to unpack when I first arrived. Brian asks if I want to put things from my dresser into a suitcase and I tell him we can just pull the drawers and take them over full if that would work better. We work in quiet companionship, the three of us slowly moving small parts of my life from the first apartment that was only mine when I stop and stand in front of my purple estate sale couch.

"I don't think we have room for that right now. I didn't take Emmy's car seat out so we're already a little full," Brian says, staring at the brightly colored fabric. "We can go drop off what we have and come back for it, though."

I don't say anything as I try to consider the furniture Tommy already has in the house.

"There's no way it'll fit in your car even if you take the baby's seat out, but thank you for offering," I say. "Besides, it doesn't match anything over there. I'm going to leave it here for now. I can always move it downstairs after the renovations."

Tommy walks behind me on his way through the room and places his hands on my shoulders. He leans in from behind me and whispers, "It doesn't need to match the other furniture at our house. It matches you."

Our house. I smile at his use of the phrase. It's the first time I've thought of it as my home, too, and oddly enough I do consider it more than just a house I will live and breathe and exist in. It's not the walls that make it home, it's the people I'll share it with. At some point, my family grew. It's not just me and Fisher anymore.

My phone vibrates in my back pocket. It's like he knew I was thinking about him.

Fish: Carefree and wild Jacey is back?

Me: She's making an appearance. Not totally back, but definitely trying to be less afraid of letting her out.

Fish: I missed you. You smile more. Mom and Dad would be proud of you.

I've smiled more since meeting Tommy than I think I had in the ten years prior. He was my missing puzzle piece and he fell right into place, easily completing the picture before I realized he was sliding into my life despite a few small hurdles. There are always going to be hurdles, they're supposed to pop up throughout life, but I think having a few thrown at us during the honeymoon period has provided us with a more solid foundation. Rather than looking at each other starry-eyed for a few months, we were given doses of reality that have kept us grounded. It helps, too, that while I was secretly falling for him I had to watch him parade other women through the restaurant. I could question why he would do that, but what would be the point?

My phone vibrates in my hand again and I look down to see Tommy's name on the screen.

TStratford: You look deep in thought. Anything I can help with?

I look up and turn around to find him leaning against the bedroom doorframe, his phone still in his hands and a perplexed expression on his face. "You aren't having second thoughts, are you?"

Shaking my head, I walk toward him and stand on my toes to reach his lips. "You're the perfect height," I say, a second before his mouth connects to mine.

Chapter Forty-one

Tommy

Four months ago, Jacelyn moved to our house, Mama was released from the hospital to continue recovering, and Dad and Dale started renovating the shop we now know as TopCoat. When I say this year started out with a bang, I mean it literally.

The first decision the dads made as Jacey's personal wrecking crew was to tear down an existing wall and extend the front of the storefront by putting up half walls further back in the space.

A lot of their plans might not have come together as quickly if it wasn't for Will. He's always said he was just a handyman — he likes to do odd jobs for people around town — but he failed to mention in the time he spent with Jacey and Fisher at the restaurant that after being discharged from the Army he used his G.I. Bill to go to college for architecture and engineering. We hadn't seen much of him since Christmas, but he stopped by to see what was going on when he heard Brian had someone renting out the store next to the coffeehouse. Seeing Jacey with a hammer in her hand was all the motivation he needed to pitch in. Will said that with everything Jace and Fisher did for him throughout the years, he owed it to her to repay the kindness, because kindness matters and people too often take it for granted. The world could use more Wills.

Will's volunteerism had become central to many conversations while he and Jace worked, and on several occasions their talks turned more into counseling than a visit among friends. At his urging, she opened up to me about her mental state when she began her trek home, finally sharing with me how she didn't think she was going to be around long enough to enjoy life. The word "suicide" has never been said, but I know that's where she thought she was headed, and had been since her parents' death. She calls Fisher's need for her to come home a taste of "divine intervention," and because of that I have her in my life.

"Fix your tie. And your hair," Brian says, standing behind me and staring at my reflection in the mirror. Jacey left early for the gallery to make sure everything was exactly as she had imagined it. Fisher was meeting her there to set up the massive display of food and drinks he planned for the evening. Stella, Steph, Max, and all the kids left shortly after Jacey.

None of them know how truly important tonight is for her.

"You're starting to sound like—"

"Close your mouth, Thomas, and fix your hair." Mama bounced back quickly, but with Dad working on the gallery, she didn't want to go back to Tennessee until he was ready. I don't know if she's ever really going to be ready and I overheard Mama talking to Dale and Jenny about real estate. Honestly, I think we'd all be happier if they moved back north. My family has always been my life and I don't like that we're split up. I'm kind of a mama's boy.

I turn toward her and her eyes soften as the creases beside her mouth appear as she smiles. Mama reaches forward and fixes my tie before quietly saying, "You're going to want to look your best. It's a big night."

Mama knows.

I leave before Mama and Brian, nervously wiping my palms on my thighs the closer I get to the parking lot. I pull in the space beside Jacey's car and kill the engine. I told her I would help her find a real car once spring rolled around, and here we are. Spring.

Running my hand along Henrietta's steering wheel it's obvious to me who needed to reconsider their transportation. At least I'll be keeping her in the family. She'll be finding a new home in Jenny and Dale's barn once the Durango comes home. It's time I grow up.

"It's okay, Henri, we'll still take you out once in a while," I say, to my car. It's definitely time to act like the mature adult I pretend to be around other adults.

I hear a knock on the window and turn my head while rolling down the window. "You know it looks really awkward when you sit in your car in public and talk to yourself, right?"

"You do it, too, Max." He knows I wasn't talking to myself. He used to have a fun car, too, and a motorcycle. Now he only takes them out when he and Steph go somewhere just the two of them.

"But I also have a big kid car now, so I only talk to my baby in the garage where no one can see me or listen in on our conversations," he says. I roll the window back up as he finishes talking and open the door. His face turns serious. "You ready for tonight?"

"As ready as I can be. Is she still panicking that no one will come? She was a ball of anxiety before leaving the house. I'm hoping being here has helped calm her down."

"She seems good. When we got here she had the stereo blaring and was just standing in the middle of the room looking at the wall," Max says. I give him a concerned look, but he shakes his head. "I think it's more her making peace with how it's all come together. She went to the kid's section and was painting with Britt and Emmy when I came out here."

I laugh, because it's just like her to wear a fancy dress and get into something messy with our niece and nephew. She's been Aunt Jacey ever since Britt's declaration at the hospital all those months ago. Watching her with the kids in our family does something to me. We are both painfully aware there's a possibility it won't happen for us naturally, but it doesn't mean we aren't going to do what we can to build our family when the time is right.

I know now the right time to start a family most certainly wasn't a year ago. What's more is, the person wasn't right. We haven't heard from Sutton since Christmas, but saw her mom putting a "For Sale" sign in the window at the bookstore when we went for a walk one afternoon. Curiosity got to us, so we stopped to ask about it. She made it very clear she was happy to be done running the business. To be closer to their kids, Sutton's mom said she and their dad were moving to New Jersey. We wished her well and didn't ask for details — she didn't offer any, either. The other "For Sale" sign went up in the yard at the house next to Max and Steph shortly thereafter. It's not that we didn't want to be nosy about Sutton, but we had agreed that chapter of our life was closed. There was no need to open the wound.

Max claps me on the shoulder and we start toward the building as Brian and Mama pull in the parking lot. "It's almost time. She's going to start thinking you forgot," Max says and I smile at him.

~*~*~*~

If I hadn't seen what the store looked like before the work was done, I never would have believed it was as much a wreck as it started out as. I've stood in her shop on Main Street countless times over the last few months, watching as it transformed from the vacant space it had been for years prior to Brian purchasing it into a physical representation of the woman who walked through the door of the coffeehouse one morning and fixed my heart. She's put so much effort into making TopCoat more than just a paint and sip kind of business to draw people downtown. As soon as she let go of her worry and fear of failure, the ideas began coming in in droves. One idea after another, Jacey built a business from the ground up before the doors have even opened for the first time to the public.

With Steph's ties to the college, Jacey was able to make connections with professors in the visual arts department. Tonight, when the gallery opens and the community sees it for the first time, the walls will be covered with images of what "home" is for each of the artists who volunteered to have their work on display. Jacey asked the students about auctioning off their pieces in the future as a charity benefit, an idea she was tossing around but hadn't settled on. She wanted feedback before moving forward with the concept and they gave her more than she bargained for when they unanimously agreed the idea was fitting and they wanted to be part of it. They asked if the first pieces on display could be the inaugural auction items. The charity auction took on a life of its own at that point, with everyone working together toward a common goal. Then they shocked her when they chose the VA Medical Center as the organization to benefit from the sales. Apparently, some of the students grew up here and know all about Will and his good deeds.

Max moves through the building ahead of me, but I hold back to take it all in. The amount of pride I feel for all Jacelyn has accomplished since moving home is insurmountable. I've known her just a year, but I feel like she's been part of me for my entire existence. Our friendship blossomed slowly at first, but when we stopped trying to control everything it was like watching a rose garden change from buds to full bloom overnight. I walk through the back of the building, with its walls covered in bright splashes of color, and take in the additional work she hung since I was here yesterday.

The gallery itself is a work of art, but one part most people aren't aware of is the collection of handprints all in a row on the wall in Jacey's office. It started as a project for the kids. Britt, Emmy, and Jake were all in and out of the building during the renovation, putting their personal touches on the space — personal touches most people would have considered messes, but Jacey interjected each time a voice would begin to scold and reminded them this was a place for artistic expression. There was a lot of artistic expression happening and by the time Jace's office was completed, everyone who helped bring her dream to life had left an imprint of themselves for her to have as a keepsake. I think even the least artsy people helping out dug deep to find their inner Picasso over the last few months. Jacelyn has a way of dragging it out of the most unsuspecting characters.

It's just before six in the evening as I enter the main gallery, noting the café tables that were brought in from the coffeehouse for the night are swathed in white linens and piled with a large spread of pastries and cheese platters. Wine, bottled water, and a small selection of locally brewed beers are set up on one of the tables, but something is missing. I immediately turn to look for the coffee and, as if on cue, Brian walks through from the back with two large carafes.

"You have your PR spiel prepared?" he asks while handing me one of the pots.

"Not really. I figured I would wing it," I say. When it's clear he doesn't realize I'm joking, I laugh and smile. "I have it ready. It's going to blow you away with all the big, fancy words I use."

Her hand slides up my back and I feel the familiar fluttering sensation in my abdomen. Jacey is the first and last woman to give me butterflies, a secret I admitted to her one night as we discussed the future. It surprised her, I think, to know men do experience that feeling.

"Big, fancy words? Should I get a dictionary for all of us common town folk?" she says in jest, giving her best try at a southern accent. Though, I'm not sure how much she has to pretend these days as it seems the rest of us transplants have rubbed off on her, even if just slightly. Every once in a while, she'll say something and I hear a little unintended twang slip out.

I shake my head and kiss her temple as she presses herself into my side. My arm automatically wraps around her shoulders. "No dictionaries necessary. I'm going to try to keep it short and sweet, just like you," I say to her.

Brian rolls his eyes. "You guys are kind of gross with all this acting in love stuff," he scoffs playfully. "I can't wait until you start acting like old married people like the rest of us. Chop, chop. Get on with it already!"

He laughs loudly and throws his hands up as he walks away. Jacey and I exchange a look. She shakes her head, but winks at me as she releases herself from my grasp and walks to the door to welcome a small group of local business owners to the gallery.

An unseasonably warm April breeze works its way through the room from the open door and it reminds me of the day Brian and Stella exchanged their vows a couple years ago. It was a big day — not just because my brother married the girl of his dreams, though. It was also the day Steph and Max truly began their relationship, and the day I finally admitted to Brian that I had kept in touch with Britt's mom.

Here we are again, at the beginning of another Spring, and life is once more flourishing for us all.

I stand back and watch Jacey visit with her colleagues, her hair falling down her back in soft, loose waves that hide the freshly dyed hot pink strands beneath it. The light catches the diamond stud in her nose, and she gingerly touches the pendant I gave her at the culmination of my week off from her. I never again want to take a week off from Jacey.

While Jacey mingles and the room slowly fills to full with people from the community, professors from the college, students and their families, I feel the clamminess begin to build on my palms again. Absentmindedly, I wipe them on my pants.

"Stop that," Dad says, handing me a handkerchief. "Public speaking makes me nervous, too."

"It's not that. I wish that's what it was."

He laughs. He knows the truth, too. Just him and Mama. And Fisher.

At six-thirty sharp, I walk to the podium we placed near the partition separating the main gallery from the project area and clear my throat. The room is quiet, so quiet I swear I can hear her heart beating from where she stands between Fisher and my mama. She looks so comfortable holding Emmy on her hip that I need to take a deep breath and swallow back the emotion that hits me out of thin air and I begin.

"Good evening. I would like to welcome you to Brockport's newest business. As many of you know, TopCoat was merely a thought a few short months ago. The space you stand in tonight, was an empty shell … a blank canvas, if you will. With Jacelyn's vision, we now have one more vibrant business breathing life back into our town."

I catch her eye as I scan the room, making sure each person sees me seeing them. Then I look directly at her again as I continue.

"Tonight, we celebrate all the hard work that has been put into making dreams come true. We celebrate Jacey's desire to give back to the community she has forever called 'home'," I say, smiling broadly at her. She's set Emmy down to play because she knows what's coming next. "But more than that, she's giving a piece of herself to all of you by sharing her knowledge and her art. Please help me officially welcome Jacelyn Reilly Stratford to the business community."

Epilogue

"Do you think they were surprised?" I ask her.

"I think they were surprised we kept it a secret," she says, turning around and pulling her hair forward over her shoulder. She points to the back of her dress, "Unzip me." I comply, pressing a kiss to the exposed skin at the base of her neck as the teeth come open.

I'll admit, when Dad confronted me about marrying Jacey so early on in our relationship, I was scared. Not scared of marrying her, but afraid of what everyone who isn't family would think. According to Mama, not everyone understands how Stratford men think, and in a small town where everything is everyone's business I'm sure she stands to be correct. I work with the businesses here and have heard the rumors that go through the mill. For obvious reasons, when I started looking for the perfect ring, I didn't shop locally. Jacey and I had talked about marriage, but I wanted the asking her to marry me part to still be a surprise rather than her hearing about it from the mailman.

Fisher was the only one to see the ring — a white gold band with intricate little gold branches twined together and leaves with diamonds nestled between them, but the show stopper is an aquamarine gemstone that sits front and center — and, since their parents have passed away, Fish was also the person from whom I asked Jacey's hand. The hug he gave me nearly crushed my ribs, and I took that as a resounding yes.

I slowly unzip her dress until the slider stops and push the sleeves from her shoulders, placing my lips first to the left and then the right, as the fabric glides silently down her arms. She doesn't know, but the night I asked her to be my wife, I almost chickened out. She was stressed because she was three weeks out from the gallery opening. I was stressed because I've recently taken on more clients and the workload between me and Steph is huge. There was a part of me that thought it would be better to wait until things slowed down.

The thing is, it never slows down. Life is coming at us at a million miles an hour and, while we might get a chance every now and again to breathe through the growing pains, it's still coming at a million miles an hour. Jacey and I haven't done a damn thing slowly, not yet, and nothing has happened in order, because there was supposed to be an order to things. Jacelyn has taught me there are times when disorder and organized chaos are better than having every minute of my life scheduled.

Two weeks ago, I came home before her and made dinner — porterhouse steaks and lobster bisque from scratch, for which Fisher had given me the recipe. It was a dish their mom only made on special occasions. She walked through the back door with her shoes dangling from her fingers, closed her eyes, and breathed in deeply. I watched as a smile formed on her lips and she opened her eyes to find me standing across the kitchen in the dining room doorway holding the open ring box in one hand. In the other, I held a piece of folded tablet paper, like the one she said she was never cool enough to be given as a schoolgirl. She chose to read the note first, then took it to the counter, and put a check mark in the box with the word "yes" beside it before letting me slide the ring on her finger.

"I think the bigger surprise was that we kept it a secret for a week and didn't tell them we had gotten engaged the week before that," she says.

I watch my wife walk across our bedroom to our closet and slip the skirt of her fancy dress down her legs, pick it up, and hang it back on a hanger. I can't take my eyes off her as she quietly slips out of her sheer pantyhose, folds them, and sets them on top of the dresser. She's breathtaking as she pulls a pair of my sweats from the top of the closet and climbs into them before pushing her arms and head through one of my long sleeve T-shirts.

She sighs deeply. "That is so much better," she says. I shake my head and laugh, but silence the chuckling as I see a serious expression darken her features.

"Jace?"

"I was just wondering ... I mean, I've been wondering but we haven't talked about it recently ..." she starts and stops.

My eyebrow lifts. We talk about a lot of things a lot, so I'm not sure which thing it is we haven't talked about recently. She fidgets, lacing and unlacing her fingers and biting the corner of her bottom lip, as she crosses the room back to where I stand.

"New relationship, new living situation, brand new marriage," she says, slowly, as though she's testing the waters. I feel that clamminess from earlier again on my palms, unsure now if I want to know. "Tommy, we don't do things gradually. It's been all or nothing pretty much from the start." I nod, but don't trust myself to talk. She looks at her hands, then at me, and says, "When do you want to start a family?"

And I smile. That conversation. No, we haven't brought it up recently, not since she decided to talk with her doctor about removing the scar tissue. The last time we had a full conversation was on our way to the hospital when we went in for the surgery at the end of January. Since then, it's been comments in passing and hopeful glances at newborns who belong to strangers.

"They said we could try right away, but we wanted to give it a year before attempting, I thought?" Stepping into her space, I take her fingers in my hands and bring them to my lips. I kiss the tip of each one. "There's no need to rush. Give your body time to get back to normal. We have all the time in the world to figure it out."

"We have seven months," she blurts out, placing her hands to my face. The fear in her eyes causes my heart to race.

"We have seven months?" I repeat, questioning, as the realization of what she's saying reaches in between us and grabs hold of me. My eyes wander from her face, down her body, and back again. "You're sure?"

"Positive, Tommy," she laughs and looks down at her still very flat abdomen. "Seven months."

M.L. Pennock

Acknowledgments

There's a lot that goes into writing a book. You are fortunate enough to read the end result of months (sometimes years) of work, but, also fortunately, you don't have to deal with the behind the scenes struggles.

I started writing Tommy's book before I was done with To Have. I had ideas rolling around in my head and a few one-liners written down. Tommy was one of my favorite characters to bring to life in Brian and Stella's book, but Steph and Max took precedence and their book came second. I'm glad they did, because Tommy needed time. Tommy needed a voice that would help convey his multifaceted personality, the serious side as well as the playful. He also needed to wait for the right girl to come along.

When To Hold was published in June 2016, To Cherish was already a large document with multiple chapters and a very different outcome planned. Plans change. Truth be told, Tommy was originally going to end up making amends with Sutton and they were going to have this great little white picket fence life. The problem was, Sutton wasn't the girl for him. I think I knew that when they fell into bed together at the end of Steph's story and I breathed a huge sigh of relief because, even though I wrote her, I didn't care for Sutton one bit. She rubbed me wrong and she wasn't Tommy's missing puzzle piece.

But Jacelyn was.

Jacey was a surprise to me. I didn't expect her to be "the one" because she was supposed to be the one who put Tommy and Sutton's relationship back together. She was a surprise to my husband who got to hear all my screaming about these imaginary friends of mine when they wouldn't do the things I wanted them to do. Jace was a big surprise to my beta readers who knew who Tommy was originally supposed to end up with before anyone else read To Hold.

The thing about Jacey is, she's multifaceted, too, and fits Tommy perfectly. Together, Tommy and Jacelyn are able to rise above things put in their way, situations that are an attempt to make their relationship to falter. A lot of little things that, given time, could create a huge thing with the power to tear them apart. That's the only thing I was able to control in this book. The little things were managed.

I want to thank Ron, my husband, for continuously reminding me to manage the little things and, when I get overwhelmed by it all, to break it down and focus on the next thing. Not all the things, but the very next thing ... like breathing. Thank you for reminding me to breathe. Thank you for already reading this book twice and offering me unending support. I literally would not be able to do this without you.

Mom, Jen, Trista, Sandi, Liz, and Theresa — thank you so much for taking the time to read Tommy and Jacelyn's story and give the feedback you did. Your support means the world to me and I love you all for the help you've given me, the suggestions you've made, and the errors you caught.

A huge thank you to Joe Pompili for selling me the rights to use his original photograph of the Erie Canal bridge and downtown Brockport, NY, for the cover and promotional material for To Cherish and an extra special thank you to Heather McCoy with 315 Designs for taking the image and creating a simple, yet stunning, cover with it.

And to you, reader. Thank you for taking the time to read this book and give Tommy, Jacey, and the entire family a sliver of your time. I hope you were able to find a place for yourself in my Brockport.

About the Author

M.L. Pennock is a former journalist turned author. She attended Alfred University, earning a Bachelor of Arts in English and communication studies, before going on to earn a Master of Arts in communications from SUNY College at Brockport. She lives in Central New York with her husband and three daughters.

M.L. Pennock is the author of the To Have series.

Visit facebook.com/mlpennock or mlpennock.com for more information about what she's working on next.

M.L. Pennock